ARCANE 1

RISKY GOODS

JAMI GRAY

Copyright © February 2021 by Jami Gray
All rights reserved.
Risky Goods - Arcane Transporter
Celtic Moon Press
ISBN: 978-1-948884-42-6 (ebook)
ISBN: 978-4-948884-44-0 (print)

Cover Art: Deranged Doctor Design
www.derangeddoctordesign.com

WHAT READERS SAY...

About Arcane Transporter:
"Taking a refreshing approach to fantasy magic, this fast-paced, economical thriller is told from a highly likable perspective." —Red Adept Editing

About PSY-IV Teams:
"This story is an emotional roller coaster, from betrayal, anger, fear, love..." —InD'tale Magazine

About the Kyn Kronicles:
"...a fantastic paranormal action novel is quite possibly the best book I've read this year. I could not put it down, and had to exercise serious self-control to keep from staying up all night to finish it." —The Romance Reviews

About Fate's Vultures:
"...if you like your characters with a bit more bite, with secrets, with hidden agendas, and all those sorts of things, and your worlds are a far more deadlier place, then this is for you." —Archaeolibrarian

ALSO BY JAMI GRAY

ARCANE TRANSPORTER

THE KYN KRONICLES

PSY-IV TEAMS

FATE'S VULTURES

Caught in the Aftermath

Fear the Reaper

BOX SETS

ACKNOWLEDGMENTS

2020 was a wild year and I wouldn't have survived it without my dedicated pit crew.

Wizards of all things Jami - Ben, Ian, and Bren

Ever dependable GPS - DeAnna, Camille, Dave, Diane, Joanna, Monica and Nana.

Glorious interior and exterior artwork - Kim and Tanja at Deranged Doctors, and Sarah and Lynn at Red Adept Editing.

For an always exciting race - you, my awesome readers!

Thanks for sticking with me through the sharp turns and bumpy roads, and a couple of wrong turns. At least we can all throw our hands up and enjoy the ride when we hit the straightaways!

If you're in control, you're not going fast enough.

- Parnelli Jones

CHAPTER ONE

"IF YOU'LL FOLLOW ME, Ms. Rossi." The concierge sketched a brief bow before leading my client, Sabella Rossi, under the arched hallways and across the tile floors to the reserved conference room. I tagged along, unsurprised by his deference. After serving as Sabella's driver and part-time body-guard for the last couple of weeks, I'd grown familiar with the hushed reverence she generated. It went hand in hand with her being the Giordano matriarch and current head of the oldest Arcane Family. She fit our surroundings at this luxury hotel, her timeless beauty and grace underscoring the old-world elegance and architecture. Even I had to admit the woman and the scenery were worth a second, and probably even a third, look.

The concierge stopped by a double set of wooden doors inlayed with wrought iron. He pulled open the one on the left and inclined his head as Sabella swept past. He waited until I cleared the threshold before letting go of the heavy door. It shut on a near-silent rush of cool, scented air with a barely discernible click. On the heels of that soft noise, my skin prickled in visceral warning of activated magic. Thanks to my recent study of magical signatures, I recognized it as a warding spell, probably meant to ensure that what happened in this room stayed in this room.

And what a room it was. Tall, arched windows peered into a meticulously kept inner courtyard and let in the bright summer light. Strategically placed potted greenery added color to the swath of cream-colored walls and marble floors. Intimate seating areas were scattered along the room's edges, the plush chairs angled around low side tables. An unlit stone fireplace dominated the room's far end, and a table of burnished wood sat directly under a wrought-iron chandelier with faux candles suspended from the intersecting gothic arches.

As we crossed the floor, an imposing man near the table's head rose from his high-backed chair and met us halfway. A welcoming smile broke through the austere lines of his face and warmed the depths of his sharp gaze. "Sabella, thank you for coming."

Sabella reached the head of the Cordova Family. "I could hardly refuse such an interesting request, Emilio." She exchanged cheek brushes with him.

My heart dropped with an unsettling mix of dread and anticipation when I heard the man's name. *Please, please, don't be here.* I sent my frantic wish toward whoever might be listening and did my best to check out the rest of the room without being obvious about it. As Emilio guided Sabella back toward the table, I swore I could hear the sound of that divine being up there laughing their ass off at my expense. My gaze stalled on the dark-haired, infuriating man standing off to the side, half-hidden by a wooden screen that subtly obscured a table covered in refreshments. His gaze met mine, and the polite mask he wore didn't falter, as if the kiss we'd shared three weeks and two days earlier had never happened. Not that I was counting.

A heartbeat passed, then two as I stubbornly held Zev Aslanov's stare. It wasn't as easy as it sounded. Zev was the Arbiter of the Cordova Family, and that title generally sent most people scurrying for cover. I, of course, was not most people. Nope, I was pissed. So even as my pulse skittered and my temper went from a simmer to a burn, I tucked my messy drama behind a coolly dismissive blink.

His lips curled the tiniest bit, and despite the distance between us, I caught a smug glint in his eyes. With undeniable audacity, he silently acknowledged me by raising his coffee cup in a mocking salute, while the man and woman next to him watched.

Arrogant, sexy jackass. Fine. If he wants to play, let's play.

Returning Zev's smirk with one of my own, I added a head tilt and shifted my focus to the pair standing with him. The light-haired man to Zev's left appeared to be in his early thirties, and based on his grin, he was highly amused by our exchange. In contrast, the icy sophisticated brunette to Zev's right wore a slightly puzzled, if irritated, frown.

Sabella's soft laugh drifted through the room and reminded me of why I was there, and it wasn't to entertain Zev. *Mind on the job, Rory.* The reminder didn't ease the sting of my wounded feminine pride, but it set my mind back to the task at hand. Deliberately, I turned my attention to Sabella. She and Emilio were chatting in low voices as they moved toward the table. I followed in their wake, keeping a careful distance to give them privacy.

Sabella caught sight of Zev and lifted a hand in greeting. As Emilio pulled out her chair, she turned to me and, with a small, frustratingly knowing smile, waved me off toward a nearby chair. Behind her, Emilio—the man Zev answered to and one of Arcane society's notables—looked from me to Zev, his speculation clear, before he ensured that Sabella was situated and then reclaimed his seat.

Stifling a sigh, I went and sat in the nearby armchair as Sabella greeted the table's other occupants. Then I settled back to watch the drama play out. This wasn't my typical scene, but as an independent contractor intent on carving out a sterling reputation as a highly qualified Transporter to the magical elite, I was quickly becoming familiar with it. Package delivery and protection became nuanced when you were your own boss.

For instance, that day, my package was Sabella. She'd been asked to mediate a Family discussion, one of the "tedious responsibilities"—in her words—that came with her particular position in the Arcane world. Her requested presence was a proactive move by the involved parties to guarantee no one came away bloodied or dead, especially since Arcane Families tended to fight down and dirty. Normally, such responsibility would belong to an Arbiter—as they were the Families' answer to judge, jury, and executioner, not that the last role was ever admitted out loud. However, Sabella indicated that this particular Family dispute required a neutral party.

According to my contract, I was to make sure she remained unscathed regardless of the resolution. In plain English, I was there to haul her ass out if things got ugly—a highly probable outcome considering that this was a Family issue. I had no idea why Sabella felt I was up to the task, but considering what she was paying me, and the fact that I liked her, I was willing to give it my best shot. Later, when I wasn't worried about bloodshed, I'd overanalyze her reasons for including me.

There was an underlying tension in the room that left me twitchy, but I did my best to appear unassuming and attentive. I scanned the other two faces already seated at the table. While I recognized Stephen Trask, head of the Trask Family and CEO of a teetering biotech research company known as

Origin, the other person remained a mystery. Still, the presence of Stephen, Emilio, and Zev did not bode well. Or perhaps that was simply residual paranoia on my part, considering how Zev and I first met.

Difficult though it was, I resisted the urge to check on what Zev was doing. Not that I had to wonder for long. The hair on my arms rose as a coffee cup appeared in front of me, held aloft in a familiar hand. "Here."

Ingrained manners overrode my need to ignore him. I met his chocolate-dark gaze and took the cup with a polite "Thank you."

Our fingers brushed, and the momentary touch sent a tremor skimming along my skin. I hid my reaction by aiming my attention at those gathered at the table. Undaunted by my clear dismissal, Zev took the chair next to me. A long moment passed, both of us studiously watching the table's occupants exchange small talk.

I was taking a sip of coffee when he spoke without looking at me. "I've been meaning to call you."

Miraculously, I managed not to choke on my drink. Instead of calling bullshit, I made a noncommittal sound and kept my eyes riveted on the table, not on the six-foot-two slice of sexy darkness looming at my side. It was harder than it sounded. He shifted, angling toward me in such a way that it would be not only telling but rude, too, if I chose to ignore him. Intent on maintaining my dignity and acting like a mature adult, I turned and looked at him.

It was a mistake. He was studying me with a small frown and a disconcerting intensity. His angled jaw was covered in perpetual scruff that merged into the neat Vandyke that surrounded his full lips and sinful mouth. His shoulder-length black hair was tied back at the nape and did nothing to downplay his rakish air. It wouldn't have surprised me to learn it was a deliberate move on his part, a silent dare to every woman to unleash the wildness ruthlessly held in check. He fascinated me more than was healthy, and that same fascination was what had initially gotten me in trouble in the first damn place.

Three weeks, two days. The reminder was a weak leash, but it worked.

"You're pissed." His voice was low, keeping the conversation between us.

"No, I'm not." It was a blatant lie. We both knew it, but instead of calling me out, he continued to hold my gaze with unflinching patience, waiting for the truth. Because I hated games, it didn't take me long to relent. "Fine, I'm pissed. I don't like being played, Zev."

His wince was so small I would have missed it if I hadn't been watching closely. He shifted, his hand rising as if to reach toward me, but instead, he curled it into a fist and dropped it to the chair's arm. "That was not my intention."

Strangely, I believed him. Zev was many things, but a liar wasn't one of them. "It doesn't matter."

"Rory, I —"

Before he could finish, someone rapped the table with their knuckles, cutting off our conversation and regaining everyone's attention.

"Shall we get started?" Emilio sat to Sabella's left. His question was clearly a formality, because he was quick to follow it with, "Thank you for coming today."

As the murmurs faded, the couple who had been talking with Zev earlier at the refreshment table claimed a pair of chairs behind Stephen, which put them across from Zev and me. The brunette waited to catch Zev's eye, then she launched a sultry smile. My green-eyed monster woke with a lazy blink, but Zev's reaction was not what I expected. He stiffened, dipped his chin in acknowledgement, and then shifted the tiniest bit until he was angled toward me.

What was that?

At his unmistakably dismissive move, the brunette narrowed her startling light eyes and stared at me with an uncomfortable intensity. With no idea of what the hell was going on, I gave her a polite smile then turned back to watch the table at large and sipped my coffee.

With everyone seated, Emilio spoke. "Before we begin, does anyone object to Sabella reinforcing our privacy ward?" When nothing was said, Emilio turned to Sabella. "If you wouldn't mind...?"

"Of course." She traced a sigil on the table.

Magic rolled over my skin like a scouring pad as she bolstered the ward. I fought back a shiver at the irritating sensation. Clearly, no one would be leaving this room until Sabella allowed it, so I decided to slow my caffeine intake.

"Thank you." Emilio turned back to the table. "For the purpose of this meeting, it is important to note that all parties involved have agreed to abide by Sabella's decision pending the outcome of this conversation. All details discussed will remain confidential. Stephen, Leander, do you have any objections before we move forward?" Both men at the table shook their heads. "Good." Emilio sat back. "Sabella, the floor is yours."

Sabella sat in her chair like a queen on a throne, one hand on the folder in front of her. "It is my understanding that all three involved families—Cordova, Trask, and Clarke—wish to uncover those responsible for the recent deaths surrounding the Delphi project."

What the hell is the Delphi project?

Both Stephen and the burly blond, who I assumed was Leander Clarke, nodded while Emilio simply watched. Sabella turned to Stephen. "To be clear, the Delphi project was central to your biotech research at Origin and was led by Lara Kaspar, correct?"

"Yes." Arrogance rode Stephen's voice, and his face was set in hard, disgruntled lines. His gaze flickered to Emilio and back to Sabella. "She was not only our head researcher but the driving force behind the initial phases of the project as well. I now believe her death should be considered part of this discussion."

Emilio's hand curled into a fist before he relaxed it. I didn't find his reaction a surprise considering Lara Kaspar was his ex-sister-in-law. Well, dead ex-sister-in-law. The distinction was important, as an ex wouldn't command the same response as a dead ex.

"Noted." Although Sabella's expression remained unchanged, her voice carried a sharp edge. "Now, allegations about who is behind these deaths have been bandied about—hence, my involvement. For the purposes of this meeting, we will focus on known facts, not rumors."

She opened a folder similar to the one she'd handed me when I arrived on her doorstep to escort her to this meeting —a folder I hadn't had a chance to go through. I made a mental note to remedy that as soon as possible. Sabella began flipping through the pages then looked at Stephen. "Let's start at the beginning. Origin employed Dr. Kaspar, a high-level Fusor mage, to assist with a project that involved neurotechnology, correct?"

"Yes," Stephen said.

"When did you first realize Dr. Kaspar was selling research results to LanTech?"

Leander stiffened in his chair but remained quiet. Temper moved over Stephen's face like an incoming storm, and his voice was clipped. "Close to seven months ago."

Sabella went back to studying the papers in front of her and, without looking up, asked, "And what steps did you take to rectify the situation?"

A muscle in Stephen's jaw jumped, and he glared at Leander. It was obvious Stephen had a truckload of resentment to unload. "We immediately revoked Dr. Kaspar's security clearance and confiscated her research."

When Stephen didn't say anything else, Sabella's hand flattened on the papers in front of her. She lifted her head and pinned the belligerent Stephen in place with a shrewd look. "Is that all?"

Red rode Stephen's face. "Once we had verifiable proof of Dr. Kaspar's NDA violation, we requested a meeting with LanTech's legal team to discuss the ramifications to the Delphi project."

I couldn't help but wonder just what those ramifications entailed, considering the fact that Stephen's company, Origin, specialized in biotech research, and Leander's rival company, LanTech, worked with magic-infused technology. *What could the two companies be working on that's big enough for both men to risk not only their professional reputations but their families' honor as well?* My imagination spun up enough conjecture to give anyone—mundane or Arcane—nightmares.

"I want to reiterate what was stated at that meeting," said Leander. "Yes, LanTech had a similar project in process. No, it had not reached the advanced stage that Origin claimed to have achieved. Dr. Kaspar came to us, offering information. We were unaware that her information was illegally obtained. She assured us it was her intellectual property. As our lawyers pointed out, we cannot be held accountable for her indiscriminate actions."

Stephen looked as if his head would explode. He slammed his fist on the tabletop, rattling nearby cups and pens as he looked daggers at Leander. "You stole our research to bolster your thrice-cursed experiments." At his outburst, shadows deepened along the edges of the room, and I thought I heard whispering.

As the surrounding shadows thickened, magic rasped

against my skin, adding to my growing unease. My own magic rose in an invisible response, a sensation akin to armor sliding into place. Out of the corner of my eye, a faint shimmer of blue sparked. Next to me, Zev leaned forward. His hands, lined with a subtle glow of magic, were held in a casting position. On the other side of the room, the brunette and blond did the same as they prepared to defend those seated at the table. Their reaction exposed them as Arbiters.

Red-faced, Leander shoved back his chair and braced his hands on the table. Outside, an eerie wail tore apart the calm summer and hard winds slammed against the windows, rattling the glass in their frames. Inside the conference room, the uncomfortable press of magic rose in sync with the two men's aggression. I wasn't sure if Leander was going to launch himself at Stephen or upend the table. I scooted forward to perch at the end of my chair, just in case I needed to jump between Sabella and Leander.

Before the trembling threat could snap to life, Sabella's sharp "Enough!" sliced through the tension-filled air, cutting both men off at the metaphoric knees.

The wind outside disappeared as if a switch had been flipped, and the whispered-filled shadows snapped away into nothing. The intense burst of Sabella's power ripped across my already stinging skin. I swallowed down a hiss of pain.

"I will happily seal both of your tongues if you two cannot behave," Sabella said.

It wasn't an idle threat. She could turn them both into jackasses fairly easily if she wanted to, which I thought would be amusing and highly satisfying. But I was doomed to disappointment when Leander, with clear reluctance and ill grace, retook his chair. Stephen locked his jaw so tight the bone showed white beneath his flushed skin. Neither one dared to disobey.

"Now," Sabella said into the taut silence. "We are not here

to rehash this argument. It has already been accepted that Dr. Kaspar, prior to her death, did violate her NDA with Origin by promising to deliver various pieces of her research to someone purporting to represent LanTech. In an effort to unlock the hexed drive containing this information, someone made an attempt to kidnap her son, who, as her heir, had the ability to unlock the security hex on that drive. That attempt was tracked back to LanTech by Jeremy's guardian, Emilio Cordova, who also noted that a separate retrieval team had been hired by Origin to track the drive, and they, too, went after Jeremy."

"Those supposed LanTech representatives acted on their own," Leander said, his frustration clear as he looked at Emilio. "This was recently verified by your Arbiter. Your prior decision to bankrupt LanTech cost many innocent employees their livelihoods. Your nephew is unharmed and alive."

"As are you." Unmoved, Emilio held Leander's hard stare. "LanTech is one of many in your financial portfolio. Be grateful we kept our vengeance contained to bankrupting a single company."

"And what about him?" Leander motioned to Stephen. "Representatives"—he sneered the word—"from Origin also targeted the kid. Yet his business is still standing."

"Not for long." Emilio's smile gave me chills and added weight to the whispers that Origin was perched on the crumbling edge of ruin.

I had a feeling it soon would join the rubble of LanTech. Emilio's ruthless decision to undercut both LanTech and Origin's military contracts, as payback, had scored direct, devastating hits. Lara may have divorced Emilio's brother and left their son, Jeremy, behind, but Emilio still considered her family. And if there was one rule you didn't break with Arcane Families, it was that you didn't fuck with family.

Stephen's face drained of color, leaving him pale and

drawn. "Cordova, we already offered our apologies and promised to rectify the situation. As I explained, we were attempting to retrieve our property, and what happened to your nephew was the result of a miscommunication and poor judgment."

Miscommunication and poor judgment? Really? That failed kidnapping attempt had put both LanTech and Origin in the Cordovas' crosshairs and drop-kicked me right into the middle of Arcane politics. Of course, the only one who knew of my involvement was Zev, and possibly Emilio. I was really hoping my unwitting role wouldn't be dragged into whatever mess was on the table at the moment.

"Gentlemen, need I remind you, we are not here to discuss that situation," Sabella warned. "Leander, I read the claim you submitted on behalf of the Clarkes and LanTech. You believe someone systematically targeted your former employees?"

"Yes." Leander sat back in his chair. "Of the two remaining members of the research team assigned to the Delphi project, one died under questionable circumstances, and one is currently missing."

"Origin has recently uncovered a similar pattern," the brunette sitting off to the side said, gaining the attention of those at the table.

A slight frown marred Sabella's face. "Are they fatalities or missing, Imogen?"

Imogen shared a look with Stephen before answering. "Fatalities. If you count Dr. Kaspar, Origin has lost two researchers with connections to the Delphi project. The third and final member of the research team is currently under protection twenty-four, seven."

Stephen drummed his fingers on the table and turned to Emilio. "Did you kill my researcher, Cordova?"

A slight frown marred Emilio's forehead, but his voice was

ice-cold. "As I've stated previously, I am not behind your loss of personnel. Nor do I appreciate your continued campaign to mar my house with false accusations. Killing your people gains me nothing."

"I disagree," Stephen shot back. "You've made it very clear why you've left Origin with a faint pulse and all but buried LanTech in financial ruin. It's your version of payback."

"It is," Emilio said with no sign of remorse. "In fact, the financial implications to date have been fairly satisfying, but no amount of money can repair the emotional injury you dealt my nephew. While I have no issue with ensuring that you and Leander bear the brunt of our wrath, I have no desire to target your employees."

"Don't you?" Leander said. "Eliminating the two research teams working on the Delphi project means your family becomes the sole entity with access to Dr. Kaspar's initial research— research that was key to moving the Delphi project forward."

"If we wanted to silence your researchers, we would simply offer them double their previous or current salaries," Emilio drawled, unruffled by the accusation. "As for Lara's contribution, her will was clear. Her research and any commodity resulting from that research belong to Jeremy. Any future decision utilizing that research remains with him."

"He's a ten-year-old boy." Stephen glared at Emilio. "You're his guardian. You can't tell me that you're going to ignore what you have? Her research holds the key to taking Arcane powers to the next evolutionary level."

Stunned by the ramifications of his claim, I almost missed Emilio's response. "That's a rather lofty statement, Trask. Especially as both the Arcane Council and I were under the impression the Delphi project was still in its initial stages. Is that not the case?"

Stephen sidestepped the question and blustered, "Initial stages or not, our research showed indications of—"

"Lara's research," Emilio cut in, his voice taking on a silky, lethal edge, "showed statistically minor indications of success but nothing that was worth pursuing. It will take years of dedicated research to make the Delphi serum a reality. My family is not interested in pouring money into a mythical serum that will likely never work."

Clearly at the end of his rope, Stephen all but shouted, "It does work, and we had a prototype serum until one of your or Leander's people stole it."

CHAPTER TWO

STEPHEN'S PRONOUNCEMENT dropped like a bomb, leveling those gathered at the table, but their shock didn't last long, and they ignited like a lit fuse. Leander and Stephen exchanged vicious accusations and equally vehement denials and almost came to blows. I shifted uncomfortably in my chair as the argument gained strength. It didn't take long before Stephen and Leander turned their ire and frustration onto Emilio, both equally determined to drag him into the escalating argument.

Not that it worked. With remarkable restraint, Emilio sat there, his expression inscrutable, his gaze dispassionate, as each of the two fighting men tried to talk over the other. Next to me, Zev watched the unfolding scene with an occasional exasperated headshake.

Witnessing the disintegrating conversation and the lack of reaction from the other Arbiters made me wonder if this was normal behavior for such meetings. If so, I totally understood Sabella's reluctance to play mediator. *Who wants the headache of dealing with grown-ass adults masquerading as overgrown, whining, spoiled adolescents with control issues?*

Sabella's polite mask didn't waver, but I caught the subtle movement of her hand over the table. I didn't need the accompanying brush of magic to clue me in to the fact that she was about to guarantee a civil conversation. Sure enough, Leander's and Stephen's mouths snapped shut midword. In almost comic unison, both men's spines snapped straight, and with stilted stiffness, they turned to face Sabella. Belligerence and unchecked temper painted their faces red while their hands were balled into useless fists, but they remained blessedly silent.

"Sit," she ordered without raising her voice.

They sat.

I looked down in an effort to hide my grin. Next to me, Zev shifted in his seat, and I snuck a glance just in time to catch him trying to hide the quivering edge of his amusement.

"Now," Sabella began quietly. "I do not like to repeat myself. Each of you will keep a civil tongue in your head. My time is valuable. I am not here to parent any of you through your personal grievances. You requested my presence to ensure that your three Families could come together to share information on a threat to your people."

She shared a hard look with those gathered at the table before settling on Stephen. "If I am to believe Stephen's statement, he thinks his lab has already created a possible serum. A serum that even in theory, may I remind you, threatens Arcane society as a whole. Is that correct?"

Under her glare, Stephen's bluster leaked away and was replaced by wariness. He swallowed and gave a jerky nod.

Sabella's voice turned frigid. "That is unfortunate."

Stephen paled.

"I will be sure to inform the Arcane Council of this development in the very near future," Sabella said.

Stephen turned so pale he became downright translucent

at the barely concealed threat. I didn't blame him. The idea of answering to the ruling body of the Arcane world would give anyone nightmares, no matter how much power was at their disposal.

When Stephen remained silent, Sabella continued, addressing the table at large. "Apparently, you need a reminder that when you and Leander initially petitioned the council, they decreed that the Cordovas were well within their rights to refuse sharing Dr. Kaspar's research with either of you. While the council recognized they could not force LanTech or Origin to abandon their respective areas of research, they were quite adamant that both companies were to discontinue the Delphi project. Furthermore, the council unanimously believed any results from said possible serum would be too volatile to risk."

What kind of results did the council consider "too volatile"? It wasn't a question I dared to ask now, because I was perfectly happy standing on the sidelines. However, I would be asking Sabella about it later—much later.

Sabella turned to the still sick-looking Stephen and mutinous Leander. When she spoke, her icy voice took on a lethal edge. "Now, in regards to your claim of producing an actual serum, Stephen, I have a few questions, some of which I expect Leander will also be able to address. Can I expect both of you to answer them in a clear and cohesive manner, or shall I call in an interrogator?"

She waited for Stephen and Leander's reluctant nods then released the silencing spell. Both men drew in harsh breaths but otherwise stayed mum. A heavy quiet permeated the room. Sabella left it there for an endless moment as the two Family leaders fought to gather their composure.

When the tension neared a breaking point, Sabella said, "Stephen, would you like to explain your statement."

Stephen didn't mistake her comment for a question.

"Before Dr. Kaspar's death, the Origin team had drafted a theoretical serum that would target identified sections of the brain utilized when an individual used magic. In theory, the serum would trigger a switch in a mage's brain. In the on position, it could activate latent abilities or boost existing ones. In the off position, a mage would be blocked from accessing his or her ability."

The ramifications of this theoretical serum were jaw-dropping and beyond frightening. He was talking about controlling an individual's access to magic. It wasn't just an abhorrent violation at a personal and spiritual level—it also raised a firestorm of nightmare scenarios that would tear Arcane society apart. What made it even worse was the fact that the knowledge was being pursued by Arcane society's powerful. Since I, like ninety percent of the Arcane world, wasn't one of those, it scared the shit out of me and made me wonder what other world-altering secrets were being kept from the masses.

Stephen wasn't quite done, and although he made an effort to tone it down, resentment still simmered underneath his level voice. "Based on this theory, we ran a series of experiments during our initial research phase. I'm sure they were similar in nature to those LanTech ran. While the Delphi project may be shelved at the council's request, that doesn't erase the research done to date or the documented successes."

"Successes with rats," Emilio cut in derisively. "Rats who were dead within days after scientists flicked your so-called mental switch and basically caused a magical overload that turned their brain matter into soup."

The graphic image made me flinch, but Stephen ignored Emilio and stayed focused on Sabella. "Based on those initial results, and despite the setback of not having access to the remainder of Dr. Kaspar's research, we continued to move forward with our limited resources. A few weeks ago, the Origin team believed they'd created their first potentially viable serum, and shortly thereafter, that sample disappeared."

Sabella's hand curled into a fist in her lap. "You moved forward with the project in clear disregard of the council's position."

A muscle ticked in Stephen's taut jaw, but he gamely replied, "Our research showed we were on the right path."

As a defense, it sucked. I doubted the council would consider that a good enough excuse for what basically amounted to sedition on his part.

Leander, who remained silent up to this point, leaned forward, his eyes alight with something uncomfortably closed to zeal. "Sabella, some lines need to be crossed. For decades, Arcane society has searched for a way to harness our abilities in an effort to provide stability to our society. If we can understand how our abilities are accessed and what determines our magical strengths and weaknesses, we then have a chance at stopping those mages that turn violent and wreak havoc on those around them. This research is a way to find those answers and reduce the tension between those with magic and those without."

There was so much wrong with Leander's statement that my brain stalled.

Emilio didn't have the same problem. "And once we have those answers, how soon before they get exploited?"

For a moment, I was stunned by the possibility that someone like him, the head of a powerful Arcane Family, would be so altruistic.

Then he added, "Or before someone figures out how to turn it against us?"

Yep, there's the self-serving arrogance I expected.

"It's too late to shove the cat back in the bag, Cordova,"

Stephen said. "It's obvious word about the Delphi project is out. Why else target the research team? Whoever is behind these deaths is intent on using the research for their own agenda. To salvage the situation, it's in our best interests to stop that from happening."

Emilio glared at Stephen. "There would be no situation to salvage if you hadn't gone against the council's decree and created the damn serum in the first place."

Stephen's mutinous expression remained, but he didn't bother denying Emilio's accusation.

Emilio visibly reined in his temper. He took a deep breath and closed his eyes, and when he reopened them, he turned to Leander. "Since you have not yet leveled baseless accusations against my family, who do you think is behind this?"

Leander shared a look with the blond sitting next to Imogen and heaved a weary sigh. "While I have my personal opinion on who is targeting the project, our investigation has stalled. My family felt it best not to aggravate you and yours further at this time—hence our request for this meeting."

Emilio's eyebrows rose in haughty disbelief. "So you do think we're behind it?"

"No." Leander's denial escaped on a frustrated growl. "I think we're all targets of the same group."

"Not this again," muttered Stephen, rubbing the back of his neck and looking disgusted.

Leander shot him a sharp look. "You believe what you will, but I know my history."

Sabella spoke up before another argument could start. "You think whoever stole this potential serum and killed your people is working with the Cabal."

Leander's jaw took on a stubborn slant. "I do."

This sounded like a recurring conversation between him and Stephen. I waited for Sabella to wave off Leander's paranoia. Most of Arcane society considered the Cabal an urban myth, a rogue group of shadowy, power-hungry mages and scientists with money, supposedly intent on mixing science and magic into some bastardized mix in an effort to rule the world. Typical evil-villain shit. If the Arcane history books were to be believed, the Cabal started back when the original twenty-seven Arcane Families shipped out to the new world, but the group didn't really flex its muscles until the world wars, when biological and chemical weapons and all sorts of sick shit became reality. Of course, history claimed they were defeated and nearly destroyed, but information I'd recently acquired made me question that account. So when Sabella gave a grave nod, my breath escaped in a quiet rush as dread curled around my spine.

"Sabella, you can't be taking his claim seriously," Stephen said incredulously.

"Why wouldn't I?"

He raised his hands and shook his head, dumbfounded. "Because we all know our history. The council wiped out the Cabal the last time they dared to stand against us."

"Leander's theory holds weight. Collectives like the Cabal have deep roots," Sabella said. "Roots that can go dormant only to come alive again when least expected." When Stephen looked like he was about to interrupt, she stopped him with a raised hand. "Maybe it's not the Cabal, but if the only ones aware of this possible serum and the results of the Delphi project are at this table, it limits our possibilities, does it not?" When no one argued with her, Sabella's tight smile remained far from amused. "Whether they call themselves the Cabal or not, I would not be surprised at the existence of a group intent on using the Delphi project to benefit their needs. Such a threat has always been a grievous concern when we've considered such projects. It is also one of the leading reasons why both Origin and LanTech were strongly advised by the council not to push forward with this research. Advice both of you chose to ignore, and now here we are."

"With all due respect, Sabella," Leander said, "as much as the council's caution may be warranted, they are slow to change, and that is not exactly conducive to survival in today's world."

"It is also a well-worn argument that will find no resolution here," Emilio cut in as he drummed his fingers on the table and studied the people around him, an expression of grim acceptance on his face. He looked at Sabella. "Leander is right—we need to determine if we are being targeted and, if so, by whom. As for Stephen's stolen serum, it must be found."

"As the serum is based on Dr. Kaspar's research, it belongs to your Family, Emilio. So once it's found, then what?" Sabella asked.

His lips curved in a merciless smile, and his gaze swept over the other men before returning to her. "We can discuss options with the council." When Stephen looked ready to argue, Emilio added, "Until then, we must find the serum and identify who has it and who is killing the researchers. Once the killer is known, we eradicate the threat."

Sabella turned to the others. "Is this a viable solution to the problem?" She got a round of nods. "Good. Seeing how all invested parties are currently in this room, I suggest we create an investigative team of your Arbiters and my representative to find our quarry."

Gazes turned my way, filled with speculation. The unexpected attention hit like an invisible punch, and heat rushed to my cheeks. While the Arbiters in question didn't blink under the scrutiny, I felt nervous in a way that left my palms damp. I did my best to hide my apprehension at being lumped in with the others and managed to keep my face impassive. My grip on my cup was so tight I was surprised it didn't shatter.

"Your representative?" Stephen studied me with a disbelieving eye.

"Yes, mine." Sabella's voice was hard. "Rory Costas. She will ensure that everyone plays nice and that there are no further miscommunications or poor judgment calls." That not-so-subtle dig left a tic in Stephen's clenched jaw. "She will also bring the serum to me, where it will stay until the council reaches a decision."

I will? I was glad someone had faith in my ability to keep Zev and company in line while holding a world-altering potion safe, because I didn't think it would be easy.

When no objections were voiced, Sabella continued. "Rory, Zev, Imogen, and Bryan"—she indicated the blond next to Imogen—"you understand your assignment?"

"You would like us to work together and track down whoever killed the LanTech and Origin researchers," Imogen said.

"And track down our missing employee, Neil Pasternak. " Bryan looked at me then back at Sabella. "We're also to retrieve the serum if it exists."

"It exists," snapped Stephen.

Bryan merely tilted his head in acknowledgment.

Then it was Zev's turn. "Once the killer is ID'd, do you want them taken into custody or dealt with?"

Leander, Stephen, and Emilio shared a look. Then Emilio said, "Use your discretion."

Zev nodded, Imogen looked excited, and Bryan appeared bored. Meanwhile, I was edging toward panic with a healthy dose of resentment. The last thing I wanted was to get involved in something that would carry long-term consequences. Unfortunately, the contract I'd signed with Sabella meant as her employee, I went where she directed, even if that meant babysitting a trio of intimidating kick-ass Family enforcers.

I am so fucked.

"As important as it is to identify who is behind this, it's equally important to recapture the serum and any leaked data related to the Delphi project." Sabella tidied the pages and closed the folder. Her gaze held mine for a second before she continued issuing her directives. "During this investigation, all data and the serum—should it be found—will be turned over to Rory, who will then bring it to me. If any of you fail to do so, you will answer to the council." Her gaze shifted to the silently waiting Arbiters. "Understood?"

The warning in her one-word question came through loud and clear. The trio of Arbiters voiced their agreement. I sat there wondering just how big a bus Sabella had just thrown me under.

Orders given, she continued. "This matter needs to be resolved quickly and quietly. How long do you need?"

Since this was well out of my bailiwick and silence seemed to be my best option, I kept my mouth shut. Zev turned to Imogen and Bryan. After a quiet back-and-forth, he told Sabella, "A week, maybe two, depending on what we find out."

"Good." Her smile was reminiscent of the Cheshire Cat when she turned back to those at the table. "Shall we plan to reconvene in a week's time to see where we stand, ladies and gentlemen?"

And that fast, the meeting was over, and I was once again working with Zev and, by unwanted extension, the Arcane Families.

This sucks.

CHAPTER THREE

AS THE GROUP at the table rose and began to disperse, Zev stood, turned to me, and extended his hand, a small smile playing around his lips. "This is nice."

"Is it?" Not wanting to be rude, I took his hand, got to my feet, and let him lead me a few feet away to the side of the room.

His fingers tightened on mine—not enough to hurt, just enough to keep me in place. "Yep, because now you have no choice but to talk to me."

"It wasn't like I was avoiding you." *More like you were dodging me.* I didn't miss the sideways looks the other two Arbiters gave us as they headed our way. I gave an experimental tug against his hold, but he didn't let me go. "You know how to reach me."

"I do, but I—"

"Zev." Imogen curled a hand on Zev's free arm with familiarity. It was a clear demand for his attention, and in case I missed that little possessive marking, she also invaded his personal space and all but shoved me out of the way.

Not keen on being dragged into the middle of whatever

these two had going on, I once again tugged on my hand, but Zev refused to let me go. Instead of making a scene, I resigned myself to playing the awkward observer.

"I'm looking forward to working with you again." She ignored me and leaned into Zev, boldly brushing her lips against his cheek.

He pulled back from her uninvited touch, his grip tightening on my hand. He shifted closer to me, the unexpected move adding a modicum of space between him and Imogen. Zev's smile carried a cool edge, and even I couldn't miss the warning flash of anger in his dark eyes. "Not sure I can claim the same."

Imogen's unusually light eyes flickered to me, reflecting a hard and calculating glint. When she turned back to Zev, her sultry demeanor carried a mean bite. "You never did like to lose."

Zev's cool expression dropped into the subarctic zone. "I never considered it a loss—more of a lucky escape."

Yikes. I did my best to hide my wince at his cutting remark even as my sympathy fluttered to life.

That sympathy didn't last long. Imogen's eyes zoned in to where his hand held mine then rose to pin me in place. "You aren't an Arbiter." Since it wasn't a question, I didn't answer, and true to mean-girl form, she kept poking. "Why would Ms. Rossi believe your presence is required?"

"Feel free to ask her yourself." This time, when I tugged on my hand, I got it back.

The last of the little quartet strolled up and deliberately stood between Zev and Imogen, leaving me facing all three at once. *I should probably get used to this.*

Bryan ignored the unfriendly vibes zinging around and cheerfully said, "Hey, I don't mean to be rude, but I've got something I need to take care of. Any chance we can meet later so we can get this show on the road? Maybe even multitask and make it a business dinner? I know this great mom-and-pop taco shop where we could talk."

"Later works for me," Zev said.

"I'll need until six to clear my schedule," Imogen said.

When Bryan looked at me, I said, "That works."

"Great." Bryan's smile gained a bit of charm. "You have a number so I can text you the address and time?"

"Just send it to me," Zev cut in. "I'll get it to her."

In an effort not to snap out something highly inappropriate, not to mention unprofessional, I bit my tongue and barely hung on to my polite expression. I also didn't miss the flash of temper in Imogen's eyes before she quickly doused it with cool disdain.

As for Bryan, he simply raised a brow while amusement danced in his eyes. "Consider it done. Until tonight, then." With that, he headed to where Leander waited for him.

Deciding it was in my best interest to follow Bryan's example, I aimed a patently false smile at both Zev and Imogen. "If you'll excuse me..."

I didn't wait for their responses but headed straight for where Sabella was talking with Emilio. Whatever was between Zev and Imogen, they were welcome to it. I had enough to worry about without adding their drama to my plate. Nor did I appreciate whatever game Zev was playing. Not that I minded being the salt in a wound, but a heads-up would have been nice.

I felt Zev's gaze on my back as I moved closer to Sabella. Not wanting to interrupt her, I stopped a few feet away. A movement at the door caught my notice, and I looked over in time to see Bryan's exaggerated eyebrow raise as he tilted his head in Zev and Imogen's direction. Amused, I rolled my eyes in response. He flashed a grin then disappeared through the doors. His attitude made me think I had one less drama llama to deal with.

Impatience gnawed at me. I wanted Sabella to finish up because I had some questions for her. They mainly revolved around the Delphi project, but an even bigger concern was what exactly she thought she could achieve by assigning me the role of Switzerland. Unfortunately, the answers would have to wait until we were alone and could talk without the worry of being overheard. Reluctantly, I set my curiosity aside.

With nothing else to occupy my attention, I gave in to temptation and snuck a look at Zev and Imogen. He stood in front of her, his arms folded, his jaw tight, and a frown darkening his face. Imogen either didn't care about or didn't recognize the signs of his impending temper. She held her position in front of him, standing so that there were only a few inches between them. When she started to jab her finger into his chest, his hand shot out, catching her wrist and forcing her to still. With her back to me, I couldn't see her face, but her spine went ramrod straight. She jerked on her arm. Zev let her go and stepped around her.

Not wanting to get caught watching, I quickly looked at the floor, trying my best not to acknowledge the spark of jealousy that ignited a dull ache. A single kiss twenty-three days ago did not justify harboring a green-eyed monster. Nor was such an emotion smart when, for the next two weeks, I was tasked to work with all three of them and my assigned role was to be neutral. *Yeah, that's going to be a serious challenge.*

I could feel Zev closing in like an approaching storm, and I tuned in to Sabella's conversation, hoping she was close to being done. Relief hit me when she turned to me and asked, "Rory, are you ready?"

Eager to make our exit, I answered, "Whenever you are, Ms. Rossi."

She patted my arm but smiled at the somber man next to her. "Well, then. Emilio, I won't say it was lovely, but it was entertaining." She reached out and squeezed his hand. Then she turned to Zev, who had stopped at Emilio's side, and studied his expression before wrinkling her nose. "Zev, I'm sorry."

He raised a brow. "For?"

Sabella didn't look over, but she did tilt her head just the slightest bit in Imogen's direction. "I know it will make things uncomfortable."

"For her, maybe, as she's never been able to separate business from personal," he said, his voice indifferent. "But not for me."

His comment left an uneasy tremor in its wake, but I shook it off.

"Still"—Sabella patted his arm—"I appreciate you accepting this assignment."

His dark eyes sparked with humor instead of the expected temper. "Did I have a choice?"

Sabella's amusement floated through the room on a light laugh. She gave his arm a squeeze and let go. "Not really, but then, I'm sure you knew that before you agreed to come." She didn't give him a chance to reply. "Regardless, thank you for indulging in an old woman's whims."

"Whims?" His voice carried an indulgent note, turning an accusation into a familiar tease. "More like machinations."

Her answering chuckle was soft. "Tomayto, tomahto. At least this way, I am assured of answers instead of more questions."

He inclined his head. "We'll endeavor not to disappoint."

She patted his arm one last time. "I'm sure you won't."

I wondered if I was the only one who heard the underlying threat beneath the friendly comment.

CHAPTER FOUR

I WAITED until we'd left the hotel in our rearview mirror before I braved a conversation with Sabella. It wasn't ideal, as my attention would be split between our conversation and the road. Normally, this would be an easy task, but I'd quickly learned that *easy* wasn't a word associated with being Sabella's driver. My first lesson occurred on our initial foray while I was driving her home after dinner with friends. When I realized we'd picked up a tail, I offered the standard choice—flight or fight. The choice was hers as she was, after all, the client. She assumed they were simply pesky paparazzi, so our ride home had included an unanticipated high-speed race through late-night streets. Fun for me, stressful for her.

I enjoyed leaving them in the dust, but afterward, I wondered if Sabella's assumption had been correct. Yes, our mysterious chasers could have been overzealous camera-carrying gossipmongers, but considering the feathers I was ruffling at the time, I had my doubts. Especially as they'd been a bit too sneaky about their approach and stubbornly persistent in sticking to our bumper.

In the end, the answer didn't matter because that initial

assignment with Sabella netted me a long-term contract as her preferred Transporter when she was in town. Well, Transporter, sometimes bodyguard, and pretty much full-time girl Friday. Three weeks earlier, after carefully reviewing the contract with an Arcane Guild lawyer, I'd agreed to take Sabella on as my client. If it had been anyone else, I would never have signed on the dotted line, but Sabella could make or break the professional future of a relative unknown like me. Although I had a few contacts from my days with the Arcane Guild, they could never build my reputation as fast or as solidly as Sabella could.

Our contract allowed me to accept other jobs when she wasn't keeping me busy, not that the issue had come up yet. Immediately after the papers were finalized, she was called back to Italy unexpectedly and had only returned to the Valley a mere week before. So taking on this proxy role as my first officially assigned task was akin to letting myself be thrown into the deep end without a life preserver. No doubt, it was going to hurt.

Once we were safely on our way, Sabella proved that despite our limited interactions to date, she had me pegged. "Now that we're away from inquisitive ears, dear, ask your questions."

I hovered between curiosity and frustration, all my questions tangled in my mind. In an effort to unravel the mess, I started with the most basic. "Why?"

Fortunately, Sabella understood the ambiguous context of my question. "Because I need an impartial set of eyes and ears."

Okay, I can see that. Unlike everyone else in that room, I had nothing at stake in this mess. *But still...* "You want *me* to run herd on a trio of Arbiters?"

"Yes." Her confirmation emerged in a perfectly calm voice.

I, on the other hand, was far from calm. "They're Arbiters, Sabella." Stressing the title in an effort to impress upon her just how daunting the task was, I did my best to rein in my panic. Contemplating dealing with the magical heavyweights of powerful Families was bad enough, but I also had a secret to protect. "I'm a Transporter. Unless I'm in a vehicle and they're not, when they turn on me, my chances of survival are nil."

"Don't be silly," she said, waving off my concerns. "They won't kill you."

"Right, because what's a little maiming between acquaintances?" I muttered, thinking I'd better make sure I had a set of wheels on hand for an emergency escape. *Maybe a rocket launcher or two to give myself a head start.*

She chuckled and patted my shoulder. "There, there, dear girl." The leather creaked as she sat back. "I never pegged you as a drama queen."

"I'm not a drama queen. What I am is realistic." I snuck a glance in the rearview mirror and caught her grin. It was clear she found my concerns amusing. I sighed. "You do realize that each of those three is used to answering to one person and one person only: the head of their Family. They have no reason to work with me."

"Then it's good that they don't have a choice, isn't it?" Her humor slid away, and her voice gained its familiar unyielding tone. "They will not disrespect or harm you for no other reason than that you are my agent."

If being her proxy meant something more than a label and a target, maybe I could believe that. Unfortunately, that protection might be put to the test if the Arbiters discovered exactly what I could do.

But she wasn't quite done. "Besides, it's not like you're completely defenseless, is it?"

My hands tightened on the leather-wrapped steering

wheel as she arrowed straight to the heart of a topic we'd only danced around—my magic, a rare and highly sought power that could easily be abused. It was a secret I'd kept close for years, but recent events had forced it out of the shadows, and now Sabella was one of two or three people in the know.

With that reminder, I ignored a lifetime of reticence. "Being a Prism doesn't make me indestructible."

She made a thoughtful hum. "Tell me you read the journal I sent you."

I nodded. I'd read it so many times that I now considered it my own personal sacred relic. If she wanted it back, I wasn't sure I could hand it over. Hungry for information on a magical ability that had been buried in the annals of time and mostly erased from the history books, I'd devoured the pages written by a female Prism who'd lived during the last world war. She had served as an allied spy while partnering with another covert agent, this one a Family-connected illusion mage. The journal was written in such a way that I still didn't have a name for her or her partner. It was just one of many missing details that drove me crazy.

"It's not exactly a how-to manual," I said. *No matter how much I wish it were.* "And while I may be able to hold one Arbiter at bay, if that changes to facing down all three at once, the odds aren't in my favor."

And despite whatever was between Zev and me, in our previous interactions, he'd asked questions I refused to answer. That turned the odds of my current predicament from concerning to worrisome. Even if Zev didn't betray me, the other two might. Yes, being a Prism meant I could withstand most of what an Arbiter could throw at me—magically. And on the rare occasion that fate smiled on me, I might even be able to redirect a magical attack back to its originator, but should they team up or decide to switch to a relentless physical assault, their combined strength would most certainly crack, if not shatter, my magic-repellant armor.

And that wasn't the only concern. Thanks to the journal, I was all too aware that being a Prism was a rare ability, often coveted and, more often, ruthlessly exploited. It was clear in her writings that the more powerful members of the Arcane society had been relentless in their hunt for those who could wield what they perceived as immunity against magic. Not only did they want to harness such a rare power, but they also would go to unimaginable lengths to coerce Prisms into becoming their personal shields against magical assassinations. Because of that, Prisms had been targeted until they were almost extinct. Or so the journal claimed.

Unfortunately, it was a believable claim. Before Sabella's journal, the only time I'd heard even a whisper about Prisms was in a chance meeting with a schizophrenic street tramp when I was a kid.

"You worry too much, Rory." Sabella hauled me out of my head and back into our conversation. "I sincerely doubt Imogen or Bryan would risk censure from their Families, let alone from me, by turning against you."

I didn't miss the fact she'd left out Zev and the Cordovas, and I wasn't sure I shared her confidence. I stifled a sigh as I passed a slow-moving car. My power was nothing like hers, the depth of which thrummed against my skin even when she wasn't doing anything more dangerous than breathing. I didn't have that kind of intimidating strength, and it was my ass on the line, not hers. Which meant that if, say, Imogen was determined to get her licks in, I'd have plenty of reasons to worry.

Before I could argue further, Sabella added, "Besides, I'm sure Zev would take issue should they turn on you."

A disbelieving snort escaped me before I could stop it. "You sure you want to make that bet, Sabella?" Stopping at a red light, I glanced to the mirror to catch her eye. "Aren't you the one that warned me that his loyalty belonged solely to the Cordovas?"

Amusement lined her face, but her eyes were diamond sharp. "Which is exactly why he wouldn't allow anything to happen to you."

Yeah, that makes complete sense... not. "I'm not following you."

"There are three Families intimately involved in this situation. However, the Cordovas are the ones currently in control, and that is not something I see changing anytime soon."

On that we could agree. "Which leads me to another question. Why on earth did the others think it smart to target Emilio's nephew in the first place?"

"Ego, greed, arrogance," she said. "Just one of those is enough to blind someone to logic. More than one..."

"Makes them stupid?"

Her laugh was soft but sincere. "Very stupid, but the Trasks and the Clarkes have a vested interest in ensuring that the blame for disregarding the council gets dumped somewhere other than on their doorstep."

I thought of the failed kidnapping attempt of Emilio's nephew, Jeremy, and agreed. The light turned green, and like the crack of a starting pistol at a drag race, I and the drivers in the surrounding lanes hit the gas, each of us determined to take the lead. *Welcome to Phoenix traffic.* Once I broke free of the pack, I set my own pace, a mere four miles above the posted limit and a hair under the guaranteed ticket range.

"Okay, I can see that," I said, but under all the anger in that room lay something older and deeper than the current situation. "There's more to this than claiming dibs on this research, isn't there?"

For a long moment, quiet reigned. It was long enough to make me wonder if I'd overstepped. Finally, she spoke. "You once told me that you thought soap operas were based on Arcane Families, and you were not wrong." The slide of material over leather whispered through the car as Sabella shifted in her seat. "Yes, there are a great deal of past grievances lurking under this mess, but what you witnessed today is mainly the result of Stephen feeling humiliated and helpless."

"I'm sure that's the result Emilio intended."

"Rest assured, Emilio's results are always intended." There was a wisp of melancholy in her voice, but it disappeared as she continued. "Unlike Leander, Stephen never quite grasped how to diversify his business ventures effectively. He's too much of a control freak, a flaw that is costing his family dearly, considering that Origin is their main financial stream."

"So I've heard." Traffic began to thin as we headed toward Sabella's home in Fountain Hills.

"Is that so?"

Her question contained a hint of disdain that triggered old resentments, but I kept my voice level. "Hey, I read the business section as much as the next person. There were rumors that the Cordovas had undercut Origin's military contracts, which I assume are worth a substantial amount of money."

"*Substantial* would be accurate," she said.

"Then Emilio's tactic did as intended and scarred the Trask Family finances."

"That's one way to put it. But more importantly, Emilio exposed the faults that lay beneath Stephen's poor leadership choices."

"Yet he did bankrupt LanTech," I pointed out.

Completely unruffled, she said, "Of course, but unlike Origin, LanTech is just one moneymaker of many for the Clarkes. It wasn't difficult to shift the majority of their staff into other companies."

I was surprised by her willingness to share the inner workings of Family-owned businesses but couldn't resist pushing my luck on getting more details on the Family drama. "Emilio doesn't strike me as someone who would limit his retribution solely to the bottom line when someone has kidnapped his heir apparent."

"Blood is easy to wash away, and finances can be rebuilt, but reputations?" Sabella's chuckle carried a dark edge. "That's a stain that lingers. By forcing Leander and Stephen to forfeit their government contracts, Emilio has ensured that the negative echoes will be heard for years to come. Not only does it mar their professional reputations and relationships, which will take years to rebuild, but it also guarantees that they're banned from any future profits or advancements tied to Lara's research. It's an elegant move meant to have them think twice before crossing the Cordovas."

In the hierarchy of the Arcane Families, reputation was king—or queen, as the case might be. Sabella's voice held a note of admiration for Emilio's strategy, which prompted me to ask, "So Emilio's not behind the deaths of the research teams?"

"That's for you and the others to answer. I'm sure I don't need to remind you to be careful, dear. Leander and Stephen are using the investigation as a smoke screen. It would not surprise me to discover that either one or both of them is considering manipulating the investigation's findings to create their desired outcome."

It didn't take a mastermind to understand that Stephen and Leander wanted the serum back. I turned into Sabella's ritzy neighborhood, Eagle's Nest, and slowed to a stop at the gate securing the community's entrance. After powering down the window, I punched in the security code on the keypad. When the gate rolled back, I pulled through and hit the button to raise the window.

"You haven't asked about Leander's theory of who's behind the missing serum," Sabella said.

There were a lot of questions I hadn't asked, and the distance to Sabella's house was quickly shrinking. I looked in the rearview mirror and found her watching me. "You mean regarding the Cabal?"

"You sound as if you don't believe they exist." Her eyebrows rose in amusement.

I do? My polite voice must have been getting better because honestly, I was pretty sure they did exist. And because I got the impression she was testing me in some way, I decided to share my thoughts as we bypassed the elaborate mini-mansions neighboring Sabella's home. "Actually, it's easy to believe that at some point in Arcane history, there was a group of mages that decided they didn't agree with the majority's belief on magic and how to use it. Add in the rise of science with man's need to mess with everything, and a philosophical split in our society is pretty much a foregone conclusion."

"You've given this a lot of thought, then?" Sabella's curiosity came through loud and clear.

I managed a shrug. "We're human, regardless of how we identify ourselves. We not only question everything but have some undeniable urge to control it as well—including something as unexplainable and intangible as where magic comes from and why some can wield it and others can't."

"So you think the Cabal is a generational group of like-minded magic-wielding scientists disgruntled with the status quo and intent on world domination?"

I choked on a laugh at her dramatic oversimplification. "Maybe, but I think the modern-day version is more apt to be a group of well-funded scientists and fringe mages intent on using magic to increase the corporate bottom line. It's just the thought of how far they're willing to go and what they're willing to risk that makes the idea so frightening."

"I've said it before, and it's worth mentioning again, Rory —you are too young to be so cynical." She sounded aggrieved.

I didn't bother to argue as I slowed to a stop at the foot of Sabella's long, sloping drive and the gate guarding it. "Whoever they are, whatever they want, I do think there's probably a real group calling themselves the Cabal." I lowered my window again, this time to lean over and input Sabella's private code. When I finished, the gate began to roll back. I sat back and met her eyes in the mirror. Maybe it was the light, maybe just a reflection of her emotions, but her normally hazel eyes appeared green. "My question is, if they do exist, why hasn't the council taken care of them?"

Something moved in the depths of her gaze, but her slow smile carried a thousand and one secrets, none of which she shared. "Oh, that answer is actually quite simple."

Sure it is. I turned back to find the gate fully retracted. I put the BMW in gear and began heading up the drive. The wheels bumped over the uneven surface of the pavers as we bypassed the stately saguaro standing sentry.

"If the council went around wiping out all those who threatened the Arcane status quo, there wouldn't be much of an Arcane society left."

And doesn't that sound properly demoralizing? At the top of the drive, I pulled to a stop. The courtyard was surrounded by a three-car garage and Sabella's two-story architectural beauty of a home. Even in the baking heat of the late afternoon, the panoramic view rising beyond the terraced landscaping was breathtaking.

I turned to face Sabella. "So how does throwing me into the mix help with this mess?"

She leaned forward and patted my arm. "You, my dear, are going to be the voice of reason."

"Me?" Not surprisingly, it came out a bit panicked.

"Yes, you."

"I'm not sure being a mediator is in my contract."

"I am," she said with irritating calm as she settled back and gathered her purse.

Taking the hint, I got out and opened her door. She gracefully exited the car. I waited for her to lead the way to her front door, but she didn't. Instead, she faced me, keeping the door between us. "You did read the contract's fine print, didn't you?"

I had. In fact, that "fine print" could be boiled down to one word in the last section of a five-page contract. The word *requested* had required hours of argument with the Guild-associated lawyer.

Holding her gaze, I repeated the section verbatim with a not-so-subtle emphasis on the word in question. "You mean this fine print? 'I accept that my position may require additional responsibilities outside those of Transporter, and I will fulfill such *requested* responsibilities to the best of my abilities as long as I am associated with Sabella Rossi-Giordano. Failure to do so, without just cause, will be grounds for termination of contract.'"

She gave me a beatific smile. "Yes, dear, that one. Consider this a requested responsibility."

As much as I wanted to snap, "Request denied," I didn't. I wasn't stupid, just frustrated. "Fine. I'll be your proxy."

"Thank you." She fairly glowed with satisfaction as she finally moved out of the narrow space.

I closed the door and followed her through the wooden half gate set in a curved wall. "As much as I appreciate the crash course in Family dynamics, I have another question for you."

She didn't turn around but continued up the smooth stone walkway that led to the glass-paned front door. "Of course you do." She pushed the door open, stepped inside the mix of stucco and river rock that she called home, and motioned to me. "Come in."

I stepped into the cool air of the foyer, and for once, the endless stretch of marble tiles and trestle-beam-lined ceilings soaring above barely registered. "What happens when you turn the serum over to the council?"

She set her bag on the entry table situated under a mirror. "That decision will be up to them."

Although not unexpected, her answer added to my frustration. "And you trust them with something that dangerous?"

She met my gaze through the mirror. "Who would you have me give it to? Emilio? Stephen? Leander?"

"What about just destroying it?" The few clues I'd picked up from the meeting indicated that the Delphi project was more volatile than anyone wanted to admit. That was not a surprise if someone was going around mixing magic and science into a nifty easy-to-inject serum that acted like a magical light switch.

She turned to face me with a glimmer of sympathy that was there just long enough to settle my ruffled feathers. "The genie has already left the bottle, my dear."

Yeah, that's what I thought.

She continued to study me, her gaze sharp. "You realize that throughout this investigation, it's almost certain you'll run into delicate information."

"I know." There was no missing the underlying implication. "I won't share."

"I know you won't, dear. Why do you think I hired you?" She tilted her head toward an archway leading to the kitchen. "Would you like something to drink?"

I checked the time and grimaced. "Unfortunately, I'll have to pass."

"Ah, yes, the dinner meeting." She frowned and held up a

finger. "Will you wait a moment? I have something I want to give you."

I nodded and watched her walk deeper into the house. She wasn't gone long. When she came back, she held out what appeared to be a polished stone on a gold chain. "Wear this for me?"

I kept my hands at my sides. "What is it?" That wasn't a simple piece of jewelry—not with the low buzz of magic emanating from it.

"A scrying stone." Sabella dropped the stone in her palm and let the chain curl around it. "I'd like you to use it to keep me updated." She held it out in silent demand.

Slowly, I reached out and took it, trusting my ability to ward off any unexpected surprises. Not that I thought Sabella would do that, but I needed to be cautious. "Why not use email or phones?"

"I'd rather our conversations stay private," she said. When I continued to hold the stone in my palm like it might try to bite me, she gave a small laugh. "It's just a scrying stone, Rory, I swear. Nothing more. Simply hold it, focus on me, and we'll be able chat. It also works in reverse. Think of it as a private instant chat, if you will."

Since my magic wasn't reacting, and oaths were not light things, I undid the clasp and put it on. The stone was warm as it settled just below my throat. "Thank you."

She nodded. "Enjoy tonight."

"I'll do my best." I turned to leave but stopped with my hand on the door. Without looking back, I said, "Just promise me if the Arbiters take me out, you'll return the favor."

Her laugh filled the foyer. "Of course I will, Rory. I like you."

CHAPTER FIVE

AFTER LEAVING SABELLA'S, I returned the borrowed BMW to the Arcane Guild's aptly named showroom. Half mechanics' garage, half vehicular nirvana, it took up the top floor of the Guild's parking garage and was locked behind dual layers of electronic and magical security. Any type of wheels needed to complete an assignment could be found in the stunning collection of automotive art and deceptive junkers. I thought I'd lose my access to the showroom when I hung out my own shingle, but thanks to the addendums in Sabella's contract, and her personal friendship with the Guild director, I still had access to all the pretty toys.

After handing off the keys, I reclaimed my precious beauty, a rebuilt 1968 Mustang Fastback. Won in a street race with an overconfident college student who had more money than sense, the Mustang was my most prized possession. Her stunning coat of midnight-blue paint was graced with white racing stripes on the hood that covered an engine with five hundred fifty-one horses. Even better, the college student had managed to incorporate modern conveniences into the classic interior, like a kick-ass stereo system and dual security system that used both electronics and wards, benefits I totally reaped.

Once inside, with the air conditioning beating back the triple-digit heat typical for June, I swiped my phone's screen and brought up the texts that had arrived during my drive back from Sabella's. First up was one from Lena, my roommate and best friend, letting me know she was on her way home and was contemplating swinging by our favorite sushi place.

I sent back a quick, *Can't, have dinner meet*, which got a *Your loss* reply.

I moved on to the next text. I didn't recognize the number, but a search of the address that made up the entire text confirmed it was the mom-and-pop taco place Bryan had mentioned. After a check of the time and a bit of mental math, I figured the six-thirty time was doable. I sent a curt *OK* and then, despite knowing the folly of making assumptions, I took a second to add the number to my contacts as *Zev*.

I moved to the last text, a string of numbers from an unknown phone. Excitement stirred. I shifted screens, opened an incognito internet window, went to a site I'd memorized, and typed in the numbers. A map popped up, and at the top, a timer was counting down.

"Dammit." Stinging disappointment snuffed out my momentary buzz as I closed the browser window.

Chances were slim to none that I would be able to get my racing fix and make some easy cash with that night's event, considering my upcoming dinner meet with the Arbiters. Not to mention that indulging in my slightly illegal pastime when Sabella was in town and I was on call wasn't the best idea in the world. I would just have to wait for the next race. My inner speed demon whined.

Before I could delete the text, the phone rang. I answered. "This is Rory."

I spent the next ten minutes negotiating a courier assignment for the following week. By the time I set my phone in its holder and pulled out of the garage, my demon was pouting in the corner, leaving me alone with my thoughts—not always a great place to be, unfortunately. Especially when those thoughts bounced from the twist and turns of Family dynamics to the terrifying dangers of a viable Delphi serum before sliding into the stomach-spinning speculation of what existed between Zev and Imogen.

Even though I considered myself a fairly well-adjusted woman with a healthy self-esteem, Zev still managed to rattle me like no one else. Part of Zev's allure was in witnessing how he protected those he considered his, no matter the cost. That kind of deeply rooted loyalty and commitment was the ultimate fantasy, especially for someone who'd grown up on the streets with no one to call family. But I also felt an undeniable attraction to the man. Hell, most females would find it hard to ignore the unspoken challenge presented by a sexy six-foot-two package wrapped in dark and dangerous. The relentless pull both fascinated me and pissed me off, which meant most of our interactions came with an edgy bite. Even when I'd managed to scrape up some maturity and ignore it, he obliterated all my good intentions, somehow knowing exactly which buttons to push to drive me nuts. And then, like an idiot, I'd had to go and kiss him.

Worst decision ever. Well, maybe not the worst decision, but definitely not my smartest move.

I didn't really have an excuse, but when he'd sat across from me, all taunting temptation, and dared me to take a risk, I couldn't resist. Instead of being smart, I accepted his dare, only to have him blow my mind and set my body on fire. When we pulled back from the unexpected implosion, both of us were jonesing for more, but then he'd called me trouble and walked away.

Now that I'd had three weeks and two days to think about that kiss and the possible long-term ramifications of getting involved with a man like Zev, I wondered if it wasn't only me who'd been thrown off kilter by the whole situation. Not that it really mattered in the overall scheme of things, because both of us were nothing if not professional. There was no way Zev would let something as trifling as physical attraction interfere with fulfilling his responsibilities to the Cordovas. As for me, a little unsettling rose-colored lust would keep me on my toes, but with my fledgling reputation and business to protect, I couldn't afford to let him get in the way.

As for whatever it was between him and Imogen, that was none of my business, no matter how much my green-eyed monster grumbled otherwise. My role was to gather the facts and ensure that the investigation was thorough, not stand between Zev and his overly possessive ex-girlfriend. *Too damn bad my heart isn't as practical as my brain.* I knew myself. If Imogen continued to ignore Zev's obvious brush-offs, I'd eventually give in and slap her back a step or four. Sometimes badass individuals needed protection, even one as badass as Zev. Regardless, chances were high that my heart would end up bruised, but I'd survived worse, so I would survive this.

Resolute, I tucked away all my messy emotions and made the turn into my condo's parking garage. I pulled into my assigned space and noted that Lena's sleek two-seater was crouched nearby. I collected the file Sabella had left with me and got out. Even in the dim depths of the underground garage, the heat was smothering. By the time I made it to the elevator, I was already sweating. The elevator's air conditioning was feeble at best, and by the time I stepped out on the eighth floor, I was so ready to get out of my work clothes and into something cooler.

I unlocked our door then swept through and called out, "Lucy! I'm home."

I walked into the open space of our kitchen and living room and then tossed my keys onto the kitchen island. They slid across the slick surface and came to rest against a pile of neatly stacked mail. Leaning against the counter next to the fridge was Lena, holding a tray with three sushi rolls. Her hair, a mix of red-gold and browns, was currently tamed into a French twist. Considering the tailored slacks and sleek blouse, she hadn't been home long.

"Hey, bitch, what's up?" She popped the last bit of rice-wrapped goodness into her mouth.

I dropped the file on the counter then took a seat on one of the barstools, giving a heavy sigh. "It's been a day." I eyed the sweating glass of tea on the counter next to her. "Pour me one?"

Her eyes narrowed, speculation sharpening their gold glint. "What happened?"

As Lena knew all my dirty little secrets, I didn't even consider dodging her question. "Sabella and Zev." As his name left my mouth, I winced and braced for impact.

It didn't take long to hit. "Oh my God, Rory. We talked about this!" The plastic rattled against the counter as Lena lost her casual pose and all but tossed her sushi aside to stand there with her hands on her hips and disapproval written all over her face.

I scrubbed my face, dropped my hands, and blew out a hard breath. "Yeah, but this was not my fault."

She gave a disbelieving huff, turned, and opened the fridge. "What happened?"

While she pulled out the pitcher of tea and poured me a glass, I gave her the basics of how Sabella had set me up as a proxy mediator in a family dispute. I was careful not to reveal anything about the Delphi project or the serum, which wasn't easy.

As soon as I mentioned Leander Clarke, her spine stiffened, but she didn't turn around. "The Clarke Family is involved?"

Considering Lena's mom was an excised daughter of the Clarke Family and a First Nation shaman, I wasn't surprised by her reaction. "Yep, seems they held shared interests in LanTech."

"And they're okay with you mediating a bunch of Family fixers?"

"First, I wouldn't call Arbiters fixers—more like judges, juries, and when needed, executioners."

She shot me a look over her shoulder and rolled her eyes. "As I said, fixers. And this doesn't worry you?"

"Of course it does. It's just that in this case, with multiple families involved, Sabella thought it best to use someone impartial."

"You sure that was her intention?" She handed me the glass of tea.

Lena's distrust of the Arcane Families was deeply ingrained. At thirteen, in an effort to escape the politics and machinations of the Clarke Family, she'd basically turned herself into an orphan by disavowing any claim on the Family and then joining the Guild as a curse breaker.

"For the most part, yeah." I pulled out the chain with the polished jasper agate and laid it on the counter. "She did give me this."

Lena used one polished nail to snag the chain and dragged the necklace over to her. "A scrying stone."

I picked up my glass. "She wants a secure way to stay in contact."

Lena's gaze met mine, her worry evident, but all she did was make a noncommittal hum.

I looked back at the innocent-looking piece of jewelry. "Could you...?"

"Make sure that's all it's meant to do?" Lena finished dryly.

It was nice to know my paranoia wasn't completely unjustified. "Yeah, because it's the other part that worries me."

She bent in, bracing her arms against the counter. "The other part?"

"I think she wants to see what I can do."

Lena picked up the chain and held it so the stone dangled above her other palm. Gold glints began to glow in the depth of her eyes as her magic flared. Sitting as close as I was, the flashover of her power set the hair along my arms on end. A red gold glow twined around the stone, climbing the chain like ivy.

Time ticked by like it was being dragged through honey, but only a couple of minutes passed before her magic faded and she held the necklace out to me. "As far as I can tell, it's clear."

Maybe the amount of relief I felt at her statement should have worried me. I reclaimed the necklace and undid the clasp. "Thanks."

She watched me fasten the chain around my neck. "I'm not sure how confident you should be in my assessment." Her gaze lifted to mine. "This is Sabella we're talking about. From what little I know about her skills, she could easily bury something in there that no one would be able to detect. Well, until it was too late."

"You're right." The stone settled just below my throat, the weight warm. "But I don't think she wants to harm me."

"There are worse things than being hurt, Rory."

"I know." After reading the journal, I was all too aware of the threat the more powerful members of the Arcane world posed for me and why. But it was getting harder and harder to keep my secret.

She tilted her head and studied me. "Yet you don't seem concerned about continuing to work for her."

"Oh, I'm plenty concerned, but it's not like I can refuse."

Nor did I want to refuse her, if I was being honest. If someone I had no connection with was hunting a killer armed with an experimental drug and some corrupt agenda, maybe I could bury my head under a pillow and let others handle it. But Zev was involved, and I just didn't have it in me to trust Bryan or Imogen to have his back.

Her eyebrows rose. "You sure about that?"

"Breach of contract, steep financial penalties, yada yada yada." I propped my chin in my hand and studied the face of the closest thing I had to a sister. She knew me so well—I had to give her some truth. I softened my voice and turned serious. "Honestly, even if those weren't considerations, I'd probably still agree to this."

That got me a sharp response, "Why? You're not normally a glutton for punishment."

No, I wasn't. In fact, up until recent events, I'd gone out of my way to avoid gaining unwanted attention. "I need to know what I can do."

Skepticism was alive and well in her voice. "I'm not sure that pitting your untrained abilities against a group of hard-core mages with hidden agendas is the best way to learn about being a Prism."

"Probably not. But with Sabella's weight behind me, it's the best chance I'll get while still being able to leash Zev and the others to some extent."

Lena pushed up from the counter and reclaimed her glass of tea. "I don't know, Rory. If one of them wants you or is ordered to acquire you, I don't think the threat of Sabella would be enough to stop them."

Lena could very well be right, and in an effort to reassure her, I said, "Sabella is not someone you want to fuck with."

Unfortunately taking calculated risks would be necessary if I wanted to secure my future as a Prism. If there was one lesson to be gained from the journal Sabella had given me, it was the importance of knowing my own power. And thanks to the disturbing lack of information on Prisms, there were some things I couldn't do without help. It was just a matter of recognizing that trusting that help only stretched so far.

She stood across from me, studying me silently for what felt like forever but was probably just a few seconds. "There's something more to this, isn't there?"

I didn't say anything, which in itself was an answer. She shook her head and looked down at the glass in her hands, her mouth pinched with worry. Nothing I could say would ease her concern, so I stayed quiet.

When she finally looked up, her eyes were hard, matching her voice. "You'd better watch your back."

"Always do." It was an easy vow to make because I knew this whole situation was one misstep from disaster. Then, to ease the tension, I gave her a cocky grin and lifted my glass in silent toast. "Besides, if they do go after me, I know you've got my back."

That earned me a wry twist of lips and a dryly amused, "I'm a Key, babe, not a miracle worker. Cursing them won't bring you back from the dead."

CHAPTER SIX

FIVE MINUTES before the scheduled dinner meet, I turned my Mustang into a parking lot behind a boarded-up storefront across the street from the taco shop. Well, maybe calling it a *lot* was being generous. It was square, surrounded by a metal fence, had pitted asphalt, and didn't require a fee. I recognized the matte black Harley parked between an older Impala crouched low to the ground with an in-progress paint job and a battered but well-cared-for SUV.

Looks like Zev beat me here. I pulled my Mustang into the empty space on the other side of the SUV and got out. I hit the button activating the electronic security and, to ensure that no one messed with my baby, sent a tendril of my magic out to trigger the personalized wards as an additional precaution. If anyone tried anything funny, they'd be seeking the services of a curse breaker, and Keys did not work cheap.

The taco shop was in an older neighborhood that bordered the trendier revitalized section of downtown, so my well-worn jeans and a faded concert T-shirt fit right in. I waited for a break in the evening traffic and jogged across the street. There wasn't much to the place. A mismatched collection of sun-faded tables and chairs were clustered under an awning, and just beyond those was the shop itself.

I crossed the patio, stepping aside for a couple of guys in construction vests with their hands full as they made their way to one of the empty tables. I caught sight of Zev and Bryan already seated at another table. Returning Zev's head tilt, I went to order my food. The shop held a narrow counter space up front for customers to place their orders. A young man and an older woman were taking orders in a jumbled mix of English and Spanish. Behind them was a pass-through large enough to reveal the well-oiled dance of the four-person team working the kitchen. Tantalizing spicy scents drifted through the opening and made my mouth water.

It didn't take long before I had three barbacoa tacos in hand and was winding my way through the patio. When I got close, Zev waved me to the empty spot next to him. I settled in, noting that the jeans-and-T-shirt motif extended to both Bryan and Zev. Apparently, I wasn't the only one who'd had a chance to change out of work clothes.

"Hey, glad to see I'm not the last one here," I said.

"Imogen likes to make an entrance," Bryan said before taking a bite of a taco.

Not sure how to take that, I concentrated on arranging my food before I dug in. The rumble of conversation washed around us like white noise—not overwhelming but enough to make holding a private conversation difficult. Neither Zev nor Bryan appeared concerned as they continued their casual talk between bites. I listened with half an ear, as I didn't have much to add, and enjoyed my food.

Then, to prove Bryan right, Imogen made her appearance. I had to give credit where credit was due—it was definitely an entrance. But that wasn't hard to pull off in this crowd, especially since she hadn't changed from her expensive heels, tailored slacks, and silk shirt that she'd worn at the meeting earlier that day. She stuck out like a well-polished sore thumb.

Around us, conversations stopped, and some brave but deluded fools managed to fill the air with wolf whistles. Imogen ignored them, her attention focused on us. Her gaze swept over our table, and both men gave chin lifts acknowledging her presence. Since my mouth and hands were full of taco, I did the same. Her eyes narrowed, and her mouth curled into something perilously close to a sneer. Either she didn't like her reception, or she didn't like the ambience. Deciding not to court her drama, I went back to my dinner.

"Gentlemen." Imogen stopped by the empty chair between Bryan and Zev and pulled it out. "Rory." She put a hand on Zev's shoulder as she sank into the chair.

Sitting as close as I was to Zev, I didn't miss the slight jerk as he moved his shoulder out from under her hand. I caught her flash of sly satisfaction as she dropped her hand and carefully brushed invisible crumbs from the table. *Yeah, this is going to be fun.*

I wiped my mouth with my napkin and then returned her cool greeting. "Imogen."

Apparently oblivious to the underlying tension, Bryan stopped just before taking a bite of his taco to ask her, "Are you going to grab anything?"

She shifted in her seat so she could cross her legs. "It smells delicious, but I'll pass, thanks."

He shrugged. "Suit yourself." His shell crunched as he took a healthy bite.

Imogen's gaze swept over the other diners on the patio, and when it turned back to the table, a small frown marred her forehead. "I was expecting something with a little more privacy."

Still chewing, Bryan gave her a closed-mouth grin, and his blue-green eyes took on a faint shimmer. An uncomfortable brush of magic swept over my skin, and I barely held back a shudder. The white noise of surrounding conversation cut out as if a switch had been thrown, locking us in a curiously quiet bubble. Even more surreal, the construction workers who'd been eyeing Imogen suddenly turned back to their meals as if she'd never existed.

Hmm.

Bryan swallowed and asked Imogen, "Better?"

She inclined her head. "For now."

Bryan shook his head and was about to take another bite when he caught my gaze. Whatever he saw made his smile reappear. "I know that look."

Taking the bait, I shot back, "What look?"

"The one that says you're trying to figure me out." His watchful eyes belied his light-hearted tone.

Recognizing this as the test it was, I nudged my plate back a few inches so I could put my elbow on the table. I wiped my fingers on my napkin, then I braced my chin in my hand and studied him with mock seriousness. "It's too easy."

"That's what they all say." That surprising comment came from Zev, and I choked back an unexpected laugh.

Bryan sent him a one-finger response and turned back to me. "Come on, Ms. Costas. Tell me what I am."

Ignoring Imogen's eye roll, I decided to play. "Illusion mage." He made a motion for me to give him more, so I did. "Since no one's screaming in fear and trying to claw their eyes out, Nightmare is out."

"You going to work your way through all the illusion classifications?" Zev settled back in his chair, studying me with dark eyes.

"Nah, that would take too long," I said.

Mage classifications could get cumbersome with their nitpicking. At its highest level, most magic was commonly split between a Mystic ability—one that utilized psychic phenomena—or an Elemental ability, which was fairly self-explanatory. Those abilities were then divided into mage classifications, which were further defined by a core set of common designations separated by razor-thin differences.

So when it came to illusion mages, outside of Nightmares —who could manipulate people's deepest fears into reality— there were Mirages and Charmers. The difference between the two was minor but distinctive. Mirages could render themselves invisible. The stronger Mirages could spread that invisibility to include people and things around them—a handy trick until someone unaffected walked into them. Charmers could create illusions so realistic they could interact with the physical world, making it difficult to tell what was real and what wasn't. If a Charmer turned someone invisible, for all intents and purposes, that person was invisible. Charmers, in my opinion, were tricky bastards who should be avoided at all costs.

I studied the people around us. A couple on their way to a nearby table passed behind Imogen, and she shifted the barest fraction. I turned back to Bryan. "Mirage."

Bryan gave me a slow clap. "Brava." He leaned forward, bracing his folded arms on the table. "My turn."

Refusing to squirm under his stare, I held his gaze, fairly confident my secret would remain safe—at least from him and probably from Imogen. The one who really worried me was the silently intense man sitting next me. Zev had been up close and personal when I used my magic, and he made it clear he had questions. I think the only reason he hadn't unearthed his answers was because the truth about Prisms was buried deep in the dusty tombs of history. So long as he didn't decide to start channeling a whip-wielding archeologist, my secret should be safe.

"Sabella's a connoisseur, which means you can't be some ordinary Hagatha."

Imogen gave a delicate snort at his comment but we all ignored her. As Bryan started his guessing game, I could feel Zev's attention sharpen.

Bryan kept going. "She's all but made you our chaperone, which means there's more to you than meets the eye."

"Call it what it is, Bryan—she's our babysitter." Imogen's taunt carried a bitter bite.

Knowing she'd keep up the snark until she got a reaction, I gave her one but not the one she expected. "If Sabella felt you all needed a babysitter, I don't think any of you would be sitting here right now, do you?"

Her lips thinned, and her eyes sparked as she folded her arms. I had no idea what type of magic she held, but I sent up a silent prayer it didn't involve fire because if her glare was any hotter, I'd be sporting one hell of a burn.

"Down, Imogen," Bryan murmured as he leaned back in his chair. "Sabella made it crystal clear that we're to treat Rory as her eyes and ears. Since I know the Clarkes aren't the ones picking off researchers, I've got no reason to bitch."

Imogen turned her displeasure on Bryan. "Is that an accusation?"

He gave an unconcerned shrug. "It is what it is." He turned back to me, leaving Imogen to fume in silence. "Since I'm not aware of any Costas associated with the local Families, I'm going to guess you're tied to the Guild in some way, so my first guess is Sentinel."

It actually wasn't a bad guess, all things considered. The Arcane Guild was a mercenary storehouse that housed five publicly acknowledged crews, each one specializing in particular areas. There were the Hounds for tracking and retrieval, Keys for decryption and curse breaking, Spiritualists, who encompassed necromancers and mediums, and Sentinels, who handled personal and professional security. Then there were the Transporters, speed demons like me who made secure deliveries. In addition to those five were the two who eschewed the limelight—Scouts, who were spies, and Blades, who were assassins. It was a weird family and one I called mine, even if I recently and officially had left them behind.

I gave Bryan an unconcerned smile. "Nope, not a Sentinel, but I appreciate the vote of confidence."

He cocked his head. "But you are with the Guild."

I shook my head. "Not anymore. I'm an independent contractor. Any more guesses?"

He drummed his fingers on the table. "Key, then, right?"

I shook my head, actually starting to enjoy this.

Zev bumped my shoulder with his. "Just tell him, or we'll be here all damn night."

I shot him a disgruntled glare that bounced off his titanium hide.

Bryan gave in. "Tell me."

"Transporter." I had the satisfaction of watching his face go blank in disbelief.

"Transporter?" He said it like it was a foreign word.

"Yep, one of the best actually." If I didn't toot my own horn, no one else would.

Imogen laughed. When she caught all of us looking at her, she waved it off. "I'm sorry, but why would Sabella consider a driver important enough to help us?"

Her question carried all sorts of scorn and wiped out my amusement. I felt my face harden as a cold relentlessness filled me. "Transporters are much more than drivers, Ms. Frost."

Imogen's haughty expression didn't waver. "Really?" she purred.

I didn't need the vindictive light in her eyes to know what was coming, but it was the only warning my magic needed before it snapped into place. Ice formed on my uneaten taco and quickly spread over the table. Zev and Bryan both cursed, grabbed their uneaten food, and sprang to their feet, getting out of the way of the spreading freeze. I held Imogen's gaze and stayed relaxed in my seat even as her power pounded against my magic's invisible diamond-hard shield. It held the brunt of her attack at bay, but my skin still pebbled as wisps of blood-freezing cold seeped through. The painful chill settled against my flesh. It hurt, but it wasn't debilitating. And it was definitely not the result Imogen intended. The pressure increased, and my magic undulated in response. As much as I wanted to flex my recently learned offensive skills and redirect her attack, I refrained. There was no sense in revealing all my secrets, not when the surprise of them might save my ass later.

When I continued to remain unaffected, the smug arrogance of the woman across from me changed to consideration, and a wariness seeped into her narrow-eyed gaze.

"Dammit, Imogen," Zev hissed. "Knock it the fuck off."

A hint of red rose in Imogen's cheeks, but the relentless pressure of her power disappeared, and so did the thin layer of ice. Remarkably, it left no traces behind. One moment, it was there. The next, it was gone as if it had never existed. No water stains, no dripping food, nothing. *Yeah, okay, turning someone into a human Popsicle is impressive. It also means I need to watch my ass around her. Great.*

The men retook their seats while Imogen and I continued our stare down.

"Right, so we all know we can handle ourselves, then," Bryan said.

"It appears so," Imogen said and finally looked away.

"Good." Bryan set his arms on the table and leaned in. "Then let's get down to business."

CHAPTER SEVEN

FOR THE NEXT THIRTY MINUTES, safe within the bubble of privacy, we shared facts and our grandstanding took a back seat. I mainly listened as the other three talked. During my brief stint at home, I'd managed to skim the file Sabella gave me and noted the basics of the case, but I hadn't had time to review them in depth. I planned to correct that.

The Delphi project had initiated with Origin and Dr. Kaspar's research. Only after she began sharing her research did LanTech create its own team, and then the race was on. Of LanTech's two-person research team, Chloe Sellares and Neil Pasternak, one was dead and one was missing. The investigation into Chloe's unexplained death remained open but was currently stalled, partially due to the fact that no one could find Neil.

In a disconcerting twist of circumstances, after Lara's death, Origin had also been left with a two-person team that recently dwindled to one—Jonas Gainer's badly burnt body had been found dumped in an alley a few days earlier. The surviving Origin scientist, Dr. Kerri Michaels, was currently being kept under watch by the Trask Family security—headed by Imogen.

Between the questions surrounding Chloe and Jonas's deaths and the disappearance of both Neil and the serum, it was clear there was something more than coincidence at play. We agreed that finding Neil before he joined the list of LanTech's dead should top our to-do list, but to do that would require retracing his last known steps. Although Bryan shared that the Clarkes had already taken that route and found nothing, he did reluctantly agree that it should be done again on the off chance that new eyes might find something that had been missed.

That settled, we turned to Dr. Kerri Michaels, the lone survivor. The fact that she was still breathing triggered a cynical debate about her possible culpability. Things were getting heated when Imogen stated in coldly polite tones that Kerri's initial interview and subsequent background search had provided no indication of involvement. In an equally polite yet frigid voice, Zev pointed out that Kerri was our one and only accessible source at this point, which made our upcoming interview list short and to the point. Bryan and I watched avidly from the sidelines as the other two stared each other down. Finally, Imogen relented and reluctantly agreed that a follow-up interview with her would be added to our action list.

Bryan chose to wade into the volatile undercurrents and redirect the conversation with a reminder that time was of the essence, not just for Neil's well-being but for our overall assignment as well. A decision quickly followed to split into two teams. Fortunately, Bryan chose to partner with Imogen. I wasn't sure who was more grateful, Zev or me. If I hadn't been convinced that Imogen would do her best to screw me, I would have offered to be her partner, as it would ensure that the team's Family obligations were evenly balanced. But no way in hell would I take that chance after witnessing the dirty looks, snide comments, and icy temper tantrum.

We put together a plan. That night, Imogen and Bryan would retrace Neil's steps, something that had been on Bryan's agenda initially. Meanwhile, Zev and I would go through Jonas's house. This arrangement gave us something tangible to do that night while allowing each invested party a chance to retrace previous investigative steps. The next morning, Zev and I would meet with Chloe's parents. Bryan offered to arrange the meet since he was the one working Chloe's case and had already established a relationship with them. Zev accepted, and we finalized our game plan with the intent to find a commonality among the dead, the missing, and the breathing, but it was clear from everyone's grim looks that no one was holding out much hope.

The last of the sun's light was fading from purple to the indigo gray of early evening, and the heat was slowly receding under the incoming night when our dinner meet drew to a close.

"Check in tomorrow?" Bryan asked.

When everyone, including a watchful Zev, turned to me, realization hit—Bryan was talking to me. It was disconcerting, to say the least, but I had a job to do. "Let's touch base by four, see where we're at. If we need to get together then, we can choose a place."

Some of the underlying tension eased. It made me wonder what they'd expected from me. I would ask Zev about that. He was a safer bet than anyone else in the group.

Bryan looked at Imogen, who gave him a nod. "Right." He rapped his knuckles against the table. "If we're done here..."

When he got an assortment of positive responses, he leaned back and got to his feet. His magic swept out like an invisible tide, taking the silence with it. Noise from the surrounding conversations and nearby traffic rushed to fill the void. Once again, no one blinked as we reentered the other customers' reality. The casually deceptive display of Bryan's ability was a stark reminder that I was punching above my weight. It was worrisome, but not enough to have me looking for an escape route. Well, not yet. Life had taught me early on how to survive in a world filled with bigger fish who had sharper teeth. When it came to evading those predators, I wouldn't hesitate to fight dirty because it was my only way of ensuring my survival.

Goodbyes were exchanged and numbers shared to make future communications easier. Well, Bryan said goodbye. Imogen gave Zev a not-so-subtle look as she bade him farewell and pointedly ignored me before following Bryan into the night. Amused at the petty move that screamed jealous ex, I pushed back from my seat and stood. My stiff muscles complained, so I did a spine twist, unlocking the kinks. Then I picked up the plate with my uneaten taco and empty cup to take them to the trash. Next to me Zev rose and did the same. I turned, the movement sending my crumbled napkin rolling across the paper plate. It was stopped by the uneaten taco, which hadn't shifted even the slightest bit.

That's weird.

I adjusted my hold and then poked the taco. The corn tortilla shell shattered like brittle glass and collapsed. Despite the fact that Imogen had blasted it with ice more than a half hour earlier and it then sat undisturbed in the Arizona heat, a chill still emanated from the pieces.

Trepidation stole my breath, and the plate in my hand jerked. "Holy shit." The curse came out in a near whisper.

Zev caught my plate as it wobbled. "Careful."

I looked at him, not caring that my shock was easily read. "It's still frozen."

His dark gaze searched my face, his thoughts hidden. "Imogen didn't get to her position on looks alone, Rory." He didn't wait for my response, just tugged the plate out of my hand and walked it to the trash bin, leaving me staring at his back.

You are so out of your league, girlfriend.

I couldn't afford to forget that. I was starting to wonder if Sabella's belief in me was sorely misguided, because Lena's suspicions about Sabella's true purpose behind my involvement were gaining teeth.

What the hell did I sign up for?

By the time Zev returned, I still hadn't found an answer. We made our way off the patio and toward the street. Even the touch of his hand at my hip as he nudged me ahead of him couldn't drown out my rising worry.

We were waiting at the light to cross the street when he said, "Rory."

I blinked and realized he'd asked me something. "Sorry, what?"

"Do you want to follow me or ride together?" When I simply stared, he added, "To Jonas's address."

Right, the investigation. Before I could answer, the light changed. Together, we crossed the street and headed down the poorly lit sidewalk to where we were parked. "Where does he live?"

"Over by the Reserve." He stepped around what appeared to be a pile of blankets. "It might be a waste of time. The file indicated that nothing out of the ordinary was found there or at his office at Origin."

"But," I said as the lump of blankets moved, revealing one of the many who called the streets home.

"But," Zev agreed, ignoring the street sleeper as he headed toward the lot.

I slowed, dug into my pocket, where I had a twenty stashed for just such an occasion, and stopped to tuck the money into a weathered fist. I returned the gap-toothed grin before catching up to where Zev waited at the lot's entrance.

His gaze shifted from the man huddled in the worn sleeping bag to me. "You do realize that was exactly what he wanted."

"Cynical much?" I strode past him, heading to my car.

He stayed on my ass. "Realistic. If he has friends nearby, you just confirmed that you're worth cornering for more."

"Or I just gave him enough to fill his stomach."

Either way, I wasn't really worried about it. If his friends were foolish enough to come after me, they'd learn better. Not to mention, if they got by me, they'd have to get through Zev, and the outcome of that was almost guaranteed.

"You don't have a very high opinion of people, do you, Zev?"

On dark eyebrow rose. "I only think highly of them if they've earned it."

That reaction was... well, I wasn't sure if it was sad, depressing, or haunting, but it stung. We were almost to my Mustang when the hair on the back of my neck rose in warning, but my magic stayed inert. I stopped, my abrupt move bringing Zev to a halt at my back. Using him to block my movements from anyone watching, I angled a bit to look behind us, but Zev's chest and shoulders were in the way.

"What?" He started to turn his head.

I pressed my hand against his chest. "Shh." I let my gaze drift over the shadows pooling under the weak amber light spilling from the lone pole in the far corner. My hands rose to his shoulders, and I used them for balance as I got on tiptoe. The move let me see behind him, but it also put my mouth close to his ear. "We're being watched."

His hands went to my waist, the heat of them searing through my T-shirt. To anyone watching, we looked as if we were having an intimate moment. Zev lowered his head, his breath falling over the curve where my neck and shoulder met, and my grip on his shoulders tightened.

"We interrupted a deal." His lips brushed my skin as he spoke at a barely audible level. "By the dumpster."

It was a fleeting touch, but it rushed through me with unexpected force. For a moment, I lost my concentration. My lashes fluttered as my body shivered in a reaction that had nothing to do with Zev's magic or mine. With a shaky breath, I angled my head enough to see the bulky shadow of the dumpster perched against the brick wall. Sure enough, the darkness shifted into two huddled figures doing their best to not attract our attention. Since my magic wasn't scrambling in defense, I figured we were safe enough for the moment, but there was no way I was leaving my Mustang there.

I dropped down until my feet were flat against the uneven ground. Zev didn't let me go, so I slid down the front of his body. Mine gave an enthusiastic cheer and clamored for more, all but melting against him. My hands drifted down to rest against his ribs, right between what felt like number six and seven of a possible eight-pack. I tilted my head back and got caught in his glittering stare, my thoughts fracturing for a second before I managed to slap them back together.

"Follow me?" It came out husky.

That glitter in his dark gaze got brighter, and the fingers at my waist dug in then relaxed. "Where?"

At his question, it hit me that our exchange could be interrupted on multiple levels, but I shook off the ill-timed thought. "The Guild. I'm not leaving my car here."

His head dipped, and then his mouth brushed mine with a fleeting touch that sparked a cascading storm. Before I could tumble into it, he drew back and let me go. "Probably for the best." Despite the grit in his voice and the gleam in his eyes, he stepped back.

The minute breathing room gave me a chance to gather

my composure, I, too, stepped back, but not before I snuck in a quick stroke over those abs. His soft inhalation was barely discernible. My hands curled into fists, holding tight to the faint sensation of muscles flexing in reaction. "Right. So let's hit the Guild, I'll drop off my car, and then we can ride over to Jonas's."

I dug my keys out of my pocket and then disarmed both the alarm and wards before Zev moved to his bike. I turned on my heel and got my door open, dropping into my baby. I pulled out of the lot with Zev on my ass. Then I spent the entire fifteen-minute trip to the Guild giving myself a stern talking-to. Unfortunately, it didn't do me much good. By the time I pulled into the garage and parked, the part of me inexorably drawn to Zev was pouting and defiant, while my more practical side was shaking its head in exasperation.

Zev pulled up alongside me, the throaty rumble of his bike filling the near-empty garage with a bone-rattling sound. I locked my car and headed over. He was twisted in his seat and bent over the side of his bike. When he straightened, his black helmet with its equally dark face shield turned to me.

It was the only warning I got before he tossed something at me. I caught it and realized it was another helmet. Only under the light could you tell it was a deep blue, so deep that it appeared black. I put it on as I got close to his Harley. It was a beautiful beast in matte black, made to intimidate. Much like the rider driving it. Together, they painted a stunning picture that kick-started more than my rebellious hunger.

I got on, tucking in close, my thighs bracketing his hips and my arms sliding around his waist. His scent, an enticing mix of sandalwood and male, left my recently lectured hormones cheering. My practical side threw up its hands in defeat and stomped away in disgust. The position of the pillion seat was just high enough for me to see over Zev's shoulders, even pressed up against his spine.

The click of a mic was the only warning I had before Zev's voice curled through the helmet's built-in speakers. "Ready?"

"Yep."

Taking me at my word, he rocketed out of the garage. There was an art to riding pillion on a bike, one that required trust that the person driving wouldn't splatter you all over the road. I had no problem giving Zev that kind of trust.

As he sped through the night-slicked streets, I could feel my face stretch in a teeth-baring grin. Zev might not be a Transporter, but it was clear he was one with his bike. Riding with him was exhilarating, and the only way it could be even better would be if I were driving. I was pretty sure that wouldn't be happening, so I settled in and enjoyed the ride.

Caught up in the leashed power of the bike and the rider, I let that innate ability that made me a Transporter flare to life. Magic and speed wove together until moving with Zev was as natural as breathing. Time slipped away. Attuned, I closed my eyes in pure bliss and trusted Zev to get us where we needed to be.

All too soon, Zev slowed. I forced my eyes open to see that we'd hit a neighborhood. As our speed eased, so did my magic until it was tucked away and that unique sense of connection dissolved into nothing but memory. Now that we were no longer racing the night, it was safe enough to unwind my arms and sit up. Before I could let go, Zev caught my hand. Heeding his silent request, I kept my hands on his hips, my chest to his spine.

He made a few turns taking us deeper into the quiet neighborhood. While the street was veined with the lines of patched asphalt common to older neighborhoods, the ranch houses all showed signs of proud ownership. I loved neighborhoods like this. They were reminiscent of simpler times, when residents weren't sitting on top of their neighbors or trying to squeeze mini-mansions into lots meant for modest homes. Homes sat back from large front yards, guarding decently sized backyards. I was pretty sure no one was overly concerned with a homeowner's association here, but still, no one parked on the street. The driveways were filled with SUVs, sedans, and vans. Not exactly the scene I pictured for a single male who pulled in good money doing research for Origin.

The growl of Zev's bike caused a couple of dogs to respond, but that was the extent of our passage. He pulled into the driveway of one of the smaller brick-faced ranch homes, triggering a security light. He stopped the bike in front of the narrow carport tucked on the side. A color-filled planter sat in front of a low brick wall that divided the home from the street. When Zev pulled off his helmet, I did the same and handed it over. He locked them to the bikes and led the way around the front. Following the walkway sandwiched between another brick planter and the home's blue shuttered windows, we slipped by the darkened front window and the bistro set.

Unconcerned with curious neighbors or potential security, Zev pulled open a wrought-iron security door. A muted set of beeps broke the quiet, and then he was stepping inside. I followed him in as he flicked on the light in the entryway.

I was turning to close the door when what lay just beyond the entryway in the living room to the right came together. I paused with my hand on the door. We were not the first visitors. "Wasn't the alarm on?"

"Yeah."

"Uh. Weird." Although it hadn't been much of a deterrent for whoever had come before, I closed the front door.

Zev only grunted and moved to the edge of the living

room. He used his foot to nudge aside a broken frame, revealing the cracked tile underneath. Broken glass scraped across the hard floor.

I went to stand next to him as he studied the rampant destruction. "Must be the housekeeper's year off."

"More like someone had a hell of tantrum."

Deep scratches marred the polished wood of the built-in shelves surrounding the torn-up drywall where the TV probably once sat. Now the television was facedown on the floor, cracks visible in the plastic back. A couple of the top shelves were crooked and barely holding on, but the rest were mixed in with the wreckage strewn across the floor. I looked at what remained of the shelves. It was almost as if someone had come through and cleared them in one brutal swipe, leaving behind broken piles of debris.

The furniture hadn't fared much better. The couch and cushioned chair looked as if massive claws had gone digging for gold. Stuffing from both pieces was scattered throughout, and tattered material hung on cracked wooden frames.

Oddly, the mess appeared to be more for destruction's sake than an actual search. Still, I couldn't stop myself from asking, "What were they looking for?"

"Same thing as us, probably. Whatever they could find." Zev kicked the debris that had spilled over into the hall that led farther into the house, clearing a path. "Come on."

I followed, picking my way through the mess. A repulsive smell crawled its way down my throat, growing stronger as we approached the kitchen. "You think they found anything?"

Zev stopped where the kitchen opened to the hall. He turned his head toward me, his nose wrinkled. "Hard to tell, but we're going to check through this mess anyway."

Oh joy.

The kitchen was a putrid mess that matched the devastation in the front room. One of the two fridge doors hung crooked, the contents spilling out into a nauseating jumble on the floor, clearly the origin of the suffocating stench. "Ugh!" I slapped my hand over my nose and breathed through my mouth in an effort not to lose my tacos. "I'm going to go over there." I motioned down the hall, desperate to get away from the smell.

I left Zev behind and headed farther in. The hall was strangely untouched, and as I worked my way back through the bathroom and two bedrooms, it was like walking backward through a progressively frustrated search. There was a violence to the destruction in the kitchen and living room that didn't exist in the back bedrooms. The farthest room, which also happened to be the smallest, was the office. There was no computer on the desk, and I assumed it had been taken, most likely with the initial search instigated by the Trasks.

I moved to the leather chair behind the uncluttered desk, sat down, and started pulling out drawers to rifle through the contents. When Zev's presence hit the doorway, I spoke without looking up. "Was there anything in the file about what was on Jonas's computer?"

"Did you not read it?"

Ignoring his note of censure, I said blandly, "Sabella gave it to me just before the meeting. I haven't had time to study the details."

"No, his computer came up clean."

Okay, moving on. "How possible is it that whoever was here before us found something?"

"Hard to tell, but considering the escalating destruction, I'm thinking they didn't find anything either."

I looked up as he moved to the two-drawer filing cabinet topped by a printer and a half-dead plant. "So, what? Third time's the charm?"

"Something like that." He opened a drawer and began

rummaging through the files. "According to Imogen, lab protocol required Jonas's notes to be stored on Origin's local network under high-priority security. When they examined those notes, there was nothing unusual or unexpected in them."

"And you think he'd keep information like that here?" I tugged on the bottom drawer, and it only opened a couple of inches. It was stuffed with papers.

He half turned from the file drawers and motioned back toward the front of the house. "Obviously, we're not the only ones who considered that."

"Why would he do that?" I yanked on the stuck drawer, but all that gained me was a sharp screech of wood. I tried again, and this time, I earned a few more inches. When I realized that Zev still hadn't responded, I looked up.

He had a file in his hands and was frowning, not at the file but at me. "Because I'm willing to bet both research teams crossed more lines than they're admitting."

Well, at least we were on the same page there. "No doubt, but so far, Origin is the only one admitting to creating a possible serum." I started fighting the stubborn drawer, determined to get it open.

"I don't think Trask was the only one with the serum."

"What? Do you think the teams were working together?" At his silence, I looked up to find him still frowning at me, his face dark.

When my gaze hit his, the forbidding look eased, and his lips twitched. "Why do you say that like it's hard to believe?"

I gave the stupid drawer one last hard yank, and it finally gave up the fight. "Because LanTech and Origin were so keen on one-upping each other that they risked everything by going after Jeremy, even knowing the Cordovas wouldn't forgive or forget." I shook my head and began flipping through papers, skimming them for anything noteworthy.

They were frustratingly mundane, a mix of billing statements and random correspondence, nothing that screamed top secret lab information. "Besides, even today at the meeting, it was clear there's no love lost between Leander and Stephen."

"So? You think that because they hate each other, it would stop them from working together on something that would set them up for life even as it fundamentally shifted the existing status quo?" He folded his arms. "Especially if they controlled the serum that created that shift?"

I sat in the chair and studied him. "But the council said that anything resulting from Lara's research belongs to the Cordovas."

His eyebrows rose. "Rory, if they created a serum that could either restrain or boost magic of any mage, what would stop them from using that against the council to get what they wanted?"

"The rest of our society wouldn't stand by for that."

"Wouldn't they?" The way he asked the question left me feeling foolishly naive. Before I could respond, he turned back to the drawer, thumbing through the files before continuing with a ruthless practicality. "If they had access to a weapon that would bring down even the most powerful, why wouldn't they risk it?"

Zev pulled out a file and flipped through it. He had a point, even if I didn't want to admit it, which sucked big-time. Zev was crushing all my altruistic hopes for humanity under his cynical boot heel.

"Is this how things work when it comes to Families?" I asked, thinking I might have to seriously reconsider my future, maybe look into finding a tiny island somewhere to hunker down until this storm passed.

He put the file back, shoved the drawer closed, and went to the next one. "Maybe not all, but in this case, when it comes to the Trasks and the Clarkes, definitely."

I scrunched my nose and shoved at the sticky drawer. It barely moved. "That's depressing."

"That's life."

"Still depressing." I kicked the bottom drawer in frustration and left it. "There's enough paper here that we could be going through these files forever." It was a mind-numbing thought.

Zev left the filing cabinet and moved to the shelves, stepping carefully around the handful of books on the floor. "Yeah, I think this is a dead end."

I sat back in the chair. "Well, it's safe to assume one thing."

Zev looked over his shoulder. "What's that?"

"Jonas knew something."

"I think the fact that he was turned into a crispy critter was proof of that."

Yeah, that's definitely telling. Something from the Prism's journal teased my mind. I reached for it, but it slipped away. "What about Jonas's body?"

"What about it?"

"Anything on it? Wounds? Signs? Magical traces?" As soon as I asked the last, that memory drifted back. There had been a brief entry about how the Prism had been able to pick up lingering traces of a broken spell on a dead man. I'd need to go back and reread it to see if there was a chance that I could pick up something the coroner couldn't. *I have to try, right?*

Zev turned and braced his shoulder against the edge of the shelves, his brow furrowed in thought. "The autopsy report didn't indicate anything unusual."

I took my first deliberate step out of my safe little box. "You think we could get in to see it?"

He studied me, his dark eyes unreadable. "Maybe. You want to share why you want to see him?"

I tried to shrug, but it felt awkward. "We're going back over everything, so why not that as well?"

"Because that's an image I'm not sure you want to carry."

An unexpected warmth blossomed as I recognized that he was trying to protect me. *People don't protect things that don't matter, right?* "I think it's necessary."

"I'll set it up under one condition." He left the bookcase and came over to the desk.

I waited.

"You tell me the real reason why you need this."

Unable to look away, I knew I'd have to give in order to get. "I'll tell you if it works."

He held my gaze, and it was a long moment before he finally nodded.

I wasn't sure if it was relief or nerves that made me happy I was sitting, not that it mattered. "Right, then. I think we can call this a bust." I pushed up from the chair and rounded the desk. I didn't get far because Zev stood in my path, refusing to move. I stopped in front of him and decided to go on the offensive. "What?"

He stared down at me for a long moment, his thoughts hidden. "I hope you know what you're doing, babe."

I swallowed at the thread of concern I heard and hoped so too.

CHAPTER EIGHT

I WALKED out the door and back into the warm night, leaving Zev to reset the alarm, even though it was obviously a pointless deterrent. I was halfway down the walk when I lost the sound of his footsteps. I turned to see him looking at his phone. "What is it?"

"Bryan." His fingers flew over the screen. "We have a nine o'clock appointment with Chloe's parents tomorrow morning." In my back pocket, my phone vibrated. "I just sent you the address."

"Thanks." I waited until he started forward again then led the way back to his bike. "Now what?"

When we were standing next to his bike he said, "Now, you and I are going to finish our conversation from earlier." He unlocked the helmets and handed me one.

I considered my options as I took the helmet, my movements automatic as I put it on and secured it. I wasn't sure this was the right time to discuss what had happened between us and his lack of follow-through, but then again, when would be? He got his helmet on, swung onto his bike, fired it up, and walked it back. Once he'd it aimed down the drive, I hopped on and wrapped my arms around his waist. Since there was no nice way to start our conversation, I stayed quiet while he headed out of the neighborhood.

"You have every right to be pissed," he said, his deep voice filling the helmet's speakers in toe-curling stereo. "But I wasn't blowing you off."

My knee-jerk reaction was a snarky, *Yeah, right*, but I didn't say it out loud. I was way past an age when that would have been a logical response. Besides, truthfully, I wasn't angry with him so much as disappointed. But arguing semantics on a speeding bike didn't seem smart.

"I'm not pissed."

"Aren't you?"

"No," I said. And because the helmet offered an illusion of distance, which made it feel safe to risk being bluntly honest, I decided to go for broke. "Disappointed, yeah, but not pissed." I should have stopped there, but in full-on maturity mode, I kept sharing. "Honestly, I kind of expected it." And I had, just maybe not for the reasons he expected.

He jerked, and against my chest, his spine turned into a rod of steel. "What the hell, Rory?" he said sharply. "You think I'm that big of a dick?"

Okay, maybe being mature is overrated. The rock-solid path underfoot just turned spongy. I fought the urge to squirm. "I never thought you were a dick, Zev."

"But...?" he snapped.

Dammit, I knew this was a bad idea. But it was obvious he was determined to go there, so I went along, because if we didn't clear this up, it could impact both the investigation and the team dynamics and not in a good way. "But you made me an offer. It's clear that you didn't expect me to take you up on it. When I did..." I trailed off, letting him fill in the blanks.

A muttered curse echoed through the helmet. "So you thought what? One kiss was enough, even though it damn near gelded me to leave? Or that once I had time to think about getting involved with you, I decided you weren't worth it?"

Wow, okay, then. Instead of focusing on the little kernel of beauty buried in what he'd said, I concentrated on the note of hurt in his voice. I had to admit it sounded shitty when laid out like that, but it was hard to deny the underlying truth. Whether I liked it or not, that insecurity existed in me. What he'd said was scarily close to what I thought.

I didn't want to answer, but in keeping with my promise of no games, I cleared the lump from my throat and mumbled, "Something like that."

A minute passed as we rode through the pools of amber light thrown by the streetlamps above, both of us far from relaxed. We swept through an intersection and he slowed, easing to the right and turning into a dimly lit parking lot in front of a closed grocery store. He parked the bike at the far end, away from the scattered cars and out of the path of any wandering late-night customers. I unwrapped my arms from around his waist and sat back as he braced his feet against the pavement and turned off the bike. Still sitting on the bike, he yanked off his helmet and hooked it on a grip.

I carefully removed my helmet so I could hear him and eyed his stiff back warily. "Zev?" I said, my voice small and quiet. "What are we doing?"

Instead of answering, he reached back. "Helmet."

I handed it over. He hung it next to his, then he reached back and grabbed my hand. I curled my fingers into his as he swung off the bike. Despite the humming tension between us, he gently pulled me with him until I followed. When we were both standing, he used his grip to tug me close. He didn't let my hand go. Instead, he pressed it flat against his waist. Off-kilter, I put my free hand on his chest. Under the soft cotton, his heart beat steadily against my palm. I tilted my head back to find him watching me, his expression a mix of frustration and hunger. His hands went to my hips and held tight, keeping me pressed against him. My body melted without my permission.

"Three weeks, Rory."

I blinked at the low, rough rasp of his voice.

"For three weeks, I've thought about you and what you're hiding." I opened my mouth to protest but he talked over me. "I've been doing my damnedest to get free of my obligations so I can make time for you," he growled. "After hauling in Theo Mahon and dealing with the fallout from the Thatcher fiasco, I got hit with this mess. I meant what I said—I wanted to call you. Thing is, I didn't think it would be fair to call only to have to hang up minutes later."

Trepidation and joy speared through me, but reality kicked in, and so did caution. "I would've taken a couple of minutes if that's what you had to offer, Zev."

"I get that." His gaze held steady. "But first, you're hiding something from me, something that scares you shitless. I can tell you to trust me, but you won't do it because, trite though it is, trust comes with time. Time I wanted to spend with you but just didn't have. So when you walked into that room today, I was fucking thrilled because it meant you would be part of whatever this was with me. Not an ideal way to pursue things, but right now, I'll take it."

If it hadn't been for this investigation, I would have imitated a monkey and wrapped myself around him after that little spiel. "Um, I'm not sure we can." When he frowned, I added, "I'm supposed to be the neutral party here, and if we start things now, questions will be asked, valid questions."

He didn't rush to answer. Instead, he took his time to think, which I appreciated, so I waited even as worry crept in. Finally, he said, "I get that you're establishing your reputation, and working with Sabella is key to ensuring that."

"It is," I agreed, not sure where he was going with this.

One of his hands left my waist. He brushed a finger along my jaw. "I respect that this job is important to you, but I'm not willing to miss out on whatever this is between us. So I have an offer for you."

Half-mesmerized by that delicate touch, I murmured, "I'm listening."

Amusement lightened his eyes, and his lips curved up the tiniest bit. "Starting tomorrow, when we meet to go see the Sellareses, we'll keep things professional."

"Okay." I drew the word out because clearly I was missing something.

His amused expression deepened, but his voice remained serious. "After this case is done, all bets are off, and we see where this leads."

I wanted to jump all over it and opened my mouth to do just that, only to close it as logic interrupted. This assignment, this position that Sabella had put me in, was tricky as hell, and Zev and I were bound to butt heads. Not to mention the little fact that I was hiding what I was. Based on our past interactions, that omission was going to bite me in the ass and maybe leave my heart broken.

"Zev, I..."

His finger left my face as he dropped his hand to mine and squeezed. "Take a risk, Rory."

He had no idea what he was asking, but his pull was strong enough to drag me under. "Yes."

"Good." He brought my hand up and pressed a hot, open-mouthed kiss against my palm.

"Zev." My protest was faint, mainly because I could barely speak past the hungry need that erupted. "That's not professional." We were standing so close that I felt, more than heard, his huff of laughter.

"I said, starting tomorrow." A wicked smile broke free.

"Tonight, it's just you and me. I want to spend time with you."

Hearing him say that eased the sting of three weeks of silence. I gave in to temptation and cupped his jaw, indulging in the skin-shivering rasp of his close-cropped beard against my palm. I wanted so badly to throw responsibility to the wind and drag him to the nearest flat surface, but I couldn't.

His dark chuckle indicated that he read my desire loud and clear. "Not like that. Something that won't get us in trouble."

Right, and that would be what? I fought through the haze of anticipation and need in search of something safe we could do that wouldn't end up with us sprawled on a flat surface in a tangle of limbs. A half-formed idea came to me. "Ever watch a night race?"

"How is that staying out of trouble? Those aren't exactly legal."

He was right, but the one I had in mind would serve a dual purpose. "First, this one skims that line, as it's outside city limits and is by invitation only."

His amusement was replaced by speculation. "You driving?"

I shook my head. "Not this time."

"And second?"

"Second, it's a long shot, but it might help with the case."

"How?"

And here's where I could lose him. Arbiters were used to working within the back rooms and halls of the Arcane Families, not down in the streets, where power wasn't decided by magic and money but by might and fists. My idea had sparked during our discussion at dinner, but I hadn't felt comfortable mentioning it, mainly because my investigative experience was laughable when compared to the three Arbiters. But if Zev meant what he said about getting to know me...

Be honest, Rory—it's a test.

I dropped my gaze to hide my wince. That chiding internal voice was partly right. It was a test of sorts, but it was also a good place to cull for clues. Night races were a hotbed of gossip—not just discussions of who was sleeping with whom but talk about what was going down in the streets as well. A couple of the regulars were more in the know than others, and if we were lucky, we might run into them.

Without looking at Zev, I said, "This crowd is eclectic enough that we might hear things, like, maybe about a new drug, one that offers a magical boost."

He didn't say anything for a long moment. When I finally looked up, he held my gaze and said, "You're thinking someone might have taken the serum to the streets."

I managed a half-hearted shrug. "It's not much of a stretch."

"Maybe, maybe not," he said absentmindedly as if still thinking things through.

I wasn't sure what was holding him back from making that connection. "Look, I think it's safe to assume that whoever is behind this needs to know how it works on something other than lab animals, right? Especially if they're trying to upset the status quo. What better way to prove their threat has teeth than by making an initial run on those no one will notice but who will still create visible results?"

Headlights swept over us as someone pulled out of a parking spot and headed toward the entrance. Zev watched them leave, and I watched him, easily reading the doubt in his face. I tried to douse my disappointment. "I told you it was a long shot."

When he turned back to me, he said, "I'm not sure I agree with your assessment, but if there's a chance you're right, it can't hurt."

It wasn't a glowing endorsement of my deductive skills,

but I'd take it. "Good." I patted his chest and stepped back. "Don't worry, I won't let anyone give you a hard time." I pulled my phone out of my pocket and turned to his bike. "I'll pull up the route and see how long it's going to take us to get there."

He stayed at my back, his arm reaching around me to the helmets. "Don't make me sound like a condescending ass." He pulled mine off and handed it over.

Holding my phone in one hand, I took the helmet with the other. "But you do it so well."

With both hands full, I was left wide-open for his sneak attack. His hands were at my waist, spinning me around, and before I could blink, he gave me a hard kiss. It was brief but carried a hell of a punch.

When he lifted his head, I read frustration, exasperation, and wry amusement in his expression. "I wasn't trying to downplay your concern. It's just that I'm not sure our target would think along those lines."

Granted, being a villain wasn't my natural inclination, but doing a test run with the serum seemed to me like a fairly straightforward evil action. "Why not?"

"Because there's the flip side of taking the serum to the streets. Say they did use it and it worked. Think about the havoc that would create. Word of something like that would've spread like wildfire." He let me go and got his helmet.

"Not this soon," I pointed out. "Jonas's death and the stolen vials was—what, a few days ago? If they go with the street-run test, they would've only had the last day or so to make it work. Which means any unusual occurrence would be hours old. Too recent to make its way above street level."

He paused in the midst of putting on his helmet and gave a grunt. "I hadn't thought of that."

I flashed him a grin. "That's why I'm here. To make sure you don't miss anything."

His grin disappeared behind his helmet.

I tucked my phone into my pocket, freeing my hands so I could get my helmet on. Head shield in place, I retrieved my phone, got behind Zev, and then pulled up the race's location from memory. Zev kicked the bike to life as the map scrolled across the screen.

Noting the travel time, I wondered if Zev would be willing to switch seats as I could definitely cut that time in half. A hysterical image of Zev sitting bitch made me snort. *Yeah, that will happen—never.* To be heard over the bike's rumble, I triggered the in-helmet speakers. "It's going take a couple hours to get out there."

"Send it to me."

I did as he asked, and while he set up his GPS, I put my phone away then wrapped my arms around his waist. It took us about fifteen minutes to get clear of the residential streets before we hit the highway that would take us out beyond the suburbs and edged along the pristine desert beauty that belonged to the First Nations. If history had gotten anything right, it was leaving swaths of untamed lands to those who valued both its natural and cultural gifts. Not that the original Arcane Family settlers had much choice, since they'd landed on the shores of a land already claimed by the First Nations. Those families were quick to recognize how vital the First Nations people were to their continued existence and set a solid groundwork that meant that hundreds of years later, the two powerful cultures were able to coexist peacefully for the most part. Not to say there wasn't friction between them, but wielding almost equal power, magically and politically, kept the two groups from tipping the scales too far in any one direction. It also meant that the Traditionalists, those who possessed little to no magic, were caught in the unenviable middle.

Moonlight soon replaced streetlights, and the farther out we went, the less traffic there was until it was just us and the road. As the ride smoothed out, I eased my hold on Zev and sat back, leaving my hands on his hips. If it had just been me, I would have forgone the helmet in favor of feeling the wind in my hair, but this was Zev's bike, which meant respecting Zev's rules. There was nothing in the world like being behind the wheel of a finely crafted car built for speed, but it didn't provide the same visceral rush that existed when it was just me and a bike. Although I had to say, sharing it with Zev was a thrill in itself.

"So tell me something." Caught in the helmet's confines, his voice surrounded me with an illusory intimacy.

"Something," I said. When his laugh filled my ears, I couldn't have stopped my grin if I wanted to. "What do you want me to tell you?"

"How often do you do this?"

"This what? Chase down murdering madmen or go for a ride with a dangerous man?"

"Is that what I am?"

"As if you need reassurance."

He gave another dark chuckle. "Neither of the above. I meant racing."

Ah, this must be part of his get-to-know-me quest. "When I can. Generally, I stick to those races that are less likely to require bail or an overnight stay in lockup."

"Like this one?"

"Yep, like this one. Races like this are set up by private, anonymous sponsors. They deliberately choose spots that tend to be in the middle of nowhere, which lessens the chance of legal interference."

"And the invitation-only part?"

"Invites are based on reputations. The better your driving reputation is, the more likely you are to receive one." Unlike typical street races, which were all about showing off shiny decked-out rides and thumping chests, night races were more about people pitting their skills against equally skilled others.

"So you're not in it just for the glory of saying you're the best."

Catching the sardonic note in his voice, I laughed. "Partially, but it's also for the money."

"Were you ever caught?"

Hypersensitive to potential judgment, I was relieved to hear only curiosity in his question. "Once or twice when I was younger. It didn't take me long to figure out how not to repeat that experience."

"And your family was okay with this?"

I paused. If he was real about his intentions, it was time for me to open the door and let him in. "I lost my family when I was young and basically grew up in shelters and group homes. Being out past curfew was kind of a time-honored tradition. By the time I joined the Arcane Guild, I knew how to evade the cops."

"But you didn't stop racing."

"Is that a question?"

"No. I'm thinking that expecting a Transporter not to race is like expecting a combat mage not to fight."

I had to chuckle because his assessment was spot-on. "No, I didn't stop racing—I just got choosier about which races I accepted. The Guild doesn't do sides, so it had no problem with me racing so long as I didn't get caught."

"Because getting caught—"

"Was bad for business," I finished.

The Guild's members couldn't care less which side of the line people stood on, so long as they upheld their end of the contract and paid for services rendered. It was all about business, after all. That straightforward simplicity had held tons of appeal to a preteen used to running wild on the streets. An appeal that hadn't faded until I grew older and wiser.

"Did you always want to work for the Guild?" Zev asked.

Truthfully, the answer was no. But as soon as I realized I had an ability no one spoke about, I knew my survival would hinge on cultivating skills that could hide me in plain sight. Since admitting that would lead to questions I wasn't ready to answer, I stuck with, "As soon as I realized they were my best chance at honing my skills, yes." Needing to get off this treacherous path, I turned his question around. "Did you always want to be an Arbiter?"

It was his turn to pause. "I'm not sure you can call it a choice."

I wondered if the hint of wistfulness I heard was simply my imagination. "Why's that?"

"Being an Arbiter was kind of a given. Not only did I grow up alongside Emilio and his brother, Alan, but my skills are also a natural fit for the role."

I remembered how Emilio's nephew Jeremy had called Zev uncle, and knowing that being a Family's dark horse meant dealing with problems in the most direct, generally lethal, way made my heart ache for him just a bit. It couldn't be easy finding that delicate balance between love and duty. "It must be difficult."

"Difficult?"

"Being both feared and loved."

He was quiet for long enough that I worried I'd way overstepped my bounds. I was gathering up the courage to apologize when his low voice came through the speakers. "Yeah, it is."

There was a darkness in his admission that hurt to hear, and before I could rethink, I leaned forward and hugged him, offering what comfort I could. "It's good they have you."

Before things could shift to awkward, I let go and sat back, forcing my voice to lighten. "All right, so before we hit the race, a couple of ground rules."

"Rules?"

Grateful that he was following my lead, I said, "Yep. You just maintain your dark and moody persona and let me do the talking."

"Who are you calling moody?"

Even though he couldn't see me, I rolled my eyes. "If you go in being all you, everyone will shut up tighter than an over-torqued spark plug. We need gossip. You are definitely not the gossiping type."

"And you are?"

"Nope," I answered cheerfully. "But I'm a known face, so casual conversation is a given." I raced through a couple of possible approaches before settling on what would hopefully be the easiest one for him to pull off. "You are going to be Felix, a visiting Hound out of California with a side interest in racing." Hounds were the retrieval specialists for the Guild, which would explain his presence at my side. Hounds and Transporters tended to gravitate toward each other thanks to the nature of their assignments, and it was a role that would best explain Zev's intimidating aura.

"No last name?"

"No one uses last names at these events, and when they do, ninety percent of them are fake."

"But not yours."

"No," I said, ignoring the unhappy vibe in his comment. "Not mine." After all, I had a reputation to maintain, and in the racing crowd, everyone recognized my name.

CHAPTER NINE

It was just after midnight when the dirt road we had followed for the last few miles ended in a flat section of desert filled with an eclectic mix of vehicles gathered in a rough oval. The darker shades of cliffs formed a horseshoe ring around the area. I had Zev park near the far side, away from the milling figures lit by the glow of bonfires and headlights. Dust and smoke filled the air, turning it hazy. Laughter, high and bright, joined the competing strands of hypnotic drumbeats and heavy bass from someone's window-rattling sound system. While a party was obviously in full swing, my goal was to get beyond the edge of the shadowed figures and over to where the drivers were gathered.

As we made our way through the gyrating bodies, Zev garnered plenty of attention, mostly female. *Big surprise.* Sweating beer bottles were thrust into our hands. I passed mine off to a gray-bearded, barrel-chested man in a heated debate about forced induction versus naturally aspirated. Past experience indicated that the discussion would graduate to the pros and cons of supercharged versus turbocharged soon.

We emerged from the motley mix of spectators and

crossed to the quieter area where firelight danced over the carefully crafted pieces of motorized art that housed the type of horsepower that made people like me drool. Unlike the races that occurred on city streets, the drivers were shooting the shit despite the rising tide of adrenaline as the start time for the upcoming races ticked closer. Caught between the crowd and the cliffs was an empty swath of desert punctuated by flickering bonfires set at intervals. Familiar with how these races played out, I knew those burning lights followed the predetermined route of the course. At the farthest point, the only way spectators would be able to identify drivers would be by their taillights.

"Rory!"

I turned to find a familiar face making its way toward me. "Gunnar." I smiled and returned the bone-rattling hug from the wiry blond scarecrow. "You racing or watching?"

"Racing, darlin'. Got my seats coming in for the sixty-eight, and they're wiping out my reserve."

Hence the need for a quick kitty. Gunnar was in the midst of rebuilding a 1968 Chevy Impala, and customizing the interior took a lot of cash. If I hadn't been such a Mustang loyalist, his royal purple beauty would have tempted me to dip into my savings.

Gunnar looked at the cars lining up at the starting point behind me. "Where's your baby, girl? I'm looking forward to seeing how those modifications of yours turned out."

I patted his arm. "Sorry, my man, but you're out of luck. I'm just watching tonight."

True disappointment dimmed his face. "Seriously?"

"Seriously."

His gaze flicked to Zev and bounced back to me. "What's with your shadow?"

"Colleague from California. He was bored and wanted to check out the race."

Gunnar lifted his chin at Zev. "Dude."

Zev returned the chin lift and stayed silent.

"So who's racing tonight?" I listened to Gunnar go through the roster with half an ear as I surreptitiously studied the undulating crowd. I spotted a couple of faces I knew, a handful of recognizable repeat attendees, but the majority were unknowns, which, for an event like this, was par for the course.

"Right." Gunner squeezed my arm. "Wish me luck. I'm heading in."

Rising on tiptoe, I pressed a brief kiss against his stubbled cheek. "Leave 'em in the dust."

Gunnar gave me his mad grin, his eyes alight with excitement, and jogged toward the cluster of drivers gathered near the starting point.

Zev closed in until I could feel his heat along my spine. Without looking at him, I said, "Come on. I'm going to go place a bet."

"On him?" Zev kept his voice low so it stayed between us.

I gave a short headshake. "As much as I love the guy, Wheelz will squeeze him out on the last curve, which means he'll dominate the fast line on the last section."

Zev stayed at my back as I made my way to a heavily tattooed woman perched on a camp table, making book. "Give me one on Wheelz, Em."

Em looked up, her teeth overly white in her tanned face. "Rory, how's it going?" Her gaze flicked to my unusually bare hands. I wasn't wearing my driving gloves. "Not driving?"

"Nope." I propped my booted foot on the seat next to her and dug out the emergency hundred I had tucked inside. "Just enjoying the action tonight." I handed the bill over.

It disappeared into the glowing can at Em's hip. "Better move it if you want a good spot, then." She handed over the blue poker chip that served as a betting slip.

The buzz of magic reverberated against my fingers as I took the clay chip. I ignored the simple charm meant to identify the holder once the race results were in. There was nothing harmful about it, unlike the spell wrapped around the collection can, making it glow like a night-light. *Reach for that, and you'll pull back burnt nubs instead of fingers.* I dropped the chip into my pocket.

Bet placed, I meandered through the spectators with Zev at my side. I exchanged greetings with a few known faces and engaged in a couple of casual conversations as I kept one ear on nearby discussions. We worked our way to the far side, my preferred viewing point, as that final rush down the straight-away tended to be the most exciting. If I couldn't feed my cravings by driving, at least I could do it vicariously. A sharp whistle caught my attention. I looked over and saw a heavily tattooed arm waving in my direction from the back of a lifted truck. Recognizing the black-and-white Mohawk and colorful ink, I took Zev's hand and began tugging him behind me as I made my way over. By the time we made it to the truck, the rising rumble of revving engines began to fill the night.

Light and shadows played over the vibrant canvas of tattoos covering the gold-skinned arm extended toward me. "Get up before you miss the takeoff." The words were barely discernible under the rising growls of the revving engines.

I grabbed hold just above the wrist, where a tangle of leather was wrapped, noting the blue cast on the other arm. "Hey, Umber," I said. Zev's hands curled around my hips, and between the two men, I was hauled up to the bed of the truck. I moved out of the way, giving Zev room to follow. I motioned to Umber's cast. "What happened?"

He stepped back, elbowing a couple of the other occupants in the truck's bed, forcing them to make room near the wheel well. "Weird story."

"I like weird stories."

Umber laughed and hooked his arm, cast and all, around the hips of the curly-haired young woman perched on the elevated hump of the wheel well. He tugged her against his chest and motioned to the open space next to her. "Hop up, short stuff."

Since I wanted to see the race and not the back of spectator heads, I hopped up. "Hey, Liv."

"Heya, Rory." Light danced off Liv's glasses, and she grinned as she lifted her drink. Unlike Umber, her skin was artwork-free and so pale it almost glowed. "Who's your friend?"

"This is Felix." I felt Zev move in behind me, his hands going to my hips, the heat he naturally generated a solid wall along my back. "He's in from California." As much as I appreciated his additional support—the wheel well wasn't that wide—his nearness was also creating a distracting amount of havoc with my libido.

Liv and Umber both greeted Zev as the music cut out, leaving behind the rumble of engines. Then a smattering of cheers broke out, indicating the race was about to start. I angled so Zev could see but didn't take my eyes off the starting point. This first race was all about the small tires, and Wheelz's ride skated just under the parameters. Eight cars, ranging from classic souped-up muscle to sleek-lined tricked-out modern racers, crouched at the line. Since this wasn't a traditional street race, where the invitation to race and acceptance hinged on the flashing of headlights, tonight's signal was a short triple blast from an air horn. Dust choked the air as the cars leapt forward before the last bleat faded.

The crowd roared, and I added my voice, my attention focused on the drivers jockeying for position. Wheelz's distinctive fluorescent-orange paint job made it easy to keep track of his progress. He deftly maneuvered his customized Dodge Hellraiser around the smaller frame of an older Toyota

Supra and took up an inside position by Gunnar's customized Honda Civic. I kept my eyes on Gunnar and Wheelz as they pulled ahead of the others. Their taillights blurred as they hit the far curve then winked out, only to be replaced by the glow of headlights as they came out into the end stretch. My heart pounded, and caught up in the excitement, I was screaming with the rest as Gunnar and Wheelz went nose to nose and blurred past us. I leaned over, trying to see the two battle it out and hit the last section. Zev's hold on my waist was the only thing keeping me from toppling to the ground. When Gunnar's brake lights sparked, I knew Wheelz had the victory. Sure enough, the crowd at the finish line went wild as the Hellraiser scorched over the line, leaving the Civic in a cloud of dust.

I threw my head back, raised my arms, and did a little celebratory dance. "Yes!" I spun around and caught Zev's face in my hands and took his mouth in a kiss. Heat and his unique taste hit my tongue and set up an achy burn. Before it could suck me in, I pulled back, dropped my hands to his shoulders, and grinned. "What did you think?"

Amusement turned his normally intimidating face wickedly sexy, but before he could answer, Umber and Liv were crowding in, yelling to be heard over the raucous din. "You going to head over to join the party or keep watching?"

Sure enough, segments of the crowd were breaking free to form again over by the finish line. I knew the next race wouldn't start for another fifteen minutes at the outside. Wheelz needed time to bask in his glory, then he'd move out so the other drivers could set up for side races that would take up the next few hours.

I turned back to Umber and Liv. "Let's hang here for a bit." In a few minutes, the crowd would thin out and tone down, making it easier to chat.

I sank down to sit on the edge of the truck's side panel as

Liv did the same next to me. Dust, fuel, and smoke hung in the air, slowly drifting up to disappear into the star-studded skies. The truck bounced as others began clearing out of the bed. Umber and Zev stayed standing, providing a welcome buffer between the hyped-up departures and the impromptu bench Liv and I claimed. Umber lifted his chin as a burly bald man pounded his back and hopped down out of the truck.

Finally, there was space to breath and, even better, talk. Only then did I turn to Umber. "Let me hear your weird story."

Umber dropped to sit next to Liv. Zev waited for another couple to clear out and then sat next to me, his foot braced near mine on the wheel well. Between the four of us, we managed to claim the side closest to the action. Only a trio of twentysomethings standing by the cab remained. They chatted in low voices with their backs to us and their beers on the roof, giving us a semblance of privacy.

Umber braced his arm along the metal edge, and Liv shifted until she was leaning against him. "It was the damnedest thing. A couple days ago, I was at the shop, waiting for my next appointment, when all hell broke loose near the back door."

"Drunken frat brats?" I asked.

It was a legit question. Umber owned Etched Chaos, a tattoo parlor near the university. His designs were in high demand, and an appointment with him and his chair required months of advance planning. At least, from the dedicated customers. Those who just wanted to claim their ink was from Etched Chaos could plan on a couple of weeks of delay before a slot opened so long as they didn't request Umber.

"Nope, some poor sleeper hyped out of his mind. When I came out, he was screaming that the rats were eating his brain." He grimaced. "He kept tearing at his face, gouging his skin and shit. Then there was the cat." He stopped, the gold of his skin turning a sickly pale yellow as he visibly swallowed.

When it looked as if that was all he was going to say, I prompted softly, "Cat?"

He blinked and shook his head as if clearing a fog. "Yeah, didn't see it until the sleeper sent me headfirst into the dumpster. I managed to block the worst of it." He lifted his cast-covered arm. "Ended up with this as a lovely parting gift. I was lying there, thinking my arm was on fire and my head was ringing. Then I got to my knees, lifted my head, and saw it. Took a few to put it all together. It looked like what's left after an animal dares to cross the street and loses. Bones, fur, blood. I didn't realize the head was missing. Well, not until I turned to revisit my lunch and saw it sitting just under the dumpster."

Under his trying-to-be-stoic expression, something close to fear rippled. I wasn't the only one to notice it. Liv pressed a kiss against his arm draped over her chest. Umber returned the gesture by rubbing his chin over her curls.

"The whole fucked-up scene was disturbing. Hell, it just felt... off. The sleeper was nearly foaming at the mouth, and his fingers were..." Umber lifted his hand, forming a claw. "And covered in gore. I got to my feet and barely had a chance to brace before he rushed me. I managed to hold him off." Umber was a low-level air mage, and his best defense was knocking someone out by launching an air balloon that basically Saran-wrapped the attacker's face, cutting off oxygen until that person collapsed. "The look in his eye..." He gave another hard headshake. "It almost made me piss my pants. There was something seriously wrong with him."

As disturbing as the incident sounded, it wasn't a far stretch to imagine. Sleepers, by nature, tended to suffer from a multitude of mental disorders. Mix that mental chaos with magic, and the results could be frightening to say the least.

I indicated Umber's cast. "I'm surprised that's all you got away with."

A ruddy color washed through his cheeks. "Yeah, well, that's why I pay big bucks for my security wards. Got 'em calibrated for both magical and nonmagical attacks. ACRT made it in under three minutes."

Arcane Criminal Response Team was a specialized unit that focused on handling magical crimes. "ACRT? What kind of magic was he throwing around?"

Umber frowned. "That's the thing. I don't know."

I cocked my head. "I'm not following."

And I wasn't. Magic was pretty obvious. If someone burned you, that was a fire mage. If someone came after you with inhuman strength and ninja-like moves, chances were that was a combat mage. If someone tried to drown you in the middle of a desert, you were dealing with a water mage. Magical skills tended to be fairly straightforward. Well, except for mine.

"There was a coat of ice on the door, but there were scorch marks along the pavement. And that poor cat looked as if it had been torn apart with claws. The way he came at me, I didn't give him a chance to get his hands on me, but I'm damn sure if he'd managed to do that, I wouldn't be talking to you right now."

I barely managed to refrain from looking at Zev. This type of weird shit was exactly what I'd hoped to hear about, just not from such a close contact as Umber. I ran a hand over the back of my neck, my mind racing. *Is it connected, or am I just drawing lines where none exist?*

I dropped my hand and curled it into a fist on my lap. "Did anyone at ACRT have a clue what his deal was?"

Umber shook his head. "I don't think so. They got there, and it took, like, three of them to get him restrained. By the time they had him locked down, he was screaming nonstop, and I swear he was bleeding from his eyes and shit."

Okay, yeah, that is definitely not normal by any definition. "I wonder what he was on?"

"Shit if I know," Umber muttered. "But whatever it is, it's bad fucking news."

The ugly suspicion crowding my brain made that truer than he knew. "Maybe it's a one-off. You know, like, a bad reaction or a bad batch of whatever he was taking."

"Maybe, but..." Umber's face darkened with unease. "You know my customers and how they talk?"

I nodded.

"Whispers are floating around, and none of it's good."

"You got something to share? I can maybe poke around for you." It wasn't an unusual offer—I'd done it before. Sometimes he took me up on it, sometimes not.

Fortunately, this time he did. "I'll see if I can pin anything down and tag you."

His quick response told me I'd be hearing from him sooner rather than later. I forced a casual smile. "Sounds good."

◆

Zev and I stuck around through the next race, but questions and worries crowded out my earlier enthusiasm. Now all I wanted to do was to get home and go over the damn file I hadn't had time to review before. Picking up on my preoccupation, Zev pulled me away from a group of mechanics, most of whom were about two and half sheets to the wind already, and started leading the way to where we'd left his bike. We broke free from the crowd, and I returned the handful of goodbyes aimed our way.

At the bike, Zev handed over my helmet before claiming his. "Talk to me."

I bit my bottom lip, worried what I said next would sound paranoid. "Do you know anyone at ACRT?"

He lowered the helmet he was about to put on. "I have a connection, yeah." He studied me. "You want to know about the sleeper?"

"Yeah." I shifted uncomfortably and looked down at the helmet in my hands. "It's probably nothing, but..."

"Better safe than sorry." There was nothing condescending or impatient in his voice.

I looked up. "It's just... ice? Scorch marks? Claws? All of that points to more than one magic-based attack, but if all Umber saw was just the one guy..."

"Then where did all that come from?"

"Right."

His gaze lifted and went unfocused as he considered. Finally, he said, "I'll reach out, see if we can get a copy of whatever report might be on file."

"You mean like an autopsy?"

He shook his head. "More like an incident report. Sleepers generally don't rate an autopsy unless there's a solid reason."

"I'd think the weirdness involved would be enough of a reason."

"You'd think. But I'm not betting on it." Zev blew out a long breath. "Come on. It's late—" He grimaced. "Early. Let's get you home so you can catch some sleep. I'll be at your place at eight so we can head over to the Sellareses' place."

I wrinkled my nose. "You're not getting in unless you come bearing large quantities of espresso."

He dropped the hand with the helmet and used his other to pull me close. Since I liked his closeness, I went with it, the soft *thunk* as our helmets hit drowned out by my rising pulse. I put a hand to his chest, my fingers curling in just a bit as if I could snag and hold him prisoner. In this position, I had no choice but to tilt my head back to keep eye contact.

He grinned down at me. "Do I get a prize if I do?"

That teasing note struck a chord deep inside me, leaving a gentle burn behind. Knowing our little window of time was quickly closing, I held his T-shirt in my fist and rose up on my toes so I could taste that sexy grin of his. It was a soft brush, a barely there touch of tongue to his lips, but my toes curled, and for a brief moment, my world lit with a beautiful glow. I drew back—not much, just enough so I wouldn't be tempted to follow that kiss up with something needier, hungrier.

"That work?" My question came out husky.

His fingers tightened on my hip, and his appreciation of my kiss was unmistakable. His voice was as rough as mine when he said, "Yeah, for now." Zev's sexy grin began to shift into an expression I was scared to name, but before it went all the way there, he pressed his lips against mine in a loud, obnoxious smooch and pulled back. "Bike, woman. Now. Otherwise, neither one of us will be good for anything tomorrow."

With the moment broken, I followed directions and let him take me home.

CHAPTER TEN

THANKS to the early-morning cop-free highways, Zev managed to get me home in record time. Since he was going to be on my doorstep in a few hours anyway, we left my Mustang at the Guild, and he dropped me off at my condo. Well, at the front lobby actually, but same diff. It was closing in on three in the morning when I walked through my door.

I shrugged off the irritating rasp of Lena's additional security wards, which she insisted on after the Thatcher mess. *Nothing like the imminent threat of unwanted Family interest to make you want to ensure that your privacy is protected.* Since I not only understood but also shared her concerns, I dealt with the annoyance of extra security.

A soft indigo glow from the under-counter lighting acted as my nightlight as I moved through the space. Lena's door was closed, no light spilling from below, which meant she was sleeping, like most normal people would be at this time. I grabbed the file I'd left on the counter and took it and a glass of water with me to my bedroom. A two-minute shower later, I was on my bed, folder open. Most of what was contained in the file was familiar, thanks to the discussion over tacos. I focused on the details about the dead and missing.

Jonas's burnt body had been found over by the university, miles away from his home. The pictures of the scene made me reconsider seeing his remains in person. His wasn't the only documented death. Chloe Sellares had died in an apparent mugging gone horrifically wrong a block away from her home. Her apartment was located near the university district, in one of the newer buildings that seemed to pop up faster than corner coffee shops. I had no idea who thought squeezing a building into every square inch equaled urban utopia.

Just for giggles, I looked up where LanTech's previous labs had been located and found them in a corridor lined with squat, block-wide buildings differentiated only by the signs on their doors. The location was almost midway between Jonas's home and the university—not a surprise if Jonas had wanted a short commute. A quick review of nearby businesses turned up a warehouse specializing in tech production, corporate offices of CharmOne Bank, and a mix of university and corporate research groups. All in all, it made sense for LanTech to set up shop there. I also looked up Origin's lab and found it just north of the university district, where innovation was quickly becoming an overused buzzword. It looked like Chloe's commute about equaled Jonas's, just in a different direction.

After reviewing the notes, I dove into the lab reports from both LanTech and Origin, and that was where my low-grade headache graduated to eye-blurring brain soup. The scientific terminology was daunting, but my handy-dandy online glossaries were there to help. Some of the more complex terms, like *caudate nucleus* or *hyperacusis*, made me regret my inattention in my college science courses. I wasn't sure why they all couldn't be as straightforward as *blood-brain barrier* or *intracranial pressure*. It would have made my reading so much easier.

By the time I finished, I wasn't sure if my assumptions were solid or just wishful thinking. The best I could decipher was that the Delphi serum was a chemical compound that acted like a switch on the part of the human brain where magical abilities lived. If that switch was naturally in the off position, it flipped it on, activating whatever latent abilities hid in the dusty corners, turning a non-magically inclined person into a mage. If the switch was already in the on position, the addition of the serum not only boosted existing abilities but also woke those that slept, turning an existing mage into a mage on steroids or, in some cases, into a hybrid mage of terrifying proportions. It was the last part that left me with concerns and questions. The official reports submitted by the research teams indicated that most of their conclusions were hypothetical, based upon early lab experiments with rats, which fit with what Stephen and Leander had shared in the meeting. But unease slipped under my skin like an embedded sliver, and I couldn't shake the feeling that the reports were incomplete.

By the time four o'clock rolled around, the words were chasing each other across the page. Giving up, I set the folder aside, turned off the light, and collapsed into sleep... only to have my damn alarm go off what felt like mere minutes later. Without opening my eyes, I fumbled around until I managed to figure out the correct combination to shut off my phone's alarm. It took an ungodly amount of effort to drag myself upright and start getting ready. By the time I walked out of my room, it was perilously close to eight o'clock in the morning. I wasn't surprised so much as resigned when I saw Zev's broad shoulders and dark hair at my counter. Lena stood in her preferred spot on the other side of the counter. The cup halfway to her mouth did nothing to hide her smirk,

I sighed. "Please tell me you have my coffee."

Instead of answering, he angled his body just enough to watch me approach and nudged an oversized cup with a familiar logo on the counter next to him. I dropped onto the stool next to him, and the tantalizing scent of warm sandalwood that was quickly becoming the bane of my existence enveloped me. Since I didn't want to give in and bury my nose in his neck to sniff him like a pathetic pup, I grabbed my coffee and took that first delicious sip. My groan was a purely habitual impulse.

"What time did you get in?" Lena asked, the smirk no longer on her lips but her amusement evident in the glint in her eyes.

"Way past sanity." I took another sip. "But it was necessary."

Lena made a suggestive hum. "I'm sure it was."

I pinned her with a glare, while next to me, Zev just grinned. "Seriously?"

Lena laughed. "You're so easy."

"I wish," Zev said.

I turned my glare from the laughing hyena I roomed with to the exasperating male next me. "You two need to grow up."

Lena's laughter faded to a snort. "Nope. Adulting is highly overrated."

Since I couldn't argue with that, I switched subjects. "What's on your agenda today?"

Lena quirked an eyebrow. "Shouldn't that be my question to you?"

I leaned over and bumped my shoulder into Zev's. "I'm with this one unless Sabella calls."

Her gaze flickered between us before dropping back to her cup, her lips in a mysterious half smile. "Right." She took a sip and pushed off the counter. "I'm finishing up a case for the Guild, doing prelims on a new assignment. Should be finished around three, but Evan's off tonight, so..." Her shrug was a little stiff. She and Evan, the Guild's top electro mage, were dipping their toes into a mutually shared attraction that they'd finally given in to a few weeks earlier.

It was my turn to wiggle my eyebrows. "Don't wait up?"

She flipped me off and headed toward her room. "And I'm out of here."

"Later!"

"Bye, bitch," Lena called over her shoulder and disappeared into her room, leaving me all alone with Zev.

Quiet settled in, stretching into a long moment as I enjoyed my coffee. Next to me, Zev did the same, his arms braced on the counter. The silence wasn't uncomfortable, but I waited until Lena's shower turned on and my brain was sufficiently fueled before starting up our conversation. "You get any sleep?"

"I had a few things to deal with when I got back, so I only got a couple hours." He studied me. "I'm thinking you got about the same?"

"Yeah, I stayed up to review Sabella's file."

His gaze swept over the kitchen, probably looking for the file that was safe in my bedroom. "Should I be worried about Sabella's file?"

I let my lips curve up and angled my head to meet his gaze. "Not unless you're hiding something from me."

He leaned in so close that all I could see was his face. "That's your thing, babe, not mine." He must have caught my tiny knee-jerk flinch, because he said in all seriousness, "Yeah, that's something we'll get to."

Please, not anytime soon. I sent the fervent prayer to anyone listening, but I was fairly sure they were all on vacation. I managed to squeak out a breathless reminder. "Professional, remember?"

"Mm-hmm." He pulled back, and I tried to subtly draw air

into my tight chest. When his eyes narrowed, I was sure I'd failed on the subtle part. "Anything in that file I should know about Chloe?"

My brain scrambled to recalibrate and found purchase on the idiosyncrasies of locations. "Her apartment is near the university. In fact, it's blocks away from where Jonas's body was found."

He frowned. "That's miles from Jonas's house."

"I know." I took another fortifying sip. "So do we know if Chloe and Jonas knew each other?"

Zev shook his head. "We don't, but we'll make sure to ask."

"If they did, it's a connection." I watched his long fingers spin his cup around in a slow circle.

"Or it's nothing, considering they're all researchers in the same field."

He played the devil's-advocate role well, but in the end, it didn't matter. One way or the other, we'd find the answer soon enough.

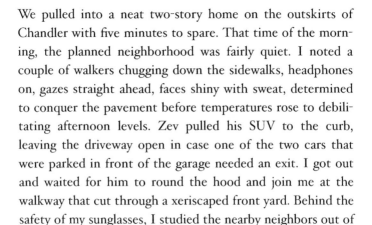

We pulled into a neat two-story home on the outskirts of Chandler with five minutes to spare. That time of the morning, the planned neighborhood was fairly quiet. I noted a couple of walkers chugging down the sidewalks, headphones on, gazes straight ahead, faces shiny with sweat, determined to conquer the pavement before temperatures rose to debilitating afternoon levels. Zev pulled his SUV to the curb, leaving the driveway open in case one of the two cars that were parked in front of the garage needed an exit. I got out and waited for him to round the hood and join me at the walkway that cut through a xeriscaped front yard. Behind the safety of my sunglasses, I studied the nearby neighbors out of habit and winced. *Holy fifty shades of beige!* Outside of the mix of one- or two-story structures, there wasn't much variation to be found on the block.

Zev and I headed to the slice of shade offered by the overhang guarding a narrow porch and the front door. We didn't get a chance to knock. The door swung open, and an older man in jeans and a button-down short-sleeved shirt waited in the frame.

Zev stopped and pulled off his sunglasses. "Mr. Sellares?"

The older man's nod was a bit jerky. "Mr. Aslanov." He turned to me. "Ms. Costas."

I came up to Zev's side, dipped my chin in acknowledgement, and took off my shades. "Mr. Sellares, thank you for seeing us."

Another jerky nod. "Thank you for being so prompt." He stepped back and motioned us forward. "Please come in."

Zev murmured his thanks and stepped aside, giving me room to enter first. I stepped over the threshold and felt my shoulders sink under the invisible weight of grief that lived and breathed within these walls. The loss of a loved one left behind heavy reminders, but when it found a space to curl up and claim as its own, it became a heavy, unmovable blanket until even the tiniest spark of hope sputtered out. Here inside the Sellares home, grief had set up permanent residence.

Chloe's father closed the door and then led us through a front room that was so neat as to be disturbing. I bet even dust didn't dare settle on the furniture. The front room spilled into an open space that was both a kitchen and a living room. A woman rose from a small, round table with the obligatory centerpiece—a candle in the midst of glass stones. A sturdy mug with steam rising from it marked her spot. Introductions were quietly exchanged and beverage offers made and then refused before Zev and I settled into padded seats across from Chloe's grief-worn parents. The sun spilled across the laughing faces forever captured in family pictures chronicling the years of toddler to young adult. Memory-filled frames lined shelves and walls, holding back the newer addition of shadows lingering along the room's edges.

Once the niceties were completed, Zev waded into the painful quiet. "We appreciate your willingness to meet with us."

Mrs. Sellares cradled her mug, a slight tremor to her hands. "Bryan said you were assisting on the investigation of Chloe's..." Her voice petered out.

"Yes, ma'am," Zev said. "We understand you've already spoken to the authorities."

"And Bryan," Mr. Sellares added.

"And Bryan," Zev amended smoothly.

"I don't know what else we can tell you that we haven't already shared." Tears pooled in Mrs. Sellares's eyes, but they didn't fall. "My Chloe didn't have any enemies. Everyone loved her. I don't know why they targeted her." Her voice shook, and her agitation rose, making her voice sharp.

Her husband curled an arm around her shoulders and held her close, but his gaze held a hard, angry light. "Chloe's death makes no sense. It was supposed to be a safe neighborhood. It's why Chloe and her roommates chose to live there."

Mr. Sellares's anger was justified. Chloe's neighborhood was safe, and if her job hadn't pointed to something suspect behind her fatal mugging, there would still be serious concerns about the randomness of the attack. On the drive over, Zev and I had discussed our approach and how much we would be willing to share. Meeting Chloe's parents, I was completely on board with Zev's suggestion of being as forthright as possible without revealing the nature of the Delphi project. Unfortunately, there was no easy way to navigate their grief.

"We agree with you." I made the admission quietly.

Mr. and Mrs. Sellares exchanged a look filled with flickering hope at finally getting answers to their daughter's death. Mrs. Sellares dropped her forehead to her husband's shoulder, probably trying to muffle her soft sob.

Mr. Sellares pinned Zev and me in place. "You're saying it wasn't an accident."

It was my turn to exchange a look with Zev, knowing we needed to tread lightly. He turned back to the Sellareses. "We have reason to believe Chloe may have been targeted."

"By who?" Mrs. Sellares turned to us without moving from her husband's embrace.

Knowing it was best to leave the explanations up to Zev, I stayed quiet.

"We're not exactly sure." Zev studied the couple. "But we believe it has to do with a project she was working on at LanTech."

Mr. Sellares frowned. "I'm not sure we'll be much help, then. Chloe didn't discuss her work with us."

But I was watching Mrs. Sellares and couldn't miss the way her eyes darkened or the way her attention shifted to her cup. I leaned forward and reached across the table to touch her wrist, and her eyes flew to mine. "Chloe told you something, didn't she, Mrs. Sellares?"

The older woman shook her head. "Not about the project."

I prompted, "But...?"

She closed her eyes and then seemed to come to a decision as she opened them again and met mine. "Chloe had some concerns about her coworker."

"Neil Pasternak?" I kept my reactions locked down, not wanting to spook her into falling silent. But when it looked like that was all she was going to share, I nudged a bit more. "Did he do or say something that made her uncomfortable?"

She nodded and shot her husband a nervous look. He was frowning, and I wasn't surprised when she let go of her mug and patted his arm. "She asked me not to say anything to you, dear heart." When his lips tightened and his jaw flexed, she continued, "She knew if I said anything, you'd step in and get involved. She didn't want that."

A silent exchange passed between the couple before Mr. Sellares looked away, conceding his wife's point. Clearly, Chloe had been a daddy's girl.

Mrs. Sellares kept her hand on her husband but turned back to me. "When she was approached to partner with Mr. Pasternak, she was both excited and nervous."

When she didn't continue, I gently asked, "Why?"

Mrs. Sellares's hand fluttered before resetting on the safety of her cup. "He was LanTech's rising star, and she'd only been there about a year. She was acutely conscious of her lack of experience, so she went out of her way to ensure that her work was stellar. It wasn't long before she was spending an exorbitant number of hours at the office. Every time I tried to get her to make time for a quick bite or a call, she had an excuse." Mrs. Sellares's gaze slid to her husband before dropping back to the cup in front of her. "I was worried something... more was happening between her and Mr. Pasternak."

I blinked, not expecting that comment. "Was it?"

She shook her head and lifted her gaze to mine. "When I asked her if she was involved with Mr. Pasternak, she laughed and said there was no way she'd jeopardize her job for"—her lips turned up in a sad, wistful smile—"and I quote, 'an old guy with ego issues.'"

"Did she share why she was putting in so many hours?"

"She was worried her lack of experience might be seen as a detriment. I did my best to reassure her that the company wouldn't have asked her to take the position if they didn't trust her skills, but it didn't seem to help."

When Mrs. Sellares fell quiet, Zev asked, "How so?"

She reached for her husband's hand, and their fingers laced together. "My Chloe is..." She stopped then started again, this time in a softer voice. "Was very detail oriented. It's why she excelled in her chosen field."

I remembered the notation in the file notes about Chloe. She was a numeric mage, so it was no surprise that she was right at home in a lab, especially when her world was all things mathematical.

Mrs. Sellares's fingers, tangled with her husband's, went bloodless. "Chloe couldn't share much about her work. She'd been required to sign a confidentiality clause when she accepted the job."

"I never did like that clause," Mr. Sellares interjected.

At my look, Mrs. Sellares explained, "Chris is a contract lawyer."

That explained the fierce fatherly worries.

"But," she continued, "Chloe slipped once and admitted that she had serious concerns about the latest reports on their project."

It was difficult not to look at Zev. "What kind of concerns?"

"She wouldn't say. In fact, she told me to forget she'd said anything at all, that she simply misspoke and was overly tired. But I know my daughter, and if she was worried, there was reason to be. She wasn't one to react without all the pertinent facts."

"Do you remember when that conversation occurred?" Zev asked.

She nodded. "It was right before LanTech announced it was filing bankruptcy. I remember feeling relieved when I heard that news. I thought that it was a sign that Chloe should move on and get away from whatever it was that was bothering her."

"And Chloe? How did she feel about LanTech closing its doors?"

Mrs. Sellares took her time to consider the question. "Relieved. She didn't waste any time putting her résumé out. In fact, she was excited because she had a couple of possible positions lined up. We were planning to go to a mom-and-daughter dinner that night, but..." Tears filled the older woman's eyes, and she blinked rapidly. A tear escaped, and she dashed it away before fisting her hand on the table. Swallowing hard, she looked at Zev and me. "I want to know why she's gone."

Her grief and anger were so palpable I couldn't resist the urge to reach out and cover her fist on the table. "So do we, Mrs. Sellares."

Her hand trembled under mine. "It wasn't an accident. I know it wasn't an accident."

"If it wasn't, we'll find out." I stopped short of making a promise I couldn't guarantee, even though I wanted to. *No parent should hurt like this.*

Mrs. Sellares gave a short, jerky nod and cleared her throat. "I'm not sure what else we can tell you that will help."

Zev shifted in his chair and braced his elbows on the table. "Did Chloe ever talk to you about Mr. Pasternak? If he shared her concerns, things like that?"

"No, but right before the lab closed, she said something about how he must be involved with someone because he went from eating at his desk and working through his lunch hour to leaving the lab and sometimes coming back late." A tiny curve eased the fine white lines around her lips. "She joked that whoever it was had to be extraordinarily unique to interrupt his obsession with their project."

We spent a few more minutes feeling out the various

corners of Chloe's life but came up disappointingly short. Until the lab closed, her life had been dominated by her job, leaving no room for anyone special. The names of her friends, as shared by her parents, matched the interview list in the file. Zev was gently leading the Sellareses through another round of questions when my phone vibrated in my pocket. I pulled it out, held it below table level, and discreetly read the incoming text. It was from Bryan, who wanted us to call him as soon as possible.

I touched the hard muscles of Zev's thigh under the table to gain his attention. He waited for a natural break in the conversation before he turned to me. I gave him what I hoped was a clear signal that we needed to go. It seemed to work, because within minutes, we were saying our goodbyes and promising the Sellareses an update as soon as we had something to share.

We didn't talk as we headed back to the SUV. I slipped my sunglasses back on, cutting down the bright glare of the late-morning sun. Two electronic beeps broke through the quiet as Zev unlocked the car.

I slid into the passenger seat, clicked my seat belt in place, and waited until Zev got in, started the engine, and the AC managed to blow cold before I said, "Bryan wants us to call him."

He thumbed the button on the steering wheel and directed the in-car system to call Bryan's number. It rang twice, and then Bryan's voice came through the speakers. "You two at the Sellareses?"

"Just finished, actually," Zev confirmed.

"Did you get anything?"

Zev and I shared a look, then I answered, "Maybe. Chloe had concerns about the project."

"What kind of concerns?"

"We weren't able to get specifics because Chloe didn't

share. The fact that she slipped and her mom remembered the slip is all we really have to work with." Then I remembered the other little tidbit. "Oh, and Chloe thought Neil had a side piece keeping him busy during his lunch hour."

"I'm not so sure it was a side piece." Bryan's voice was grim.

I aimed a frown at the stereo while Zev glared and demanded, "What do you mean?"

Bryan said, "I'm sending you an address. Come over and see for yourselves."

CHAPTER ELEVEN

THE ADDRESS BRYAN sent took us to the area behind the university and along the shores of the man-made Salt River. Why anyone thought a river in a desert was a good thing was beyond me, but the city planners had wasted no time shoving high-rise condos and corporate centers onto every inch of the shore, interspersing their showpieces with the occasional park that allowed visitors to enjoy the river. Narrow streets wound around half-constructed high-rises and spilled us into what at first appeared to be an industrial park. Since identifying numbers were either missing or on awkward spots on the buildings, Zev slowed so I could try to pinpoint the one we needed because the GPS was no longer helpful. It had declared our arrival at the intended location, but all we saw was a mixed collection of older one-story cinderblock buildings and newer two- to three-story office spaces.

I twisted in my seat, doing my best to make out the numbers scattered on either windows or doors as we cruised by. "There's 2111, 2113... the last one's blank, so maybe 2115?"

Zev pressed the accelerator, and we hit the next set of

buildings. This grouping was the older one-story variety and would probably disappear over the next few months as progress rolled relentlessly forward. We'd gotten about halfway down the structure when I found a new number. "Hold up!" Without looking away, I reached out and hit Zev's arm. "That looks like 2205." Spotting a narrow drive ahead, I said, "Turn in here. I'm betting it's on the back side of one of these."

He turned, and we followed the pitted asphalt around a beige-on-beige building that had seen better days and found ourselves in a narrow parking lot. Dusty trucks and beat-up sedans filled some of the spots, while tarp-covered trailers and one golf cart occupied a few others. Spaced along the building's brick back side were roll-up garage doors paired with metal doors, both decorated with rust and dents. There were a few sun-worn, dust-chipped, barely legible black numbers. In some weird attempt at improvement, it looked as if two painters with different colors—startling white and puke beige—had started at opposite ends and met in the middle. A cement block fence decorated in black graffiti dominated the area, separating the building from the lot behind. Zev kept us to a crawl because it was narrow enough that if anyone decided to drive out, going the other way, we'd end up in a game of chicken.

I knew we had the right address when I spotted Imogen leaning against a sporty two-door car parked a couple of spaces away from a faintly familiar battered SUV. She looked decidedly out of place in her heels, tailored slacks, and shirt that was basically a silk scarf draped for decency's sake. Zev pulled into the open space next to her and shut off our SUV. In the half-open door in front of us, Bryan appeared. I didn't know if it was the unnaturally blank expression on his face or the way he held himself or what, but something was off. The feeling was so strong the hair on the back of my neck rose in warning. Slowly, I undid my seat belt, leaned forward, and scanned our surroundings. I don't know what I was looking for, but nothing obvious was out there.

Next to me, Zev paused with a hand on the door. "What?"

His terse question meant he'd picked up on my unease, but since I couldn't explain it, I said, "It's nothing." I reached for my door and blurted out the first thing to hit my frazzled brain. "I was just checking to make sure we weren't on someone's security camera." With that, I opened my door and hopped out, hoping to forestall further inquisition.

The sound of Zev's door opening and then closing echoed and was soon followed by the low-voiced exchange of greetings between him and Imogen. I rounded the hood about the same time as Zev and Imogen and caught the tail end of their conversation.

"Agreed to meet with you around four," Imogen said as Zev did something on his phone. "I gave her your number in case something changes and sent her safe-house address to your phone."

"Appreciate it." Zev tucked his phone away, looked up, and caught my raised brows. "Dr. Kerri Michaels," he clarified. "Imogen got her to agree to meet with us today."

Works for me. It would be nice to get the surviving researcher's insight on the Delphi project. Origin was racing neck and neck with LanTech on this project, and she would be familiar with Neil and his team since they were her competition. Long shot though it was, I hoped Kerri might know why Chloe had been so nervous about LanTech's progress.

As we came up to the door, Bryan stepped back, making room for us to enter. "Watch your step. It's a mess in here."

I let Imogen and Zev go first and took off my sunglasses

in preparation for the shadowed interior. I stepped inside, and when the space came into view, I let out a low whistle. "Okay, this does not look like an illicit love nest."

"I'm thinking Neil wasn't slipping out at lunch for a quickie." A few steps ahead of me, Imogen used the pointed toe of her three-inch-heel shoe to nudge what appeared to be a broken pet cage of some kind out of her path. How she managed not to break her neck navigating the debris-strewn floor in those heels was beyond me. I chalked it up to one of her superpowers.

"Clearly not," Zev murmured as he moved farther into the space.

Bryan strode across the room, stopping only when he hit the leading edge of the worst of the mess. "Not unless he was into some truly twisted kink."

Sunlight fought its way through the narrow rectangular windows along the top of the door and combined forces with the harsh bare fluorescent bulbs hanging from the exposed rafters. Underneath, three long, narrow tables filled the middle of the room. One lay on its side, and the other two remained upright but had obviously been shoved out of alignment. On the middle one, the shattered screen of a computer rested in a drunken tilt. I moved closer until I could see the broken glass that, based on the couple of intact items on the desk, had once been beakers or some kind of test tubes, maybe even those glass slides used under a microscope. Strictly old-school science-lab stuff.

Strange stains spilled across the tabletops and left their mark as they dripped over the side. The floor directly below was marred by scorch marks, which explained the nose-curling stench of burnt plastic and the scattered fragments of burnt paper among the mess. Along the far wall was a high counter with a lopsided rolling stool leaning against it. There was another computer monitor and some kind of machine whose purpose I had no clue about other than that it vaguely looked like something from one of my favorite crime-lab shows. What was obvious was that this had once been some kind of lab.

Even worse was what I spotted as I came around the last narrow table. *Oh shit.* A chill ran down my spine as I stared at the twisted remains of a wire cage, the kind that normally held a small pet, lying in the center of what used to be a containment ward. If I was reading the scene right, whatever had been held in the cage had managed to tear through the wire mesh and breach the now-ruptured warding lines. On the floor, rust-colored stains dotted with fur proved that whatever had escaped had paid dearly for the attempt.

Carefully staying clear of the broken warding sigils and fracture lines, I crouched down. Some of the savaged ends of the wire held bits of bloody fur, and stuck in the gore were two shiny pieces of something translucent. Looking around, I found a piece of broken plastic and used it to poke through the mess while I stayed outside the nulled circle. I nudged aside more pieces of broken cage and clumps of fur and found a bigger, more defined piece of the see-through material. When I used the plastic to move it, it left behind a shallow groove in the cement.

I sucked in a breath. "What the hell?"

Sensing movement behind me, I twisted to see Zev staring at the same thing, his face carefully blank. I turned back to what appeared to be an insect-like shell, which had to be as strong as titanium since it could scrape concrete. At roughly two inches long, it was veined through with virulent red. It was disturbingly fascinating. I was no entomologist, but it looked an awful lot like an empty cicada shell. Correction—a shell from a mutant cicada on steroids.

Using the plastic to point to the weirdness, I turned to look at Zev. "This doesn't make sense."

His gaze met mine, something dark and terrible working in his eyes, but his voice was flat. "It does if Neil progressed to live experiments."

"If Neil stole the beta version of the serum, why would he waste it like that? According to Stephen, there was a limited amount of the serum, right? Not to mention, Stephen indicated the beta version was missing a critical component. I can't see Neil cracking that mystery this fast, can you?" I aimed that last at Imogen, who as the Trask Arbiter was in a better position than the rest of us to answer.

She curled a hand into a fist at her side, but her voice remained clinical. "If Neil chose to use the serum, it's possible his familiarity with the research allowed him to identify the final necessary component." Her gaze went to Bryan before shifting away. She pivoted, stalked around the table, and headed toward the mess scattered behind it. "Perhaps he believes he's finalized the serum."

Part of me wanted to argue with Ms. Know-It-All that unlocking the "necessary component" couldn't be that easy if Origin still hadn't managed to do so before this mess went down, but what did I know? Instead, I focused on a more immediate worry. "What the hell was in this cage?"

Zev shrugged and handed me the broken plastic. Then he straightened and went to join Imogen's search. I pushed to my feet, my gaze searching the gloom edging the room just out of reach of the overhead light, my mind conjuring all sorts of twisted lab experiments. Maybe I should cut back on how much *Mystery Science Theater* I watched.

"Is it still here, you think?" I couldn't quite stifle a squeak of panic. The thought of some rabid science experiment lurking about made me jumpy as hell, but I seemed to be the only one with a vivid imagination.

"I think we're safe." Bryan kicked an empty file box and watched it bounce across the floor and settle against the wall. "If something was here, it would've made itself known by now."

"You sure about that?" I muttered, not expecting an answer even as I kept peering around, trying to reassure myself that the shadows were just shadows.

"Well," Bryan drawled, "since nothing tore out my throat when I did the initial walk-through and we're not under attack now, yep."

"Guys, you need to see this," Imogen said. We turned to find her standing by the far counter near a dark corner, her lips pinched in disgust as she looked at us from over her shoulder. "I think I found your lab experiment, or what's left of it." Her phone's light was aimed at the floor in front of her.

We headed over. Sure enough, crumpled in the corner was a pile of bloody fur that belonged to what looked initially like an oversized rat, but there was something wrong with it. The longer I stared at it, the worse the sense of wrongness grew. "That is a rat, right?"

Zev took the forgotten piece of plastic from me and crouched. He flipped the carcass over. I sucked in a breath while Bryan coughed and turned away. Imogen muttered something I couldn't make out, and the light in her hand jiggled then steadied.

Zev used the plastic to nudge the body into the light, exposing short fur patched with a lot of open wounds. "I don't think so."

Putrid odor hit my nose about the same moment I registered that the wounds were a mixed batch, some filled with pus, some just torn flesh. Zev used the plastic to prod the curled foreleg off the gore-covered chest. It was short and stubbed and seemed malformed. While it matched the other foreleg, it didn't match the much longer and more muscular back legs. Under Imogen's light, I could also see that the muzzle was more feline than rodent. It lay on the ground so that one ear with a wiry tuft of hair at its tip was visible. My stomach pitched at the decided wrongness of it all.

Zev's face was grim, and he said with a hint of disgust, "If I was to guess, I'd say someone magically spliced a rat and a cat."

Imogen made a noise, and Zev looked up. For a long moment, the two stared at each other, and I got the impression they knew something I didn't. Since I was still finding my footing in our strange group dynamic, I didn't confront either of them. Instead, I focused on confirming where logic was taking me. There was only one kind of mage that could take two organic compounds and merge them into one.

I looked at Bryan. "Was Neil a Fusor?"

Bryan's stony expression was an answer in itself, but he still said, "Yeah, but my understanding is that his skills were pretty basic and limited to a micro level, not complex organics."

Which I'm sure was a huge benefit in Neil's chosen career. But if Neil had held enough magic to meld living beings, the Arcane Council would have contained him long before this. At least, I hoped so, as that kind of magic was closely monitored and highly restrictive for obvious reasons.

"Well, Chloe was a numerical mage, so I'm pretty sure she's not behind this." I turned to Imogen. "What about Origin's team? Any Fusors?"

She flicked a look at Zev. "Not anymore."

First, not the answer I expected, and second, what? Then I remembered something said at the meeting. "Wait, Lara was a Fusor?"

"Lara was a multilevel Fusor," Zev confirmed. "Her expertise was at the nano level, but she was able to work at the micro level as well. It's why her knowledge was coveted."

Coveted would be a damn good way to put it, considering the Delphi project centered on neurological changes in the brain. It didn't explain the Frankensteinian critter in the corner. However, looking down at the nightmarish proof that something more might be at play made me wonder.

What if Neil finalized a version of a serum created to unlock magical potential, and since he was no longer hampered by the constraints of a monitored lab, he decided to use himself as a test subject? It was crazy, but looking at the dead rat-cat, I was starting to think Neil was a lot more dangerous than anyone anticipated, which not only moved the serum from a hypothetical threat to a viable threat but also upped the pucker factor significantly.

"I'm going to go out on a limb and guess that Neil has leveled up," I said.

"We need to find Neil and contain him." Imogen's voice was so cold I was surprised ice wasn't forming around us.

Bryan studied the dead rat-cat, his face grim. His next words confirmed that I wasn't the only one thinking about worst-case scenarios. "If he was stupid enough to use an experimental version of the serum, he may already be dead or dying."

Or about to go nuclear on a magical level. I managed not to share my fear out loud.

"Imogen's right." Zev rose. "Our priority needs to be containment." He tossed aside the piece of plastic. It hit the wall and rattled to the floor.

Something flew up with a harsh hum and darted straight at Bryan, who managed to bat it away with a sharp curse. "What the hell was that?" He shook out his arm as he stared in the direction the thing had gone.

There was the dull sound of an object hitting metal, then the dangling light fixture began to swing. Imogen aimed her phone's light at the direction of the sound. It danced over the broken monitor and glinted off of something perched on the plastic edge.

"Holy shit." Her words came out on a low breath.

The biggest cicada I'd ever seen stared back at us, its red eyes aimed right at us in a creepy insect-like way, its wings moving so fast they were a blur. The buzzing bored into my skull until it vibrated in my teeth. Before I could get my hands over my ears, a single line of blue power whipped along my peripheral vision, and the accompanying wave of magic seared along my skin. The buzzing stopped, and the cicada body toppled off its precarious perch. As it hit the floor, it bounced twice with the dull thud of a ball bearing on concrete then fell still.

Slowly, I turned my head to see Zev, just behind me, lowering his hand. His gaze met mine as the glow of magic slowly receded from the dark depths. Imogen grabbed something from the nearby table and walked past us. I turned to watch as she collected the dead insect in a jar. She lifted it up and rattled it. You could hear the insect bounce off the glass with high-pitched *tings* that were not normal. Bryan came up on my other side, rubbing at his arm.

I swallowed a couple of times until my heart rate dropped back into the normal range and finally managed a relatively steady, "You okay?"

Bryan grimaced. "Yeah, it just hit me." He stopped rubbing and lifted his arm to reveal a raised welt, but as far as I could tell, there was no broken skin. "It's nothing."

Zev went to Imogen and took the container, carefully studying it. "Looks like another experiment of some kind." A soft blue aura wrapped around the jar, sinking through glass to cover the insect. He shook the container gently, and the disturbing *tings* sounded again. "Those aren't natural wings."

Great. Mutant insect— just what we need on an already creepy assignment. I suppressed a shiver.

Imogen rummaged around on the table and found a salvageable lid. Reclaiming the mutant bug, she said, "I'll send it to the lab to have it tested, see if they can tell what happened to it." She didn't sound optimistic.

Bryan made his way to the remains of the computer. Staying clear of Imogen and her bug, I followed along. Together, we started poking through the mess.

I set a dented case aside and saw that Bryan was working a hard drive loose. "Anything salvageable?"

He pulled out a square drive that looked as if it had been left in a hot car too long and stared at it in disgust. "Not likely. I'm not sure anyone, even an electro mage, will be able to recover anything from these." He handed it over, and I realized that not only had the drive been warped by serious heat, but there were holes pocking the entire thing as well, almost as if it had been left in an acidic rain shower. Whatever had left those marks had ensured that restoration would be impossible.

Zev moved back to the other computer and spent a few minutes digging through the electronic remains. It didn't take him long to find the drive. Still in a squat, he twisted, warped drive in hand. "Same thing here." He tossed it back onto the floor.

Next to me, Bryan kicked the useless pile of electronics in frustration. A couple of burnt pieces of paper rose in the resulting puff of air, only to drift back down. I used a finger to gently snake through the remains. "They even burned the paper files."

Zev stood, his hands on his hips, as he glared around the space. "So we've got nothing?"

"I wouldn't say that," Imogen said.

We all turned to find her crouched in front of the table with the bug-filled container. Since I could barely see her, I got up and moved closer to watch her brush her fingertips across the floor. "What is it?"

She shot me a look and then turned back. "Remains of an Arcane circle."

"For...?" Zev strode over and came to a stop on Imogen's other side.

She shook her head, her arms braced on her thighs as she rubbed her fingertips together. "Not sure." She brought her fingers to her nose and inhaled. "Nothing." She rose as Zev dropped into a crouch. She looked around and found a scrap of cardboard to wipe her fingers on.

At her feet, Zev used his hand to brush aside the debris. He took his time until he had revealed a two-foot section. Marks covered the floor, some a deep black, others a mix of whatever had spilled, with a few white ones as if the concrete had been gouged out.

I had no idea what he was looking at because all I could see were scrapes that could have come from something being shoved across the floor or from whatever violence had torn through the space. No matter how hard I tried, I couldn't get the marks to match up to any known sigil. I wanted to ask Imogen if she was sure but thought better of it. No sense in pissing her off more than my mere presence already did.

Zev didn't take his attention from the floor. "Imogen, can you make sure there's no spillage?"

"Easy enough." Imogen moved to stand behind him. She lifted her arms at her sides, palms facing out.

Knowing what was about to happen, I braced just as she made a soft murmur I couldn't make out, and a white light luminesced in a precise circle, arcing from palm to palm and rising into a dome. Her magic rushed along my skin with a chill, silent breeze. Blue flames of power flickered to life in Zev's hands, but the only magic I could feel was Imogen's.

Bryan came and stood at my side, one hip against the

table, his arms folded across his chest. I barely spared him a glance, too fascinated by what Zev and Imogen were doing. From my position, I couldn't see Zev's face, so I was left with witnessing his movements.

He braced his arms on his knees and brought his hands up, fingertip to fingertip, fingers spread wide. Inside that gap, a familiar globe of indigo snapped to life and became a mesmerizing sphere of silent flame. Now I could feel the barely leashed power of his magic under a thin shell of ice, the combination of their power making my skin jump.

Tongues of flames licked up his arms, stopping just below his shoulders. Something unseen shifted—I could feel the pressure of the change like an invisible touch. He drew his hands apart, and his magic coalesced in his left palm and arm. He reached down and touched something on the floor. The flash was so bright it left me blinking away afterimages. When my vision cleared, I finally saw what Imogen was talking about.

Zev's magic stretched along the markings, his power running the gamut from navy to pale blue. The darker colors filling in areas where there were no marks to follow until the outline of an Arcane circle floated about five inches above the floor. Some of the sigils were crystal clear. There were markings for containment and a couple that I recognized for bindings, but there were others I'd never seen before. That was no surprise, as circles were generally used in extremely advanced spell work, something I didn't have much experience with considering that my magic was innate and less complex. And this was extremely advanced, which meant it fell under the Arbiters' bailiwick, so I let them do their thing.

Next to me, Bryan leaned forward. "Well, shit."

"What?" I asked.

He moved around the edges of the circle that Zev's magic

revealed, crouched at about the seven o'clock position, and looked at Zev. "Did you see this?"

"Yeah." Zev sounded far from happy.

"Neil's definitely fucking with things he shouldn't," Bryan said.

"If it's Neil we're dealing with and not something other." Imogen's attention was on the markings.

I swallowed hard. That didn't sound good at all.

"I don't think he managed a portal," Zev answered absentmindedly, shifting just a bit so he could extend an arm to point at the four o'clock position. "That one over there is incomplete. Means he was either trying to combine sigils or retracing from memory."

"Well, it's a hell of a mistake," Bryan said then winced. "No pun intended."

"But it's still a mistake," Imogen pointed out.

My brain filled in the gaps of their conversation, and I did not like the picture it painted. "So no portal to hell, then, right?"

Bryan's lips twitched. Imogen shot me a look filled with disdain, but Zev shook his head. "No portal to hell, just a twisted mess of shoddy runes."

"Which explains how the lab experiments managed to escape," Bryan pointed out. "Neil's shit at spell work."

"But someone is feeding him enough to get by." Zev did something that snuffed out the steady press of magic and flicked off the switch for the light show, leaving the space once more draped in mediocre lighting and edged in shadows.

At the same time, Imogen dropped her protective circle. The two actions happened so close together, with no verbal communication, that it was clear the two had worked together before. Even knowing my reaction was juvenile, I was bothered by that.

Zev straightened, and so did Bryan, who checked his

watch and said, "Dammit, I've got to head out. I've got something I need to take care of." He looked at Imogen. "I should be done around six. Want me to touch base with you then?"

"Sure." She turned, picked up the mutant bug jar, and headed over. "I'll get this dropped off, then I have a few things to follow up on."

Bryan turned to Zev and me. "And you two? What's up next for you?"

"Interview with Dr. Kerri Michaels," Zev said. "We'll let you both know if anything comes of it."

"Sounds like a plan."

Imogen turned to me, her eyes hard, her tone snide. "Can we assume you'll be updating Sabella?"

Refusing to rise to her bait, I blithely shot back, "You assume correctly."

Her eyes flashed, and her lip curled, but she spun away and stalked to the door. By the time Zev and I stepped outside, she was already in her car and reversing out of her spot. I put my sunglasses back on and watched her drive away while Bryan pulled the door closed. When a brush of magic hit my back, I turned to see him add the final touches to a ward.

When he caught me watching, he grinned. "Don't want anyone poking around in here."

"What if he comes back?"

Zev touched the base of my spine, a silent prod to head to his SUV. "He won't be back."

I looked at him. "So how do we find him now?"

"Now," Bryan said as he set his sunglasses in place. "After I finish my thing, I get to do some serious video watching and see if I can't track his movements."

"If that comes up empty, maybe we should check with any nearby businesses, see if they remember him," Zev said as we walked to the SUV.

I stopped at the passenger door and looked between the two of them. "What can I do to help?"

Bryan hit his battered SUV, turned, and said, "Keep Sabella happy so she doesn't get involved." He didn't wait for my response but got in and started up the car.

Zev unlocked our ride, and I opened my door with a huge sigh. I had a feeling that was easier said than done.

CHAPTER TWELVE

As Zev and I were on our way to the address Imogen had given us for Kerri, Zev's phone buzzed with an incoming text. Since he was driving, I read it aloud. "Kerri says something came up, and she wants to know if we can meet with her tomorrow morning first thing."

This made Zev frown, but he said, "See if nine works for her."

A couple of texts later, we were set for a nine o'clock meeting with Kerri. "Done." I put his phone back in the holder and settled back. "Since we've got time, maybe we should head to the coroner's, check out Jonas's body?"

Probably picking up my poorly hidden reluctance, he asked, "You sure you want to do that?"

Honestly, not in the least. I remembered the nightmares that had plagued my few hours of sleep after seeing the photos in the file, but I just said, "As this is more in line with your job than mine, you tell me. Will seeing the remains give us more than what we already have in the file?"

Instead of an instant response, he took his time thinking it through. I waited, a little antsy and unsure of what I wanted him to say. Finally, he said, "It may be better to wait until we have more information to work with or something specific for them to pursue. Right now, we're still putting the pieces together."

Relieved at the reprieve, I considered other next steps. "Should we go back and help Bryan? Since he'll be pulling video, maybe we could talk with nearby businesses, see if anyone saw Neil."

Zev had opened his mouth to answer when his phone rang. I caught Emilio's name on the screen. Zev used his Bluetooth to pick up. "Yeah?"

"Where are you?" Emilio demanded.

"Coming back from Tempe. What's up?"

There was a significant pause, then Emilio asked, "Am I on speakerphone?"

Zev shot me a sidelong glance. "Yeah."

"You alone?"

"No."

I was surprised that Zev didn't elaborate, but I wasn't surprised by Emilio's next request. "I need you to take me off speaker, Zev."

Zev's shoulders rose and fell in a near silent sigh but he popped in an earbud and did as Emilio instructed. "You're off." He paused, listening as his face tightened. "Yeah, I can do that." Another pause. "No, no bother. Got to do a drop-off first, though. That work?" Based on Zev's next answer, Emilio must have finally gotten curious. "Rory. Just finished a meet with Bryan and Imogen." A short break. "No, I'll update you when I get there." Another, longer pause. "Okay, got it. Yeah, I'll meet you there." He clicked off.

Unable to help myself, I asked, "Let me guess—duty calls?"

"Yeah. Got a situation that needs immediate attention."

Even though I was curious, I didn't push, because there

was no way he'd share Family business with me. Still, it didn't stop me from wondering what kind of situation was important enough to pull him away from this mess. "Right. So do you want me to follow up on the neighborhood canvas, then?"

"I'd rather you didn't."

I blinked. "Excuse me?"

Before my feathers could get too ruffled, he said, "I'm not comfortable with you poking around on your own." I opened my mouth to argue, but he cut me off. "Bryan will be busy getting video feeds. If Imogen was free, I'd say nab her to tag along, but she isn't, so no, let's hold off."

Torn between warm fuzzies and a need to exert my independence, I couldn't quite back down. "I think I can ask a few questions without a babysitter, Zev."

"That's not what I meant."

"Then what did you mean?"

Instead of explaining, he said, "Let's see if Bryan gets anything from the feeds. I'm fairly confident Neil kept his presence under the radar, which means asking questions is a hell of a long shot and probably a waste of time. Hence, my initial comment that if Bryan comes up empty, we move on to option two."

Frustrated with the situation—and maybe a little with Zev—I gave in. "Fine."

He shot me a look then turned back, his lips twitching. "I'll take you to the Guild so you can pick up your car."

"That works. Thanks." I looked out the window and considered how to spend the rest of the day. Updating Sabella wouldn't take long, which left the remainder of my afternoon open. I could go back through the file then maybe drive by the alley where Jonas's body had been found. It might be a waste of time, but it would make me feel like I wasn't just sitting around, twiddling my thumbs.

Zev and I spent most of the drive back to the Guild lost

in our own thoughts. As we got closer, I couldn't leave without regaining some control of this situation. "If you get free and decide to poke around tonight, call me."

"I will," Zev promised. "I'm not sure how long things will run with Emilio, but as soon as I can, I'll let you know."

Knowing that Family business would always take priority, I couldn't expect more than that. "Sounds good."

Clearly occupied by whatever was going on with Emilio, he dropped me off at the entrance to the Guild's parking garage with a distracted goodbye. Twenty minutes later, I was waiting for the elevator to take me up to my condo when my phone buzzed with an incoming text. I pulled it out and stepped into the elevator as I read my screen.

Umber was asking if I had time to swing by his shop, as he had some information to share. I checked the time and told him to give me an hour. I got a thumbs-up emoji in response.

A sharp yip greeted me as I stepped out of the elevator and onto my floor. I turned to watch one of my neighbors, Angie, being dragged out of her condo by an overly excited Yorkie and another small, long-haired pup with bright eyes, not an unusual sight, considering that she did dog walking for various tenants.

"Ang, if they catch you bringing your pups up, you're going to hear about it," I said.

Ang's rainbow-hued hair was held back in a messy knot that threatened to unravel as she aimed a "Hush" at the vocal pup. She turned to me and explained in a breathless rush, "I forgot my cup." She held up a reusable coffee tumbler. "If I don't get my tea fix, I'm useless. I figured I'd run up and be back out before anyone noticed."

"Don't let me hold you up." I waved my hands, shooing her away. "Move quick before you're caught."

"See ya, Rory," she called as she did a strange mix of a skip and a walk to the elevator.

"See ya!" I unlocked my door and went inside.

As soon the door was closed behind me, I tossed my phone onto the counter then headed for the fridge. Breakfast was a fond memory, and lunch was long gone. I wasn't overly hungry, but I needed enough fuel to keep going or I'd fade into bitch territory soon. I foraged up a combination of left-over sushi, grapes, and string cheese.

Feeling a bit more like me, I cleaned up and headed to my room. Behind a closed door, I did a quick change from business casual to casual. Afterward, I left the door closed, as there was a chance Lena would be home soon, and this check-in required privacy.

I dropped into the uber-comfortable chair tucked in the corner near the French doors that opened to my portion of the balcony and pulled out the scrying stone Sabella gave me. Since it provided a direct hotline to Sabella, I wouldn't have to rely on a circle to channel my magic. Holding it up by the chain, I once again considered the wisdom of trusting someone of her stature, because that type always played a long game. But with Lena's reassurance that nothing nasty was hidden in the stone and confidence that my own magic would deflect the brunt of any less-than-favorable intentions, I took a bracing breath and cupped the stone in my palm. Then I used my magic to nudge awake the stone's slumbering hum of power.

The two magical energies touched and sparked, spreading like lightning through my noisy brain. It took time to compartmentalize my thoughts, making sure to lock my most private ones behind the strongest mental vaults I could imagine. Bit by bit, my brain fell quiet, and as my concentration strengthened, I brought Sabella's presence front and center.

She didn't make me wait, and her mental voice filled my head, resonating with a depth our physical interactions didn't have. *"Rory, you have something already?"*

"We have something, but you may not like it."

Then I laid out the concerns raised by Umber's story at the night race, the worries of Chloe's parents, and finally, what the team had discovered at Neil's makeshift lab. When I was done, she was quiet, but there was an edgy feeling to her silence that had sweat breaking out along my hairline.

When it became unbearable, I ventured, *"Sabella?"*

That looming threat drifted away. *"Apologies, Rory. I was not prepared to have such quick confirmation that Stephen and Leander's foolhardy ventures had borne fruit."*

"I'm not exactly sure they have. There's no doubt Neil's up to something, and whatever he's messing with, it's not good, but all we have right now are assumptions, nothing concrete."

"You said your friend at the tattoo parlor..."

"Umber."

"Umber—he has more information for you?" she asked.

"That's what his text said."

"Are you taking anyone with you?"

"No, the Three Arbiters are taking care of Family business right now. I'll talk to Umber and catch them up if what he shares leads to anything interesting."

A hint of amusement made it into her mental voice. *"The Three Arbiters?"*

"It fits."

"Dare I ask who is who?"

I wanted to roll my eyes because it was fairly obvious, at least to me. Bryan was the honest but slightly gullible Porthos and Imogen the ruthless player, Aramis, which left Zev to take the noble Athos's position—and not because he was sexy as hell. Instead of turning our conversation into a book-club meeting, I decided to bring our check-in to a close. *"I need to go, Sabella."*

"Of course," she conceded, humor still evident. *"I'm going to*

be otherwise occupied and unavailable shortly, so we'll talk tomorrow."

"When I can."

"When you can," she agreed.

When I was once again alone in my own mind, I rubbed my hands over my face and blew out a big breath. I scanned to ensure that my mental locks remained undisturbed, and only then did the tension tightening my shoulders ease. I'd survived my first check-in. *Yay me!*

I sat there, legs stretched out and ankles crossed, staring unseeing at my feet, exhaustion hazing my brain. Only the sound of the lock going and Lena's "I'm home!" kept me from falling into a doze.

I pushed to my feet, went to the door, pulled it open, and leaned a shoulder against the frame. "How was work?"

Lena tossed her keys and phone on the counter. "It was work." Her hands went to her hair as she studied me and unfastened whatever was holding it all in place. "How was your day?"

I managed a shrug. "Interesting."

"Interesting good or interesting bad?" Her hands dropped as her hair fell around her shoulders. She tossed a barrette onto the counter.

"A little of both." Not ready to hash it out again, I said, "I'm heading over to see Umber."

She folded her arms and eyed me. "You have a sudden urge for a tattoo?"

Since my aversion to needles made the answer obvious, I ignored her question and asked one of my own. "You and Evan still heading out tonight?"

Her nose wrinkled as she scrunched up her face. "Yes, but he won't tell me where."

I laughed. "And it's driving you nuts, isn't it?"

Her face softened. "Yeah, it is, but damn if I don't enjoy the suspense."

Once Evan decided to go all in with Lena, their relationship was fun to watch. Before Evan had demanded a spot in Lena's life, her career took center stage. As an unacknowledged member of the Clarke Family, she made it a point to prove to anyone and everyone that she could stand on her own, no help needed. Once Evan pulled his head out of his ass, he'd fractured that focus like a kaleidoscope. I liked that for Lena.

"Well, have fun." I crossed the room and picked up my phone and keys. "I'm out of here." I turned and headed for the front door.

Lena's voice followed me. "Rory."

I stopped and looked back. "Yeah?"

All signs of teasing were gone, leaving behind genuine concern. "If your interesting turns bad, you'll call?"

God she is an awesome friend. "Yeah, girl, I'll call."

She pinned me in place with a narrow-eyed glare. "And not like last time, where you called me after the fact, right?"

She knew me too well. I grinned. "Right, I promise." I crossed my heart. "Are we good now?"

"Fine." She shooed me away with her hands. "Go forth and find trouble."

I laughed as I left, not bothering to remind her that I didn't have to find trouble—it managed to find me just fine.

———————— ◆ ————————

I opened the door at Etched Chaos and stepped into a wall of noise. Voices called back and forth, laughter rose and fell, and just above the music being pumped through the speakers was the steady hum of various tattoo machines stitching ink into skin.

Sketches covered the walls, both in vibrant color and subtle monochrome. The front had some beat-up seats clustered around a low table, their current occupants separated from the business in the back by a partial wall that ran behind the front desk, its sides open to the back, where the artists' chairs were arranged.

At the desk, a dark-haired, multipierced twentysomething male occasionally shot an exasperated look at the four young women huddled at the counter as they flipped through a sketchbook, discussing options. Since it looked as if they'd be a while, I went to the other end and flashed Mr. Impatient a grin. "Umber in?"

He sauntered over, leaned his arms on the counter, and did the head-to-toe scan most males of his age did by habit. When his eyes finally made it back to mine, his grin was all kinds of flirty. It made me want to pat his cheek and say, "Aww, aren't you sweet." But I refrained.

"You got an appointment?"

I shook my head. "But he's expecting me."

"Gotcha." He straightened and picked up the nearby phone. "Umber, your presence is requested at the desk." The echo of his voice drifted from the back.

"Be there in a sec!" Umber shouted. Less than a minute later, he was walking up to the front. Meanwhile, the indecisive women had managed to loop in the front-desk guy for his opinion on their options. Umber spotted me and gestured. "Come on back, Rory."

Fortunately escaping before my opinion could be requested, I left front-desk guy to fend for himself. After all, that was what he was paid to do. I waited until I got to Umber before saying, "Hey, you. What's up?"

"Got something I want to share." He grabbed my arm and began leading me past the busy space and into a small deserted kitchen.

I settled into a beat-up plastic seat while Umber closed the door. He pulled out a nearby chair, its metal legs scraping across the worn linoleum as he positioned it next to me. "Okay, so here's the thing..." He swung the chair around so its back faced me and straddled it, resting his casted arm along the back. "Know those whispers I mentioned?"

"Yeah." I hated it when my instincts were proven right.

"Got another one today." His face was screwed up as if he'd bitten into something sour. "Normally, I'd blow it off, but man..." He shook his head, his Mohawk bending like a wave. "Sounds just as fucked-up as the shit that happened to me. And coincidence is for idiots."

Since I wasn't going to argue with that, I said, "Okay."

"About a week ago, a couple of my customers were hitting a scene."

Translation: they went to an underground gathering with music, liquid refreshments, and illegal party favors in an abandoned building. These pop-up events weren't common, but they happened.

"They were taking a break in the back alley, enjoying a smoke, when they heard two guys going at it."

Since that term could be broadly interpreted, I figured I'd better clarify. "Arguing?"

"Well, they weren't having a good time, that's for sure." He shifted in the seat, his voice lowering. "They didn't catch much, just enough to understand that some kind of drug deal was going down, and not in a good way. The tone was dark enough to make them decide to cut their smoke break short and get back inside."

"Umber, considering the circumstances, an argument like that isn't that unusual."

"It is when the next morning some SOB turns up well-done in that same alley."

A sour taste hit my tongue. A week before, Jonas Gainer

had been found dead and burnt in an alley. As Umber said, coincidence was for fools. The story left an ugly feeling brewing in my gut.

Even knowing it was a stretch, I asked, "Another sleeper?"

Umber tugged at the gauge in his ear. "That's the thing—I don't know. Figured I'd let you find out since you've got better connections than me."

"You got an address?"

He rattled it off as I put it in my phone. It sounded familiar enough, and I guessed that when I checked it against the information I had in the file, I'd find a match. "So your customers, they didn't hear any specifics?"

He shook his head. "Honestly, even if they said they did, I'd take it with a grain of salt as they weren't exactly sober."

I looked up from my phone. Since I'd have to defend this story to the other three hard-asses on the team, I pushed. "You sure they heard what they thought they heard?"

"Oh yeah. They were freaked, even today. They kept checking over their shoulders like men in black were hounding their asses. Paranoia like that..." He rubbed his chin. "So yeah, I believe them."

Considering that Umber's nose for bullshit was pretty damn good, it was enough for me. "Got it. I'll do some poking around, see if I can figure out who ended up in the alley and why." I was fairly certain I already had the who. It was the why that I needed. "Since I'm here, you mind if I poke around behind your shop?"

He got up from his chair. "Feel free, but I'm not sure you'll find much. ACRT was all over it." He flipped the chair around and pushed it back into the table. "You think you'll find something they missed?"

I stood as well. "Don't know—just need to walk through the scene."

"You going to hit that alley as well?"

Am I? If Zev found out, he'd ream me a new one, but everyone on the team was otherwise occupied. Besides, it had been a week. What kind of threat could possibly still exist? I shoved that question aside before fate decided to take it as a dare.

"If I've got time, maybe," I hedged.

Umber studied me for a long moment, looking far from happy. "If you do, you'd better watch your ass, girl. Something wicked is out there, and it's not playing nice."

Yeah, that's exactly what I'm afraid of.

CHAPTER THIRTEEN

WHETHER MY OPTIMISM was fueled by procrastination or curiosity, I couldn't tell, but I stood in the space behind Umber's shop and hoped to find something to rationalize my presence. With evening settling in, the strongest illumination came from the security lights bolted above the door. The dumpster was toward the back, away from the street, the concrete around it strangely clear.

I let the back door close, leaving me alone. I looked to my left and saw the traffic sliding by on the street. Anything that happened back here wouldn't be obvious. I took my time studying the space, noting the newish dent down toward the bottom of the dumpster, most likely where Umber had smashed into it. There were fresh gouge marks in the pavement just a few inches from the dumpster's current position. The metal container had been moved either during ACRT's investigation or when Umber hit it. Other than that, there wasn't much else to go on. Not a surprise. ACRT would have swept through this area, getting everything they could.

I finished my walk-through as an idea played along the edges of my mind. Being a Prism was a challenge, especially when trying to discover what I could and couldn't do. Information was nearly nonexistent, so my only reference so far was the journal Sabella had given me. There was one passage where the Prism mentioned being able to pick up on magical echoes. She hadn't gone into specifics on how she did it, but I had theories—one I hadn't had a chance to test yet.

This was an opportunity I couldn't pass up. Maybe I would fail, or maybe I wouldn't. Hell, maybe I'd get something but have no freaking idea of what it meant. That was the most likely outcome. Either way, it was worth a shot. Since I could feel active magic, it stood to reason that picking up on echoes had to work in a similar fashion.

Deciding this was as private as I was going to get, I moved until I could lean back against the wall next to the door and closed my eyes. I released the tight grip I kept on the awareness that clued me in to when active magic was near. It was nowhere near as easy as it sounded. At first, I let go too much and got a body slam of warding magic that left me hunched over, trying to catch my breath while my skin tried its best to crawl off my bones and my stomach threatened to turn inside out. Umber's security was fully active. I shoved my mental shields back up so I could reconsider my approach, because this clearly wasn't working.

Magic was not easily explainable—never had been. It was personal and innate, so instinct tended to be the driving force behind a mage's strength. In my case, when I was behind the wheel and needed it, what made me a Transporter would just click on. It wasn't as simple as being able to explain a process but was more like breathing. I needed air—I took it in, let it out. It was that simple. When I connected with a vehicle, every sense I called mine sharpened, became precise. I knew, at an unexplainable level, speed, mechanics, and reaction times and could anticipate minute changes that directly impacted my performance. The Guild had taken that innate skill and honed it through the years until it was an integral part of me, like my eye color or hair.

While Prisms and Transporters both had Mystic abilities, there was a big difference between the two. Being a Prism meant there was no one to train me on my gifts. Instead, I'd been left with trial and error and the tantalizing bits and pieces shared in the journal. I had to decipher vague descriptions provided by someone who thought the basics were a given.

Unfortunately, I didn't have the first clue as to what made up the basics for a Prism, so having that magical ability was akin to working with a faulty ignition. To get my magic to work, I needed to be able to not only power the magical engine but also keep that power strong and steady. Otherwise, the magic would stall out. I'd spent most of my life trying to both build the hypothetical ignition switch with scrap metal and maintain it until I had something I could work with. During the last few weeks, I'd been diligently replacing those temporary pieces with solidly built basics until I was working with a better ignition—not quite the desired fully functioning one but better than what I'd had before. At the moment, it was just a matter of figuring out how to work with it.

I inched down that barrier between the world and my sense of magic. The uncomfortable sensation of the security wards shivered over me, but I kept at it. It took a couple more tries before I figured out how to adjust the gap. I didn't know how it happened, and for future reference, I wanted to understand that, but whatever made me a Prism clicked on, shifting my perception to the next gear. Where before active magic had given me the heebie-jeebies, now it was as if a thin layer held back the worst of it.

Okay, I can work with this.

I could feel the flow of magic powering the security

wards, and something told me that if I let my attention expand, I would be able to pinpoint individual sparks inside the building. Before that could freak me out, I throttled back on the magic, narrowing it to the alley.

When I was fairly certain the power wouldn't gun its engine and roar free, I opened my eyes. I wasn't sure what I expected, but what I was staring at wasn't it. Although night was close, the alley was lit with a soft buttery yellow. I looked around for the light source but came up empty. I stopped moving and let my eyes go blurry just enough to soften the outlines of my vision. That was when it came into focus—a living net created by a thick weave of gauzy gold undulating with a hypnotic grace. Sparks of deep green, purple, and even silvery gray erupted along the lines every now and then, but when I turned to pinpoint the flash, they were gone.

The fluid movement stilled on the net's far side then snapped like a wet sheet around a small creature. It pulsed, going from gold to sage green then back to butter before the weave relaxed and returned to its normal dance. In the glow of magic, I stared at the feral cat, who hissed at me then disappeared under the dumpster.

"Holy shit." The words came out on an airless whisper as I realized I was seeing the magical layout of Umber's security. I considered how cool this would be if I was into breaching security for kicks, but that thought was quickly swept away when the net began to flicker in and out.

Right, I need to concentrate. I didn't know what I was looking for, but I started at the far end where the dumpster sat, since that was where everything went down. I noted the flickers in my peripheral vision as I took my time studying the dumpster and the area around it. It took a minute or so before I caught on to the fact that the magical construct danced just above the ground, coming close but not touching it. It was during one of those almost-touching moments that I noticed an anomaly.

I walked closer, picking my steps carefully and staying focused on what I was watching. At first, I wondered if it was a trick of the light, but with every dip and rise, the edge of the magical net changed color, seeping into a deep gold before shifting back to the softer yellow and then repeating in tandem with the movement. It wasn't much of a shift, but the longer I watched, the more obvious it became.

Hmm. Since I had no idea what it meant, I did my best to spot any other areas where this phenomenon occurred. I wasn't sure how long it took, but by the time I identified at least three, maybe four, other instances all near the metal container, a headache had set up shop in my temples. Recognizing that I'd strained a magical muscle, I released my hold on my magic, and it drained away, leaving me dizzy.

I braced a hand on the wall near the back door to Etched Chaos, dropped my head, and began the familiar breathing pattern used in my occasional bouts of yoga. When I was sure I wouldn't stagger out of the alley like a drunk, I set out for my car at a careful pace. Once my butt hit the leather seat and my doors were locked, I started the car so I could get the AC blowing. As the cool air washed over my clammy face, I closed my eyes and took a few minutes to make sure I would be safe behind the wheel. My best bet was to go home, crash, and wait for the next day, but that wasn't going to happen. Revved up by this newly discovered aspect of my Prism ability, I really wanted to try it again, this time in the spot where Jonas had bought it. Maybe I'd get lucky and find some sort of connection.

A small voice in my mind piped up that heading in solo to mess around with something I barely understood was a sure-fire way to guarantee that Zev would jump all over my ass. I shot back with the faulty logic that what he didn't know wouldn't hurt him. That earned me a snort of exasperation and skepticism, which I firmly ignored. Then, as soon as I felt steady enough, I pulled up the address Umber had shared on my phone and headed for the spot where Jonas might have breathed his last.

◆

Both Tempe and Scottsdale were cities that had decided light pollution was worse than crime, so instead of streetlights that actually discouraged illegal behavior, people who slunk in the shadows had plenty of nooks and crannies to call their own, bathed in a dull amber glow. Which meant that by the time I arrived, the last rays of the setting sun had been replaced by a mix of grays and blacks broken by weak pools of light.

The address sat in the not-so-great area of North Tempe and South Scottsdale. A couple of miles to the south or north, I'd hit either college nirvana or high-end shopping, but this in-between place had not aged well. It was an unsettling mix of well-used apartments, older homes no longer watched over by HOAs, and strip malls long past their prime. There were budget car lots and abandoned shopping centers that had once housed bulk food stores. If the recent wave of development by the university held steady, in the next ten years, this area would be swallowed up and left unrecognizable.

But for the moment, I was loath to park my car there. I circled the block of the address, trying to find a corner store or somewhere I could park without worrying about coming back to find my baby's frame on blocks. About a half block down, near the corner, there was a well-lit lot next to a car wash that looked promising. The business was a combination of self-serve and automated roller washes, but even better, it included well-lit parking spots. There were a few people taking advantage of the wash-it-yourself stalls, and traffic was fairly steady on the nearby street.

I pulled in, got out, and made sure to activate the car's warding as a backup to the standard electronic security. Still a little light-headed but much steadier than earlier, I back-tracked to the address that matched a strip of shops, most of which were long abandoned while a few held on by their fingertips. None of them were currently open, which ensured that my visit would stay low-key.

As I passed darkened windows and barred doors, I kept an eye out for security. There were a couple cameras that I doubted discouraged much of anything. The first one had a broken casing, and the second and third were aimed down at doorways, so swinging out toward the parking lot meant staying out of camera range. I strolled past the shop I wanted, noting the tagged plywood over two large windows and the heavy-duty lock and chain wrapped around the doors. Dust and grime coated the chain, lock, and doors. If it was used for parties, no one was coming through the front, which made sense if that action was going down at the back.

I kept my head down, just in case one of the cameras got lucky, and walked steadily. I got to the end of the building and went around the corner, aiming for the back. Garbage was piled up against an overflowing trash bin, and the stench was eye watering. My gaze skittered across the scene as I breathed through my mouth and picked up my pace.

I knew from the file that Jonas's body had been found in the back, so I didn't slow as I rounded the corner. A cement wall ran down the back, and the rush of traffic from the street out front barely penetrated. The space was narrow and dark. I could see how nefarious things could occur without anyone being the wiser.

As I stared into the gloom, a shiver ran down my spine, and I briefly reconsidered my decision. I shook it off. *I'm here now, so best to just get it done.* I pulled out my phone, activated the flashlight app, and moved farther into the alley. Even though I was trying for stealth, my footsteps sounded overly loud. Broken pallets leaned against the wall, and the weed-choked pavement was littered with typical trash found in such places—broken bottles, fast-food wrappers, old flyers, cigarette butts, and other unidentified debris. I moved the light over the ground, keeping it low, and picked up the darker side of a dumpster about where I thought the address's rear entrance would be.

I angled my phone toward my torso and my feet, trying to keep the light contained. I was fairly sure there weren't any cameras back here, but I wasn't about to swing that light around and give away my presence on the off chance that I was wrong. Carefully, I made my way over to the door closest to the dumpster. A glint of metal sparked through the shadows. The door was sporting a new chain and lock, a sure sign that its party days were done. Not that it mattered because—fingers crossed—what I wanted would be out here.

I shut off the phone's light, and the shadows pooling along the wall deepened. I kept my back to the building and crouched in case someone should happen by. Squatting in the dark was not good for my nerves. I knew I was alone, but it was still hard to shake off my unease. I unfurled the part of me that could sense active magic, searching for anything out of the ordinary, and came up empty. *Right, then.* I could excuse my jumpiness on the fact I was borderline trespassing and risking a misdemeanor.

A couple of deep breaths later, I was as calm as I was going to get. This time, I didn't dare close my eyes, because that was just asking for trouble. Instead, I let them lose their focus enough to trigger my magic.

I couldn't tell if the change was quicker because of my previous foray or because of my heightened sense of urgency.

Whatever it was, the world around me shifted, the edges turning fuzzy, but this time, there was no magical net to be found. Instead of the warm glow I'd encountered at Etched Chaos, I discovered faint, filmy strands of what could easily be mistaken for smoke. They drifted in no discernible pattern and were difficult to recognize. Only the fact they rose and fell in an invisible breeze clued me in to the fact that what I was doing was working.

Sweat lined my spine as I tried to hold on to the images, a task made difficult because the colors were faded and hazy and therefore hard to distinguish. Wrapped in the night shadows, they ran the gamut from wispy gray to ink black. These... echoes, or whatever, were maybe light purple or gunmetal gray. The only reason I could tell that much was because they were accompanied by a barely discernible hum of residual magic. The tidbit of power, weak though it was, hit my magical skin like pinpricks. The sensation wasn't constant but faded in and out, much like the blurry trails. But just like at Etched Chaos, the magical waves flowed just above the ground without touching, even as their faint colors wavered. If I hadn't known to look for that specific phenomenon, I would have missed it. Especially because when the waves changed colors, they were able to blend into the shadows, giving the impression they were winking out of existence.

Those strange blips of light and dark were clustered in the area in front of the dumpster, but something about them bothered me. I couldn't put my finger on it, but I shifted on the balls of my feet, tilting my head to get a better angle. It was difficult to stare without losing the hazy focus I needed. I set my fingertips to the pavement and leaned closer. The minute my fingers touched the ground, those broken spaces sharpened and took on definition.

I sucked in a breath. *Is that a rune?*

I tipped too far forward and had to shift my foot to regain my balance. That small move jarred my perception, and I lost the image. Even as I pinned the details in my mind, frustration rose. If those were runes or a sigil, they weren't like any I had seen, which meant I'd probably need to share this discovery with Zev. And doing that meant admitting I'd gone out solo after promising not to.

Fan-freakin'-tastic.

While I wasn't looking forward to that discussion, at least there was one positive takeaway from the night's adventures —we had a connection. Whatever had happened here was disturbingly similar to what had happened at Etched Chaos, which meant the two scenes were tied together. Now it was just a matter of figuring out what that tie was.

A sharp sputter of a siren interrupted my thoughts. Staying in a crouch, I pivoted back toward the opening as my heart pulsed in my throat and adrenaline rushed through my veins. A wash of red and blue was quickly followed by the steady scream of a police siren. An engine revved, the lights veered away, and the siren began to fade as the police sped down the main road.

A heartbeat passed, then two as the realization hit me that they weren't chasing me. Since I didn't want to tempt fate, it was time to get out of there. I got to my feet and went to take a step when my head spun, and I stumbled into the wall. Fortunately, my shoulder hit first and not my head. I wasn't sure my aching skull could take much more. I kept my gaze on the ground as the dizziness pulled back. I still wasn't feeling all that steady, but this was not the spot for a nap.

I pushed off the wall and carefully retraced my steps. I kept my head down as I made my way back to where I'd parked, this time because every move sent another wave of pain, not because I was avoiding detection. The half-block trek felt endless, and by the time I saw the bright lights of the car wash, the throbbing in my head had gone from annoying to painful. I'd definitely pushed myself and my magic too hard, and getting home was going to be a bitch.

I finally made it to my car, dropped into the driver's seat, and managed to engage the locks without whimpering. I sat there for I didn't know how long, eyes closed, simply concentrating on breathing. Bit by bit, the headache backed off, probably because I wasn't upright and moving. I was pondering the wisdom of indulging in a nap when my phone vibrated in my back pocket.

Keeping my eyes closed, I braced my feet and lifted my hips so I could dig my phone out. My poor head did not like the move and protested with a warning throb. Once I got the phone out, I carefully sank back into the seat and spent a few moments holding it. When it buzzed in my hand with a reminder of an unread text, I lifted it up to face height, thumbed the screen out of habit, and finally opened my eyes.

Zev: *Where are you?*

I guessed Zev was done for the night.

My fingers moved over the screen: *Out. What's up?*

I waited for his reply, but instead, my phone rang. Seeing his name on the screen, I picked up. "Hey."

"Out where?"

Maybe it was because my head hurt and I was exhausted, so my patience was stretched thin, or maybe it was his tone, but for whatever reason, my response was sharp. "Out. What do you want?"

Silence vibrated across the line. Then in a less aggressive tone, he said, "Things wrapped up sooner than expected. I thought we could go check a few things out that we didn't have time to do this afternoon."

The last thing I wanted to do was go back out and poke around, but it was my job, so I sucked it up. "Give me about twenty, and I'll meet you at my place."

"Tell me where you are. Maybe it'll be faster if I come pick you up."

What is his deal? I pulled the phone from my ear and glared at it before putting it back up. "Twenty minutes. My place."

Before he could respond, I hung up and tossed the phone into the center cupholder, wondering how much trouble I would earn by ditching his ass that night. Since the answer was probably "More than I could handle," I started up my Mustang and headed home.

CHAPTER FOURTEEN

I FOUND Zev waiting for me when I stepped out of the elevator at my condo. Dressed in jeans and a dark T-shirt, he was leaning against the wall by my door, arms folded and a familiar frown etched on his face. That frown, laced with broody intensity and paired with that body, took him from flat-out sexy male to dangerous badass trouble. It was a good thing it was late and most of my neighbors were already in, because with him standing there smoldering like that, someone would have called security. Or invited him in.

His gaze caught mine and held it. Then, as if trapped by an invisible tractor beam, it drew me in. With each step, I could feel my balance wobble along the thin line separating our personal and professional relationships, and I wasn't sure how long I could remain steady. He was going to have questions I wasn't ready to answer, which meant I was out of time and needed to make a decision on how much I was willing to share with him.

As I got closer, I could tell something was working deep in those eyes, but the exact nature of it was beyond me. I was dead on my feet, thanks to the night's activities.

He straightened, dropped his arms, and took a step toward me as the air in the hall went electric. "What happened to you?"

What? No hello? Instead of snapping back, I broke eye contact and headed straight to the door. "Nothing. I'm just tired."

I fumbled at the lock, finally got the door open, and stepped over the threshold. I pulled up short when the pulse of warding magic raked over what felt like raw exposed nerves. Gritting my teeth at yet another sign that I'd magically overreached, I touched a warding sigil set above the light switch in the entryway and reversed the ward, deactivating Lena's personalized version of a home security system.

The disconcerting sting of magic faded and was replaced by the unmistakable weight of Zev's presence close at my back. I heard him inhale sharply like a dog tracking a scent. I kept moving forward, doing everything I could to not look like I was avoiding his touch. I heard the door close and the lock engage as I headed straight for the fridge, praying it held something cold and caffeinated. Granted, I would have preferred a high alcohol content but knew that wouldn't be wise.

I dug through the second shelf and found a can of soda tucked in the back. With my head in the fridge, I asked, "Want something to drink?"

"No."

I grabbed the can, took a quick bracing breath, and closed the fridge. Only then did I turn to face the inevitable, shifting backward until my butt hit the cabinets and the counter's edge pressed against my spine. I popped the tab on the can and took a drink, keeping my gaze on Zev as he watched from across the island. I lowered the can and curled both hands around it, holding it against my stomach while we continued our stare down. Zev didn't say anything, just pinned me in place with his look that said plenty.

He was good, because I broke about fifteen seconds in. "What?"

"What happened?" he asked.

"Nothing happened."

"Rory, you look like a ghost, and based on the lines around your mouth and the permanent wince you're sporting, I'm also betting you're in serious pain."

Damn, he's good. If his insistence hadn't been so annoying, I just might have been impressed. "I've just had a long day, Zev."

"Stood with you through longer, so nope, not buying it. Share."

"Share what? I'm tired, it's a long day, end of story." *Why can't he leave it alone? Hell, a better question would be why can't I just give him a straight answer?* It was as if I had to keep testing him, keep pushing until he did what I expected and walked away. *God, I hope he doesn't walk away.*

"When I left you, you were fine. I come back a few hours later, you look like shit. That's not right." He cocked his head. "What did you do?"

I wanted to chuck my soda at him but didn't. "What's your deal? Why are you pushing this?"

He rounded the island and closed in. Me being me, I refused to retreat, so I stubbornly held my position. Not that I had anywhere to go as Zev stopped right in front of me, braced his hands on either side of me, and basically trapped me between him and the counter. He was so close that if I even twitched my hands, which were clinging to the aluminum can for dear life, I'd be touching him.

He leaned in, the movement causing the muscles of his shoulders and arms to flex. He lowered his head without breaking eye contact until all I could see was him. "Where. Were. You?"

My heart beat like a wild thing, and I could barely get air into my tight chest. The condo could explode around us, and I'd still be trapped in his gaze. Nerves that had nothing to do with fear and everything to do with Zev struck me. The faintly hysterical thought that he was digging in, not walking away, drifted through my mind, but he was so close, too close.

My thoughts were tripping over themselves and losing their way to my mouth, but I managed to string together enough to fight back. "Why do you want to know?"

"Because partners share. That's what they do."

His comment caused a sharp ache I refused to acknowledge. It also snapped the thin thread of panic and left me nervous and defensive. "Is that what we are? I thought I was your babysitter."

His face darkened, and his voice hardened as he met my temper with his. "Don't dump that shit on me. That was all Imogen, and you know it."

I bit my lip and dropped my gaze, because he was right.

He touched my chin with a finger, bringing my head back up. Once he had my eyes, he put his hand back on the counter. His anger faded. "The more you keep dodging, the more you make me wonder what you're hiding."

"I'm not..." I cut myself off because even for me, it was too blatant a lie to utter.

His lip curled, and it wasn't in amusement. "Yeah, that's what I thought." He shook his head. "You and your damn secrets." He didn't give me a chance to finish. His gaze drifted over my face, but I swore it felt like an actual touch. "If you want whatever it is between us to survive this, you need to stop hiding."

A jolt of surprise made me twitch at his blunt comment, making me give a knee-jerk response. "Why?"

The lines on his face relaxed as amusement crept in around the cynical edges. "You get that you're admitting you're hiding something, right?"

Okay, yeah, but... "Doesn't make my question any less valid, Zev."

"Fair enough. You want it straight?"

I barely stopped myself from rolling my eyes since if I asked, the answer should be obvious. "Please."

A few more harsh lines on his face eased. "If you don't trust me enough to share something this simple, what are we doing?"

Even though what he wanted to know wouldn't stay simple, his question struck hard and true, knocking me off my high horse of stubbornness with enough force to rattle some sense into my pride. I could feel the heat riding in my cheeks as I looked at my feet and muttered, "Dammit."

Reading it for the concession it was, he waited for me to talk. I lifted my head and met his gaze. He was still here, trying. I owed him the same. "Umber called, said he had some info to share and asked me to stop by."

"So you went alone?"

"You were busy, remember?"

"You could've sent me a text."

His comment caught me off guard and left me puzzled. "Why would I do that?"

Frustration stained his cheeks red. "I don't know. So I'd at least know where you were."

"Again, why? I'm perfectly capable of working solo. In fact, that's kind of my default, remember?"

He dropped his head until all I could see was the dark-haired top. "You should've called me."

Not able to see his face and get a read on his thoughts made my suspicions rush to the fore. Maybe I needed to give him the benefit of the doubt and construe his being pushy as concern for my well-being, but a cynical little voice reminded me of one inescapable fact—his primary loyalty was to the Cordova Family.

Treading carefully, I said, "Even if something did happen, it's not like you could do anything, because Family business takes priority, right?"

When he raised his head, I still couldn't read his expression, but his voice carried an edge of resentment. I just didn't know who it was aimed at—me, the Cordovas, or himself. "Never made a secret of that, Rory."

No, he hadn't, so my foolishly wishing he'd change his mind made zero sense. My grip on the can tightened, and the faint *ping* of aluminum denting whispered between us. Carefully sidestepping that argument, I slogged ahead. "You were busy, and I had time, so I stopped by. Plus, if you were at my side, it would make Umber uncomfortable."

Zev dropped his hands from the counter, straightened, and then leaned a shoulder against the fridge. "Why? He thinks I'm Guild."

His change in stance gave me a little breathing room, and my grip on the can relaxed. "For something like this, it doesn't matter. What matters is, he doesn't know you—he knows me."

Of course, Zev—being who he was and what he was—got that. "Okay. So his information, was there something to it?"

The tension in my shoulders eased as we inched around one of the potentially heartbreaking pitfalls that lay before us. "Yeah, actually, there was. He had a couple of customers who were there when Jonas died." I took another sip of soda.

Zev folded his arms, his gaze sharp. "Did they see what went down that night?"

I shook my head as I set the can on the counter. "No, but they heard two guys arguing about a drug deal and the intensity of it was uncomfortable enough that Umber's customers hotfooted it back inside, where an underground party was happening, to make sure they didn't get caught up in it. I pressed, trying to see if the partygoers heard anything specific, and Umber said no, but they freaked even more when a body turned up the next morning in the alley behind the party's location. It didn't take much for them to put two and two together to get a close four."

"But they didn't see who was arguing?" Zev asked.

"Right."

"So all they knew was there was an argument and someone turned up dead."

It wasn't a question, but I nodded.

"Okay, a meet with Umber would've kept you busy until dinner, but"—he watched me closely—"it doesn't explain you dragging back in here at close to nine at night."

As much as I enjoyed Zev's intelligence, right then it was a pain in my ass because he was leading us back into the minefield I wanted to avoid. "After the meet, I swung by where Jonas was found and the party was held."

"And?"

"And nothing." I tried my best to sound casual but failed.

Zev dropped his arms and turned away until all I had was his back. He crossed the small space to the island and braced his hands on it while he faced out into the living room. While I couldn't help but appreciate the rear view, the tension winding between us was making me antsy. Needing something to do, I reclaimed my soda and took a drink.

Without looking at me, he said, "You know those secrets I mentioned?"

Since it wasn't really a question, I didn't answer. Instead, I braced and waited for whatever this was to play out. He didn't make me wait long.

His shoulders bunched as he pushed off the counter and

turned back to me. "I didn't forget what went down when we went after Lena."

Playing stupid wasn't going to work, so instead, I stayed quiet and did my best not to squirm under his intense gaze.

His voice was quiet but sure. "There's more to you than a Transporter, and you're not keen on making whatever it is public."

Anxiety rose, sending my stomach roiling, as I wondered how much he'd figured out.

He took his shot, watching me carefully. "As you admitted your magic is Mystic based, I'm going to take a guess that whatever ability you have, it's some sort of variant of curse breaking, and you either see magic or can manipulate it."

I swallowed hard, held mute as his shot whizzed by so close I could feel it singe my hair. I'd forgotten that I'd made that admission when we were trying to get Lena out of the Drainer's Circle. He had flexed his magical muscle to reverse the spell, but to get enough oomph to make that happen, all three of us had to work together. For that to be done safely, he needed to know if we were combining like powers or not, which led to me sharing that my magic was the kind founded in psychic abilities instead of elemental.

He wasn't done. "So tell me, how close am I?"

Too damn close for comfort. Especially since that night's little experiment indicated that he was half-right—I could see magic. I didn't know enough about the magical spectrum to know if that ability was specific only to curse breakers, the mages who specialized in the setting and breaking of curses. If it was, I was more of a freak than I thought. Manipulating magic was always given the side-eye because mages didn't want someone messing with their abilities. What I did know was that Prisms weren't about manipulating magic—they were immune to it. That difference was what made being a Prism so dangerous. Magical immunity was coveted for a variety of reasons, and most of those would not end well for the Prism—a fact borne out by what historical stories I could find about Prisms.

"Rory?"

I stared at him as panic welled. I was nowhere near ready for this discussion, but Zev was right on one point—if we wanted something beyond this, I needed to know how far I could trust him. "Before I answer, I've got a question for you."

God, am I really going to do this? Putting myself out there meant giving him information he could take back to his Family. Even if I didn't share outright, what I gave him would be enough for him to start making the right connections. It wouldn't take him long to put it all together, and then... that was what worried me. Being outed as a Prism could potentially upend my life and put me in the midst of something I wasn't ready for.

But the thing was, my secret had been seeping out for a while. Sabella knew it. Lena knew it. I was pretty sure Evan had figured it out as well, considering how I'd gone about freeing him from a spelled trap laid with sub-rosa runes, which even a Key would have a tough time breaking. Chances were damn high the Guild director knew, too, especially since I'd grown up under their aegis and hadn't left until this last year. While working for the Guild, I'd run into the occasional situation that a typical Transporter might find challenging to slip away from. Now, as an independent contractor catering to the Arcane elite, keeping the lid on my ability was getting tougher and tougher with each day. *My best bet at controlling the fallout is to control the reveal, right?*

Something of what was going through my head must have been evident, because Zev took his time answering, and when he did, it came out stilted. "Ask."

Gathering my courage, I lifted my chin, and met his gaze

head-on. "If you knew something that wouldn't hurt the Cordovas but could cause someone else harm if they knew, would you tell Emilio?"

He slowly straightened, and it was like watching a snake uncoil. I braced myself.

"Would this knowledge bring danger or harm to the Cordovas at any point in time?"

Could it? Thinking of the journal Sabella had given me and how the Arcane Families relentlessly pursued the Prism who'd written it, the possibility was there. Honesty forced me to say, "I don't know."

At my answer, his gaze dropped, and despite the heavy shadow along his jaw, I saw it tighten. A moment passed, then two. Finally, he looked at me. "If this information was not an imminent threat to the Family, then I would have no problem keeping it to myself." Before relief could get a foothold in me, he added, "But if that changed..."

He didn't need to finish. Once again, his priority was clear —Family first. As much as I hated his honesty, I appreciated it. Hell, I even understood it to some extent. If he could be honest with me, even if it might end us before we even started, I could do no less. I gathered my courage close, lifted my chin and in a low but clear voice gave him a piece of me. "Yes, I can see magic, but it doesn't matter because I have no idea what I'm looking at or what it means."

His eyes widened, a clear indication he hadn't expected me to step up. "I don't understand. Didn't the Guild test you when you joined?"

I nodded slowly. Taking the Guild assessment exam was one of the first things a person did when applying for acceptance. "But at the time, my dominant ability was clearly in transporting, so that's what we focused on." When he continued to stare at me silently, I snapped, "What?"

He blinked and gave his head a short shake. "I just... sorry.

It seems strange that the Guild wouldn't take advantage of a dual ability and train you for both. A Transporter Key would be the ultimate in security transport."

The term was vaguely familiar, but I wasn't connecting what it had to do with me, probably because my head was still a pounding mess. "What do you mean?"

"What do you mean, what do I mean?" His confusion was obvious. "Any Family would pay dearly to have access to a top-notch Transporter who was a Key. Not only would their items be safe during delivery, but they also wouldn't have to worry about cursed packages. It also means a Family would only have to worry about trusting and paying one mage for two jobs. The demand for a dual-level mage who can handle that type of security means the Guild's commission alone would be nuts. Not to mention, once you went independent, you could've written your ticket."

As he spoke, his elation came through loud and clear. Unfortunately, seeing how keen he was with his assumption left my mouth dry and my legs weak. "I'm not a Key, Zev. I just see magical echoes."

His rising enthusiasm stalled, and he frowned. "You have to be."

It was my turn to blink. "I'm not."

"You are," he argued. "You reversed the occlusion spell that hid where they had Lena stashed, not to mention the house security wards you shut down when we first got to where they were holding her."

Shit shit shit. I had done that, just not the way he thought. When we went looking for the man who kidnapped Lena, we ended up at a rental with hefty security wards. I basically bullied my way through them by using my Prism ability to short out the magical repercussions. As for the invisibility spell that kept Lena hidden while the Drainer's Circle did its deadly work and siphoned her magic and life away, I didn't reverse it—I shattered it. At the time, things had been intense enough that I hoped Zev hadn't noticed the particulars of what I was doing. Obviously, I'd been wrong.

"That's not what happened," I said.

Impatience seeped into his voice. "I was there, Rory."

"I know you were, Zev, but I didn't reverse anything."

His excitement disappeared, and a new tension settled in, dragging along a hint of wariness. "Are you telling me you can manipulate magic?"

It struck me that maybe I should have paid closer attention in my basic magical theory classes, because the way he asked that made it sound like nothing good came with manipulating magic. "No, I can't manipulate magic."

"So you're telling me you've never trained as a Key, you don't manipulate magic, but you see magical echoes, yet you still managed to break a complex occlusion spell without serious physical or mental damage?" As he laid out the pieces, I knew that quick brain of his was making the connections faster than I wanted.

Swallowing hard, I managed to say, "Yes." Then, because I was a chickenshit, I waited for him to figure it out. Part of me wanted him to put the pieces together. Part of me really, really didn't. Neither part wanted to lie outright, because he wouldn't forgive that.

He stood in front of me, the foot or so of space between us widening with each breath, as he took what I'd given him and began to fill in the blanks. Uncertain of his reaction, I watched him, braced for anything. My decision was a good one, because when his reaction hit, my instincts were the only things that saved me.

Magic ripped out of him, whipping around my arms and chest to coil into a painful strike. Just as quickly, my magic snapped into place, taking the brunt of his unexpected attack on its invisible diamond-hard shell. A hiss and a wince still escaped me because whatever he'd thrown at me was meant to leave a mark, and the fraction of time between his attack and me erecting my shield was long enough for it to hit with raw intensity. The sudden pain, emotional and physical, sparked by his attack merged into instinctual self-protection, and then it was Zev who jerked back with a pain-filled hiss as my ability didn't just deflect his attack but turned it back on him. As I watched, red welts rose along his forearms.

That fast, I lost Zev and found myself facing the intimidating Arbiter who carried out justice and vengeance for the powerful Cordova Family. Facing that man scared me shitless, but a bigger part of me was pissed off and deeply hurt.

We stared at each other, the air around us vibrating with magic and volatile emotions. His dark eyes burned. So did mine, but definitely not for the same reason. He pulled his magic back, but mine stayed put. It wouldn't do shit against any emotional damage he meted out, but if he threw anything else at me, I'd make sure to give as good as I got. Well, so long as I could figure out how.

"No, you're not a Key." His voice was as flat and as empty as his expression.

"No, I'm not." My response was equally hard.

He took a slow, careful step back, his hands at his sides, palms forward as if trying to reassure a striking cobra that he wasn't a threat. There wasn't much room to retreat, and he stopped when he hit the island. Using the same careful movements, he folded his arms and let his weight rest against the island. The welts on his arms faded.

Those cautious movements worked like a subconscious signal, deescalating my magic. It was as if with him stepping back and assuming a relaxed pose, my instincts no longer viewed him as a threat. Too bad I didn't feel the same. Though I could feel my protective armor lighten, it didn't disappear completely.

Zev continued to watch me, and this time, I didn't miss the slight glow to his eyes, a sign that he was actively using his abilities. What those were, I had yet to figure out, something that I probably needed to remedy pretty damn quickly. I knew he could connect psychically with animals, as I'd made the unfortunate acquaintance with a raptor on our initial meet. I also knew he was an excellent tracker and hunter, not to mention that he wielded his magic with a terrifying confidence, so much so that he was the one who'd managed to reverse the lethal Drainer's Circle so we could rescue Lena. Something told me that whatever ability or abilities Zev claimed as his, they were a force to be reckoned with.

The way he watched me told me he'd put the pieces together and my secret was out. Sure enough, when he spoke, his quiet accusation fell between us like a bomb. "Prism."

CHAPTER FIFTEEN

STILL DEALING with the combined emotional repercussions of his attack and his declaration, I held his gaze and my tongue.

It was no surprise when he treated my lack of response as an answer. "Does Sabella know?" Before I could respond, he grimaced and muttered, "Of course she does. It's why she tied you to her so damn fast. I wondered when it happened. I just didn't think something like this would be why." The last of his magic flickered out, but his frustration lingered. "Dammit, Rory. Do you have any idea what you've set yourself up for, aligning with her like this?"

Wait, what? "You were the one who told me I needed alliances, Zev. You made it crystal clear that if I decided to work with the Arcane elite, I needed to cover my ass." Reading his disappointment and frustration in the harsh lines of his face, I was left choking on the feeling I was missing something important. Not about to let this go, I said, "Sabella's the head of the oldest Arcane Family. Working for her is about as covered as I can get."

He swiped out a hand, his voice rising with his temper,

"Contracts aren't alliances. Contracts won't haul your ass out of trouble if some half-cocked Family member decides they need their own personal shield and won't take no for an answer. Contracts will turn on your ass once the check is cashed and the job is done. Hell, some won't even wait that long."

I really, *really* didn't appreciate the thread of dread his rant caused or the way it hollowed out my stomach. "Sabella is not going to sell me out."

His hands went to his hips, and his eyes narrowed. "You sure about that?"

If I went with my gut, yes, I was sure, but I didn't think Zev was in the right frame of mind to appreciate that insight. What I did know was that if Sabella turned on me, I might as well dig my own grave. With the power and influence she had at her command, it would only take one whisper from her to destroy my life. Just as one word of praise from her would set me up for life. Two sides of the same tricky coin. It was a risk I'd recognized and accepted when I signed the contract. But faced with Zev's gloom and doom, paranoid doubts poked their annoying heads up.

I ignored the chill breaking over my skin and folded my arms, adding a defiant chin lift for giggles. "I thought you liked Sabella."

He grimaced and looked away and said reluctantly, "I do, but do you have any idea what will happen when it becomes known that you're a Prism?" He pushed off the counter and began pacing through the kitchen. On one of his passes, I caught a glimpse of something more than frustration in his face. *Is that... worry?*

On the off chance I wasn't hallucinating, I dialed back on my belligerent tone. "Yeah, actually, I do."

At that, he spun around so quickly I wondered if he'd

given himself whiplash. "Right." Disbelief dripped from that one word. "I find that hard to believe."

Insulted pride and age-old resentment came together in a snap, and my hands curled into fists, the action hidden behind my folded arms. Through gritted teeth, I managed to say, in barely civil tones, "And why's that?"

He stalked through the small space between us to loom over me. "Because if you knew what the potential fallout would be with that information being out there, you would never have given it to Sabella. Instead, you'd have taken that information to the damn grave." He glared for a moment, and whatever he read in my face had him spinning away, tension riding his spine, as he muttered, "At this rate, you just might."

I reached for my thinning patience and barely kept hold. I stared hard at his back and said in a voice that was lethally sharp with resentment, "You do realize it's not practical to expect any mage to hide what they are forever, right?"

"It is if exposing it will cost them their life," the arrogant ass shot back. "For God's sake, Rory! You put this out there, and you'll always be watching your back."

The certainty in his voice turned my vision red. "What do think I'm going to do, Zev? Run out and plaster it on a billboard? For fuck's sake, I know how to watch my own back. I've been doing it for years without you or anyone else." It was my turn to throw my arms out in disgust. I stalked away, needing distance so I wouldn't give in to my urge to slap him. "I know who I can and can't trust."

The charged air stilled then shifted to something cold and lethal. It hit me when I was halfway to the living room and brought me to a halt. I turned to find that Zev had stopped his pacing and now faced me. His shoulders were a ridge, his hands were fisted at his sides, and a scary intensity burned in his dark eyes. "You sure about that?"

Refusing to quail under that intimidating glare, I snapped,

"Yeah, I am, since I'm standing in front of you, alive and well."

His head reared back, an expression I couldn't read rushing across his face before he wiped it blank. He took a deep breath, then another. "Who else knows?" Something in the way he asked that set off all my internal alarms and left me uncertain of how to proceed. I stayed quiet too long because he took a slow step forward and demanded, "Who else, Rory?"

Worried that my answers might lead him to do something I wouldn't be able to forgive—say, hunt down whoever's name I gave him—I asked, "Why do you want to know?"

"Just answer the damn question."

"I'm not sure I want to, not with you looking like"—I waved a hand at all Zev in his wrathful glory—"you're going to go out and kill them."

He sucked in air, pivoted, and dragged his hands through his hair. He muttered something I couldn't catch, which was probably for the best. When he turned back to me, he'd leashed his temper. "I swear to you, I'm not going to go out and kill anyone, okay?" He waited for my nod then said, "Tell me who else knows."

"Lena." I shared the most obvious first then grimaced. "If I had to guess, Evan and probably the Guild director."

"How long?"

"How long have they known?" I waited for his nod. "Lena guessed when she was in the hospital, but she knew something was up long before that—she just didn't want to pry." *Because she is my best friend and understands the nature of dangerous secrets.* "If Evan's taken the time to reflect on how I helped him out of that spelled trap, he might have an inkling." *Especially if his curiosity is driving him nuts.*

Evan was a master at uncovering information, which was not an unusual trait for a top-notch electro mage who regularly mined the dark realms of electronic data with scary ease. *Something I should have considered years ago when I went looking for information on Prisms, but too late now...*

I yanked my wayward thoughts back in line. "As for the director, I don't know if she knows or not, but considering I all but grew up in the Guild and Sylvia is scary sharp and knows how to hold things close..."

He put a hand on the counter and used his other to rub the back of his neck. "And Sabella?" Zev dropped his hand until both were pressed flat on the counter. "How'd she find out? Did you blurt it out over coffee?"

His patronizing attitude was getting old. I pointed at him. "Fuck you, Zev." His brow lowered and his chin jerked back as I stomped over and got in his face, drilling my finger into his chest to empathize my point. "I don't owe you an answer. Especially when you're treating me like I'm a witless airhead."

"You're right. I was out of line." He caught my hand and held it tight, but for the first time, his touch did nothing for me. "I wouldn't ask if it wasn't important. How did Sabella find out?"

I didn't bother pulling my hand away. "I don't know. What I do know is she is the first person who cared to share something with me about something no one admits even exists." I got on tiptoe until we were basically nose to nose and hissed, "So for that, yeah, she's got my loyalty, which she'll keep until she proves she shouldn't, because she gave me something that was fucking priceless."

"What exactly did she give you?"

I dropped back down and went to step away, but he wouldn't let me go. Instead of degenerating into a physical tug-of-war, I pulled back as far as I could go. "A journal written by a Prism."

Something changed in his expression, but I was too pissed too care. I gave another tug on my hand and he finally released it. Free to move, I stalked away from him and into the living room.

His voice, no longer harsh but curious, followed me. "A journal?"

"Yeah," I admitted as the roller-coaster ride of emotions started to slow and exhaustion crept back with a vengeance. *Why the hell was I so angry with him about this?* I spent plenty of sleepless nights asking myself the same things—how Sabella knew, what her angle was, who else knew, and what it all meant. It was enough to drive me crazy, and sometimes I thought it had.

I dropped onto the couch and curled up on one side. I wasn't surprised when Zev followed and sat at the other end. I propped my elbow on the couch and dropped my head into my hand, staring at the floor without really seeing it.

"Reading through it was the first time I realized I wasn't some weird magical genetic one-off and that there was so much more I could do with my ability." I rubbed the ache in my temple and scrunched deeper into the cushion so I could rest my head against the plush back. "Unfortunately, it also reestablished why I needed to watch my ass around the Families."

"Everyone needs to watch their ass around the Families," Zev pointed out in a bland tone.

My snort of laughter came out a tad bitter. "That may be true, but after reading what that Prism went through, I have to wonder if it's worth it."

"If what's worth it?"

"Using my ability as a Prism or even admitting what I am. What they did to her..." The barbaric scenes from the past, stark horrors etched in faded ink, had made their way into my nightmares and left me shaking in the dead hours of morning. "Why do people have to be so damn ugly?" I shook my head, my heart aching with anger, fear, and resentment for a woman I'd never met but understood all too well. Turning, I looked at Zev. "What purpose did it serve to wipe out an entire class of mages? What exactly did the Families gain from what basically amounted to a systematic genocide?" I didn't really expect him to answer.

But he did. "First, it happened a generation ago, and as much as it sucks, there's no one left to hold accountable. Second, not all Families treated their Prisms like that. Many considered them precious because they knew exactly what kind of sacrifice they were asking from those mages."

His calm acceptance rankled almost as much as the near-clinical tone. "And that makes it okay?" I asked. "Prism after Prism died shielding precious heirs of notable Families, and in return, the Families basically wiped them out of existence. Not just physically but in every way possible. All because those same Families coveted a glorified shield. How is that fair? How is that considering them precious?" The last came out harsh, and this time, I met his gaze head-on. "Here's a better question. Why would someone like you give someone like that loyalty? How do you justify it?"

Zev shifted his position, bending his knee to bring one leg to rest on the cushion while stretching his arms along the couch's back and arm. His earlier anger was tucked away, leaving him watching me as he picked his words carefully and sidestepped my last question. "Is that what you think being a Prism was—a glorified shield?"

"History speaks for itself."

"Then you're reading the wrong history."

Mild though his response was, it did nothing to soothe the ragged edges ripping through me. I could feel my lip curl in derision. "I'm so sorry. Maybe I should've been clearer. What little history that was allowed to survive doesn't paint such a rosy picture."

Again, he insisted, "You're reading the wrong history."

"Really? And where am I going to find the right history, Zev? Who's holding it? Because it sure as hell isn't public record." I didn't give him a chance to respond. I was done with his blind faith in the Families. "Do you know how much it messes with your head when you have an ability you can't explain, much less find evidence of its existence? Bad enough I had no blood family to go to with my questions, but even worse, when I went looking for information, it was nowhere to be found. I dug through books and databases, and you know what?" Caught up in my escalating resentment, I didn't give him a chance to answer and kept spewing. "There was not one damn thing to be found. At first, I didn't even have a clue as to what I was looking for, so it made sense that I couldn't find anything. Only by a quirk of fate did I even find out my ability had a name. Once I had that, I dug deeper and deeper. Yet no matter how deep I went, I came up empty. Finally, I just gave up and figured it was better to keep my mouth shut and concentrate on what I knew I could do well, because there was obviously no way I was ever going to figure out what the hell lived inside of me. So that's what I did." My eyes burned, most likely from exhaustion, and I felt hollow.

Into that resonating quiet, Zev asked, "And now?"

Confused, I frowned. "Now what?"

There was a strange intensity to him I didn't understand. "Now that you have avenues to get information on Prisms, are you planning on using them?"

I still wasn't following him. Maybe I was so tired that it was messing with my brain. "What do you think I've been doing?"

He looked at his lap as he considered something. When he lifted his head, his face was unreadable. "How real can you take?"

That sounded ominous. However, there was no way I would

wimp out now, especially with him. "As real as you're willing to give me."

"I think you're looking for your place."

My mouth snapped closed as his statement ripped through my battered defenses and scored bone. I stared at Zev mutely as my world shifted and reformed under that brutal light. Pressure tightened my chest, and tremors began snaking through me. "Oh shit."

He didn't gloat, he didn't push—he stayed quiet, letting me find my way as my self-perception rocked and resettled. It took longer than I was comfortable with because it was an old pain, etched deep by years of convincing myself I was fine on my own and didn't need anyone. But that need to belong was there underneath all the stubborn persistence of doing things myself and the shameful jealousy of wanting what others had. It lay at the heart of the abandoned child who was now a grown woman, both versions of myself still searching for that elusive sense of belonging. On the heels of that came the realization that what my future held as I moved deeper in the Arcane society would require setting insecurity aside and finding the courage to forge connections I'd never considered. It kind of felt like growing up. And it sucked. Huge.

But Zev wasn't done. "That's why I'm worried, Rory."

There was a note in his voice that hurt to hear. I blinked until Zev came into focus, the emotion on his face hard to take. He held my gaze, his dark eyes bright with worry, but under it all, I saw something else, a fragile beginning of an emotion deeper than concern and closer to an experience I never admitted to craving—love. Nascent though it was, it was a promise, and it scared me to death.

Zev leaned forward, driving his point home. "To ensure that you survive and don't end up repeating history, you need alliances, not masters. More importantly, you need to know what you can do with your power so no one can use it against you, and you can't do that alone."

He's right. He's so right. I concentrated on that instead of what I was reading in his eyes. "Which is why I'm working for Sabella."

"She can't be your only source of information."

"I know that, but it's not like I can put up an ad for a Prism tutor." Honestly, if I could, I'd have happily interviewed a cadre of Prisms to get my questions answered, but I didn't have that luxury, and no one, outside of Sabella, was stepping up.

His lips quirked as humor pushed his intensity aside. "No, but you can leverage who you know."

I narrowed my eyes. "Are you offering to help?"

"Yeah, I am."

His short answer sparked a flurry of questions, and I blurted out the first one to escape. "What about the Cordovas?"

"Are you a threat to the Family?"

I blinked. "Are they a threat to me?"

"No." His answer was quick and firm, leaving no wiggle room.

Right, then. On to the next important question. "What do you get out of this?"

Instead of being offended, he actually grinned. "Your eternal gratefulness?"

I fought through the mini heart attack his grin inspired and croaked, "Is that all?" Even as I teased, I worried, because he had to get something out of this. That was how things work. It was a cold, cynical thought that lingered with stubborn persistence.

As if he could read my thoughts, his grin faded, and he turned serious. He reached out, took my hand, and held it in his. "No ulterior motives, Rory."

I wanted to believe him, but it was hard to forget that he'd been the one to warn me that everything came with a price when dealing with Families. And for all intents and purposes, Zev was, at his core, Family. I swallowed, my fingers twitching in his hold. "Then why?" Though proud that the question had come out steady, I couldn't stop poking at the sore spot.

Instead of the expected antipathy, he responded with a painful honesty. "Because I don't want to see you get chewed up and spit out." He tugged on my hand, pulling me closer. Stunned, I let him resettle me in front of him. "Because you fascinate me. You make me laugh. You make me want to tear out my hair with how damn stubborn you can be. You can be reckless but focused. You hold yourself back but don't hesitate to put yourself in front of others. You bounce between snarky and sweet, but most of all..." He let go of my hand and cupped my face, holding me still. "I want you strong enough to survive in my world."

I licked my lips nervously, unable to look away. "I'm not sure there's room for me in your world, Zev."

"I'll make it," he growled.

Then he kissed me. It wasn't the rush of heat and fire that burned behind the flash fire of lust but something more insidious, a brush of lips, meant to tease and tempt. Unable to resist that exquisite caress, my lips parted under the intimate pressure, and a sigh escaped only to be caught by him. His thumbs stroked along my jaw, the sensation cascading farther down and leaving a trail of aching want behind. Slumbering hunger blinked sleepy eyes open and woke with an undeniable craving for more.

Wicked man that he was, he took his time, keeping it gentle, luring me deeper into his web. My hands curled into his arms, holding on as everything blurred and the only real thing was his mouth moving against mine. By the time his tongue traced featherlight over my lips, that slow ember had ignited into a driving hunger, and I was more than ready to welcome him.

We got lost in the kiss, tongues tangling, breaths mingling, bodies straining. He left my mouth and began to lay a trail of kisses along my neck as I buried my hands in his hair. My fingers slid through the long strands, relishing the sensation. He wrapped his arms around me, holding me against the hard heat of his chest, and I clutched those silky strands into gentle fists, keeping him still as I let out a soft groan. Heeding my nonverbal demand, he opened his mouth, licked at the tender skin, and drew it deep enough to leave a mark. It felt so damn good that another groan escaped me, this one a little huskier, a little needier. It was echoed by his groan as his kisses stopped and he buried his face in the crook of my neck.

I blinked blindly up at my ceiling, wondering when I'd ended up on my back on the couch. Not that I was complaining. I liked his weight against me. In fact, there were certain parts I wouldn't mind having a little more against me, but some indefinable feeling held me still as if one small move would ignite the flames into a devastating inferno.

I swallowed hard, unable to escape his lingering taste. "Zev?" My voice was so husky it was nearly unrecognizable.

"Give me a minute, babe." His mouth moved against my neck as he spoke, setting off chills that raced down my arms.

"Why?"

Fortunately, he read my question correctly and gave me a reason for the change in direction. "Because I made you a promise," he said, his voice rough with want and regret, "and I don't want to break it."

Break it, please. Despite the plaintive whine in my head, I fought back the urge to nudge him over. "Okay." The word came out breathy.

We lay there, holding on to each other as the sensual storm receded. He pressed one last soft kiss where my neck met my shoulder, and his arms tightened then slowly unwound. He braced his hands on the couch and pushed up.

I bit my lip as the move forced his abdomen and the lower portion—where goodness awaited—deeper against me. My muscles twitched with the urge to move, to make that tiny shift that would get us back in trouble. Instead, I sighed and slid my hands from his shoulders to fist against his chest. "Well, that was... we should..." I wasn't sure what to say.

"Great," he finished. From his position above me, he gave me a smile that carried a hint of a wicked promise I wanted to claim. "We should do it again, but not until we're done with this job."

I cleared my throat. "Right, because that wouldn't be professional."

His chuckle was a mesmerizing mix of regret and wry humor. Slowly, we untangled and eventually regained our positions sitting side by side on the sofa. This time, his arm was around my shoulders and my head was on his chest. It was almost as good as our previous position. Almost.

"So..."

"So..." he repeated.

I angled my head back so I could see his face. "So what do I need to know to survive in your world?"

CHAPTER SIXTEEN

FOR THE NEXT couple of hours, Zev and I discussed the various techniques and theories of offensive and defensive magic Zev insisted I needed to understand in order to refine my maneuvers. Some of it reminded me of my Guild-training days, but he took it further in an effort to ensure that I had something to work with. The conversation veered into a careful—on my part—description of what I'd seen behind Umber's place and where Jonas had died. Zev reaffirmed my assumption that what I'd been looking at was a visual echo of magical energy. He theorized that it was a natural byproduct of being a Prism, seeing how my ability was centered on magical energy. Neither one of us could explain the strange blips, but we did agree it was worth researching when we had time. That segued into a plan of how he could help me safely explore the limits of my ability once this job was over.

It was disturbingly easy to talk to him, especially when I wasn't busy hiding who and what I was. But despite my rising excitement at accessing information I'd spent years chasing, I couldn't give him everything. I held back some aspects of my abilities because, well, a woman needed some mystique. Not to mention, a lifetime of wariness couldn't be erased by an intriguing promise sealed with a hot kiss from an even hotter man.

By the time Zev walked me to the door and gave me one last kiss that would trigger very pleasant dreams, the excitement was dulled by exhaustion. It had been a long, emotion-filled day, and I was ready to call it a night. I left the light above the stove on for Lena, who was still out with Evan, and shuffled into my room. I barely remembered stripping down and falling into bed before the buzz of my cell phone dragged me out of a deep, dreamless sleep.

"What the...?" I mumbled, slapping around my nightstand until I found my vibrating phone. I touched the screen and squinted at the incoming text. Seeing Bryan's name attached, I knuckled my eyes clear as I sat up with my back against my headboard and drew my legs up tailor style.

Ramada Wyndham 1640 N. Scottsdale Rd. Rm 259 ASAP

I sent back a quick *OMW* then got out of bed. Ten minutes later, I was locking the condo door behind me and taking the elevator down to the garage. Night skies held sway, as dawn was still a couple hours away, but even better were the near-empty streets. It didn't take me long to arrive at the three-story hotel in North Tempe. The blocky construction with the Spanish tile roof hinted at age, but the clean white paint and neat landscaping told of recent renovations. Fortunately, it was one of those hotels where you could bypass the front desk and go directly to the rooms.

Noting the numbers near the corners of the buildings, I found an empty parking space near the right section. I got out of my car and spotted Zev's Harley a few spaces down, parked alongside Bryan's now familiar battered SUV. I scanned the parking lot and found Imogen's coupe, predictably parked all by its lonesome so as not to get contaminated by the more plebeian rides. *Looks like the gang's all here.*

I hit the walkway leading between two buildings and, in moments, found myself skirting a pool glittering in the shadows cast by the surrounding lighted walkways. The red doors of hotel rooms broke up the white walls that formed a U around the pool, but at the far end, soft light spilled from an eye-catching wall of windows framed in the same deep red. In front of that was a shuffling group of people wearing a variety of sleepwear clustered around the chairs and chaise lounges normally used for sunbathing.

I avoided the half-awake, grumbling group by taking the long way around the pool to get to the other side. Movement near the far corner caught my eye, and I looked over to see Bryan gallantly leading an older couple over to the others. He was bent in toward the snow-haired woman, listening. He answered, patted her arm, then turned to leave. He caught sight of me and jerked his head toward the rooms behind him.

Heeding his silent directions, I met up with him at the stairwell and followed in his wake to the second floor. We walked quickly down the walkway, and I couldn't help but note that Bryan looked a little rough. His hair was disheveled as if he'd been dragging his hands through it repeatedly, and his jaw carried a five o'clock shadow. Not to mention his blood-shot eyes. It was obvious he'd been going nonstop since that afternoon.

We met up with Imogen and Zev, who were waiting about halfway down the walkway. I checked the room numbers and realized 259 would be farther down, near the end. I kept my voice low so it wouldn't carry. "What's going on?"

"Imogen and I tracked Neil to this room," Bryan said tersely. "The night clerk confirmed he checked in the day before Jonas turned up."

At Bryan's statement, it hit me that the hotel wasn't far from the nearly abandoned strip mall I'd stopped at earlier. "Is he in there?"

He ran a hand through his hair as his eyes slid to the room then back to us. "I don't think so."

"But something's moving in there," Imogen added, all business. "With the curtains closed, we'll be going in blind."

That explained why they'd pulled people out of their rooms and hustled them downstairs. With what Neil had been playing around with, no one was willing to risk a magical attack on innocent bystanders. As we huddled, I noticed a young man slowly herding those by the pool inside, occasionally sending a worried glance our way.

Zev saw him too. "We convinced the night staff to let us handle this as Family business. If we can keep this contained, we shouldn't have to deal with the authorities."

Ah yes, the benefits of a Family connection. "So what's the plan?"

Not surprisingly, Zev took charge. "Rory, you're going to knock and see if you can get him to open the door."

I looked at him with my brows raised in silent question.

He explained, "You're the only one of us that he wouldn't recognize."

It sounded logical, but there was something in his look that warned me that there was more to this than what he'd said. Not sure if my interpretation of his intense looks was working correctly, I repeated, "You want me to knock and get him to open the door?"

"Yeah." His one-word response was flat, but his gaze said a hell of a lot more.

I frowned and tipped my head the tiniest bit to the side in silent inquiry. His chin dropped in a barely perceptible dip of acknowledgement. If I was translating correctly, he wanted me to use my ability to check for a magical threat. That I could do.

"And all of you will be where?"

"Right behind you," Zev assured me.

Imogen, who'd been silently listening up to this point, gave a snort as Bryan muttered, "Need to move, people."

Discussion over, we headed toward room 259. The Three Arbiteers took up positions along the blank wall space between the doors, leaving me seemingly all by my lonesome in front of the door. Taking a bracing breath, I released my grip on my magic, let the edges of my vision fuzz until the magical echoes began to flicker to life, and knocked.

Three things happened at once. First, I didn't crumple in pain when my knuckles hit wood, which meant no security wards were active. Second, a wash of power emanating from the motley trio to my right triggered an immediate response from my magic, which snapped into place in order to buffer the impact. Third, a violent burst of sickly red-and-gray magic surged through the cracks of the doorframe, impacted with the Arbiters' power, and erupted into a blinding burst of light while something hit the door with a resounding thump.

Unprepared, I stumbled back a step. "Whoa!"

"Rory?" Zev called in a low rumble.

I waved a hand in his direction as I blinked my vision clear. "I'm good." The last of the dancing white spots disappeared, and I realized the three watchful mages were staring at me intently. Uncomfortable under their perusal, I turned back to the door. "Something is definitely moving around in there, and it's not friendly."

"Human?" Imogen asked.

Studying the tendrils of disturbing magic licking around the doorframe, I cautiously shook my head. "I don't think so." The writhing power didn't reach above the doorknob, which made me think whatever was generating it was either a feral toddler or some kind of animal. No way could I imagine Neil running around with a toddler, but him carting around an animal seemed plausible, considering what we'd run into at his cobbled-together lab. "There's no ward on the door, but I'd advise caution going in."

Zev stepped up and, with a gentle hip check, nudged me aside. "Step back."

I did as ordered and waved a hand at the electronic keypad on the door. "Have at it."

A crystalline blue glow erupted over his hands and crawled up his arms. He pressed his palm against the pad, and small forks of lightning erupted. Coincidentally, a teeth-gritting scrape of power scored over the protective layer of my magic and left a slight but persistent ache behind.

Dammit, I should have stepped farther away. Too late now.

Zev's magic receded until it was gathered around his hands. He looked at Imogen and Bryan, and after an exchange of nods between the three, Zev grabbed the doorknob. Imogen and Bryan moved up to Zev's back. Power roiled around the three of them, agitating those ugly red-and-gray tendrils. Disgruntled with the heavy air of power, my magic thickened the protective layer, muffling the worst of it so I could stand steady under the unrelenting pressure. Since a headache was starting up, I let go of the soft-focus vision.

As I was out of the badass loop, I hung back, not anxious to get nailed by whatever lay in wait on the other side of the door. I'd leave that to the professionals. However, I couldn't help but warn Zev, "Be careful." When he turned to look at me, I could feel my cheeks heat, but I sallied forth. "Whatever it is, it's determined."

He cocked an eyebrow. "What am I looking at?"

I managed an uncomfortable shrug. "Don't know, but that impact sounded about yea high." I lifted a hand to hover midthigh.

"Got it." He turned back, his magic expanding before him as he slowly opened the door and slipped inside.

Imogen and Bryan each shot me a long look but stayed at Zev's back, leaving me to trail behind. Once inside, I slapped around the wall near the door until my palm hit a light switch. I stayed close to the door, shutting it behind me, as the soft glow of a lamp near the bed beat back the shadows.

In the faint illumination, the jumbled mess of the room barely registered as my attention was snagged by a muted grunt from Zev, a furious hiss from Imogen, and a muffled exclamation from Bryan as vying magics filled the room. Confusion abounded. A flash of indigo shot out and hit the bundle of sickly red taking up the floor space between the bed and the door. A sharp squeal preceded the ear-popping sensation of a pressure change, which left my ears ringing. There was a clash of cold and heat, and when the dust settled, Zev was in a defensive crouch, hands up in a combat pose. Imogen mirrored him as a pearlescent silver glow curled around her, and Bryan was aiming a gun at something in front of Zev.

"What the hell is that?" Bryan asked, his question echoing through the room.

I inched around, toeing what looked like a shredded pile of rags out of my way so I could get into position to see what they were staring at. When it came into view, all I could say was, "Holy shit."

Nauseating and morbidly fascinating at the same time, it was similar to the Frankenstein creature in Neil's makeshift lab except bigger and nastier. Of course, that could be because it was currently trying to escape whatever spell Zev and Imogen had it trapped in so it could rip off their faces. I could see traits of rat, cat, and maybe raccoon melded together into a monstrous concoction.

It was caught in midattack, its lower half encased in solid

ice while Zev's blue flames wrapped around it like a net. The creature was so determined to get to Zev that it fought the magical restraints with mindless intensity. It was disturbing to watch because I could see where the lines of Zev's power were slowly slicing into fur and skin, raising raw wounds. Even more chilling, there was maybe a foot or less between the foam-laced muzzle and Zev's face. Showing a decided lack of concern, Zev stayed crouched and moved a few inches closer.

"Do you have it?" Imogen gritted out.

"Almost," Zev murmured as his hand moved and a thick ribbon of blue locked on to the creature then began to wrap around that snarling snout like a muzzle. It was a visual reminder that Zev had an affinity for animals. The straining creature's jerky movements began to slow, and the lines of the blue net darkened, but the evil red glint in its eyes didn't dim. Zev moved one of his magic-coated hands toward it. It snarled and lunged, trying to sink sharp teeth into his skin. Fortunately, it missed.

"Is there something we can put it in?"

It took a second for Zev's calm question to register, but I drew back and took in the room. "Give me a minute. I'll see if I can find something."

"Make it quick," Imogen demanded.

I refrained from rolling my eyes as I skirted Imogen and Zev. There wasn't much to the room—a queen-size bed, a nightstand, a dresser, a TV attached to the wall, and the closed, deeply gouged door, which probably led to the bathroom.

Bryan was staring at the creature with clear disgust. "Better if I just kill it now."

"Let's try to keep it alive so we can figure out what the hell happened to it." Zev's attention didn't waver from the animal.

I kicked aside the shredded remains of the comforter pooled on the floor and squeezed through the narrow space between Zev and the foot of the bed.

"I think it's pretty damn obvious what happened," snapped Bryan. "Neil's been playing mad scientist, so you'd better make sure that thing doesn't bite you."

Still on a mission for a container, I spotted a mangled mesh of metal in the space between the bed and the closet. Since the bedside lamp was on the other side, shadows were deep and heavy in the narrow space. I pulled out my phone, activated the flashlight app, and aimed at the mess. "I, uh, found the cage." I picked it up, turned, and held it aloft for the others to see. "Don't think it's worth much anymore."

That was putting it lightly. The wire mesh carrier looked as if the creature had exploded out of it, tearing a hole in the side and leaving tuffs of bloodied fur on the sharp torn ends. I lifted it higher, brought it close, and let out a low whistle of disbelief. "Definitely don't let it bite you, Zev, because based on these teeth marks, I'm thinking you'll lose an appendage if it gets close enough."

"Not helpful," Zev grunted.

"Right." I tossed the useless carrier onto the bed and put my phone back in my pocket.

I turned back to the closet, slid open the door, and found it empty. *Great.* That left the bathroom. I went to the door and put my hand on the knob, and then caution kicked in. Just in case our Frankencritter wasn't alone, I touched my magic as I searched the bathroom to make sure I wasn't walking into a spell of some sort. When my power remained calm, I stood to the side, took a deep breath, and threw the door open.

When nothing rushed out, I flicked on the light. My stomach tightened. Blood spattered the counter. Towels were an ugly mix of rust and white. The mirror above the sink sported a starburst pattern marred with more red, and long cracks snaked out to the edges of the mirror. "Neil can forget about his security deposit."

Behind me, an animalistic shriek of pain erupted simultaneously with Zev's curse. Magic hit my back, and I spun around, eyes wide, to see Zev standing, hands at his hips and a dark glare directed at the floor. Imogen was pale but resolute, the silvery glow gone, and Bryan's gun was now aimed at the floor.

"What happened?" My voice came out strangely calm despite the fact that my heart was going a hundred miles per hour.

Zev dragged a hand through his hair, a disgusted look on his face. "I don't know."

I got closer until I could see the limp body on the floor, lying motionless in a spreading pool of blood. "Guess we don't need a container."

"Actually, we do," Imogen said in a coldly clinical voice. "We need to get this"—she motioned to the dead animal—"whatever it is, into a lab so we can figure out what Neil did to it."

"I'll go hit up the front desk," Bryan offered, tucking his gun into a holster in his waistband. His lip curled as he stared at the carcass. "Maybe they'll have some rubber gloves. I'm not touching that thing." He didn't wait for a response but headed out.

Imogen gave Zev a look I couldn't read. "I'm going to make a call and find someone in-house who can figure out what that is."

Zev gave her a nod, and she turned and stepped outside. When it was just Zev and I in the room, I asked softly, "What the hell?"

His voice was equally quiet. "I don't know. I almost had it calmed, then something snapped, and the next thing I know, it's seizing in its own blood." He looked at the still-open door, and I did the same. Imogen was on her phone, staring into the courtyard. "Rory."

I turned back to Zev. "Yeah?"

"I need you to look at this before they get back."

I studied the mess on the floor. "I'm looking at it, Zev."

"No." He shifted closer, his voice going lower. "Like you did in the alley. We need to know if the magic involved is similar to the other scenes you looked at."

Knowing we didn't have much time, I gave him a short nod and let my vision soften. The dull ache spiked, but I pushed through until the magical echoes lit up the room with dizzying speed. This time, they were brighter, probably because what had gone down was only moments old. The shift was so abrupt that I felt my balance tilt, but before I could fall, Zev's arm was around my waist, keeping me steady.

"Thanks," I whispered then got to work.

Even as I studied the undulating pattern, the magical traces began to fade. I held on grimly, focusing on the warped ribbons that lingered, but they kept smearing away like greasy smoke. I was able to pick out the deep blue going the stormy gray of Zev's magic, the silvery pearl shading to the white of Imogen's lingering power, and the sickly red mottled with an ugly pewter color that was slowly uncoiling around the creature. But no sigils, no runes, at least none that I recognized. And just at the edge of my vision were those strange blips where the echoes flickered in and out like an electrical short. The arm at my waist tightened in warning, and I blinked my vision clear.

"You got someone?" Zev held me so close that his question vibrated through his body to mine.

"Yes," Imogen said in a snippy tone.

Someone has her panties in a bunch. I couldn't find it in myself to care, so I took my time pulling away from Zev under

Imogen's narrowed-eye glare. Ignoring her, I crouched by the animal, resting my arms on my knees, making sure not to touch it. I studied the still body, noting that there were no obvious signs of surgery, which added weight to our assumption about Neil's Fusor abilities undergoing an unexpected boost. Following that logic, the next conclusion would be that the boost came in the form of a serum. *If Neil was willing to use a serum on himself, wouldn't he have tested it first?*

"I think it's safe to assume Neil has progressed to animal experimentation," I said.

Zev had no problem following the same logic. He turned to Imogen. "Your contact—can they rush the test results?"

"I'll make sure they do." She skirted around me and moved farther into the room, carefully picking her way through the mess.

Still staring at the pathetic lump of fur, I murmured, "If we're lucky, maybe they can tell us why it died."

Imogen snorted as she went to the door of the bathroom and stuck her head inside. "I'd think the why would be pretty obvious."

I had to give her credit—she navigated the line between condescending and mocking well. Getting into it with her was a waste of time, so I didn't bother. Instead, I thought about the similarities of the echoes here and where Jonas and the sleeper had died. Since Zev had waited until Imogen was otherwise occupied, I knew he didn't want to share my newly discovered quirk, but it didn't feel right not to get the team on the same page. Besides, seeing the similarities wasn't enough. We needed someone to be able to match the magic used here to the magic used at the death scenes. Vague suspicions filled my mind, but I didn't have enough to string them together. I needed a way to get more information and not just because Sabella would require solid proof.

The minute I added Sabella to the mix, the solution hit

me. I could use my status as her proxy to make unorthodox requests. In the initial meeting with Trask and Clarke, they'd mentioned that the serum worked on the brain, which would be what Imogen's contact would look for, I was sure. But that wasn't the only kind of forensics out there. In my time with the Guild, magical forensics had been a key component in various cases. This shouldn't be any different.

I rose, easing the ache in my calves. "Besides physical evidence, is there any way to determine if there's a magical connection between this"—I motioned to the animal—"and Chloe's and Jonas's deaths?"

Imogen turned from the bathroom and eyed me with speculation. "Maybe."

"That's definitely worth checking," Zev said, taking the hint and adding his weight to the conversation.

Imogen considered us for a long moment then slowly nodded. "I'll submit the request and have management hold off on cleaning the room."

"Thanks." Now that I'd gotten what I wanted, I could be nice.

"This is all they had." Bryan walked into the room, waving an empty garbage bag.

Imogen's nose wrinkled. "It'll have to do."

In a matter of minutes, the dead animal was wrapped in plastic. We left the room and stood on the walkway as Zev set a ward on the door. Dawn chased back the night as we talked. Bryan set the bag down at his feet, and we discussed next steps. Imogen would notify hotel management that the room was to remain undisturbed until she could get a forensics team in. She would supervise the evidence collection then accompany it back to her contact and encourage them to prioritize the results. She promised to update us as soon as she could.

Bryan volunteered to get surrounding street and security

cameras to see if we could track Neil's movements. It would make for a long day because he'd have to work his way backward. Zev and I volunteered to review the tapes Bryan had collected, as the only thing on our agenda was our interview with Kerri in a handful of hours.

"Send me the link where you're uploading the videos," Zev told Bryan. "Rory and I will work through them at my office once we're done with Kerri."

"You have an office?" I asked, taken aback. I just couldn't picture him in a corporate setting.

"The Cordova Family has a suite at Dueñas Park." He seemed amused.

Dueñas Park was a collection of multistory buildings that sat in the middle of Medina Memorial Plaza and housed corporate offices for many of the more prominent Arcane Families in the area. It was also the site where I'd taken the job that had me crossing paths with Zev for the first time.

"Right," I mumbled while they finished finalizing their plans for the day.

We exchanged promises to check in by evening with the latest so we could finish putting the pieces together and hopefully corner Neil. We headed down the stairs and through the empty courtyard to our respective rides.

Zev stayed back with me while Bryan followed Imogen to her car, where he put the bag in her trunk then turned to his SUV. As Bryan got in and Imogen backed out of the lot, Zev said, "I'll be at your place in about an hour and a half."

Bryan followed Imogen out of the lot, their taillights disappearing around the corner of the building, leaving Zev and I alone.

Not quite following, I said, "Sorry?"

He shifted his position until I was trapped between my car and him. He brushed his hand over my cheek in a fleeting caress that made my lashes flutter in pleasure at the delicate touch. "Go home, down some caffeine, check in with Sabella, and do whatever it is you need to do to get ready for our interview with Kerri. Since we're spending the day together, I'll pick you up around eight."

Somehow, without my volition, my hands found his chest. The heat of him seeped through my palms as I looked up into his face, noting the faint signs of interrupted sleep and lingering stress in the lines around his mouth and eyes. The sight tugged at my heart.

I managed a soft, "Sounds good."

He dropped a kiss to the top of my head and stepped back then waited until I was safely in my car before he strode to his bike. He followed me out of the lot, and I lost him when I had to turn west and he continued north.

As I was driving home, all the random pieces kept swirling through my mind. Just before I got home, I checked the time, noting that it was just past six, and instructed my Bluetooth system to call Evan's desk number. When I got his voicemail, I used the personal-favor card and left a message asking him to do a scan for reports on any unusual deaths in the area from Etched Chaos to North Tempe, specifically where ACRT had been called in. I also gave him the names of Jonas, Chloe, Neil, and Kerri to see what he could dig up.

It was a long shot, but it made me feel better to have someone I knew looking into things, especially a master electro mage like Evan. For me, he'd dig deep and fast and not just because he was sleeping with my best friend but because, like me, he regarded the Families with a jaundiced eye and wouldn't want a member of the Guild twisting in the wind. I was sure the Arbiters would share, with Sabella watching them, but just in case they decided to hold something back for their Families, I didn't want it to come back and bite me in the ass.

CHAPTER SEVENTEEN

ZEV PULLED up to the safe house where Kerri was stashed with five minutes to spare. Actually, *safe house* wasn't quite accurate. It was more like a safe apartment located in one of the older neighborhoods west of the university. The two-story complex was well maintained despite its apparent age, and small squares of green were broken by cement walkways. Tree-lined streets doubled as parking for the collection of economic rides characteristic of the college crowd. The shiny black SUV that belonged to the Trask security team stood out like a sore thumb.

Zev lifted his chin in the SUV's direction as we followed a sidewalk to a three-quarter brick wall enclosing the nearest garden unit and its tiny backyard, which sat directly in the line of sight of the watchers. I caught a glimpse of the parking lot on the other side and realized we were coming in from the back of the complex. *Strange, but all right.*

I glanced around, noting how quiet it was and wondering why Trask had chosen this place to stash his remaining researcher. Safe houses required heightened security, and this, in my limited opinion, was far from secure.

Zev unlocked a wooden gate and held it open as I passed through. I eased my grip on my magic just enough to test for any wards and hit pay dirt, literally. A thick layer of magic lay under my feet, covering the small yard, which measured twelve by eight feet at most. Two faded red plastic chairs sat on the cement slab of the porch shaded by the balcony from the unit above. Between the chairs, a round metal table held an empty vase covered in dust. It was not the most inviting spot in the world but was definitely protected.

Zev rapped his knuckles on the sliding glass door and waited. It didn't take long before the long vinyl slats swayed and the wan face of a woman appeared. She blinked up at Zev, her mouth forming a surprised "Oh." Then she was unlocking the door. She opened it just a few inches as if that would keep Zev out. "Mr. Aslanov?"

"Good morning, Dr. Michaels." Zev moved to the side and motioned to me. "My associate, Ms. Costas. Ms. Frost explained that you had time this morning to talk to us."

"Yes, of course." Kerri moved aside, disappearing into the shadowed interior as she kept a hand on the blinds to hold them out of the way. "Please come in."

Zev waved me forward. I stepped inside and was met with cool air carrying a lingering floral scent. Recessed lighting illuminated a modest but utilitarian sofa facing a wall-mounted TV. A pillow and a throw blanket were tucked into one corner. The end table held a couple of remotes, a phone charger, a soda can, and a half-empty bag of pretzels. Papers, notebooks, a sleek laptop, and a compact printer sat on the bar counter that split the space between the living room and the galley kitchen. A two-person dinette set was up against the wall as if trying to stay out of the way. Its surface held a collection of neatly stacked files and notebooks next to a pizza box. Clearly, Kerri spent most of her time in this space.

I stood off to the side as Zev came in and pulled the

patio door closed, letting the vinyl blinds fall back into place. Kerri paced to the middle of the room and wrung her hands, her nervousness obvious. She wore what I imagined a highly professional woman in a male-dominated field would wear. Her tailored slacks were mannish in style, but her blouse was all female, showing a hint of cleavage but nothing that would diminish her professionalism. Her sable hair was in a stylish, sleek short cut that emphasized her hazel eyes shaded in tones of gold and brown. A light smattering of freckles dusted the bridge of her nose and her cheeks, adding a youthful vibe to a woman I knew was in her late thirties.

"Um, please, grab a chair..." She blinked owlishly then turned and grabbed one of the spindle-backed chairs from the dinette set. "Here, sorry. Not a lot of options for company."

I took the chair she offered and dragged it over. "Thank you."

Zev nabbed the other chair, setting it a few feet from mine so we were both facing the couch. "Please, Dr. Michaels, have a seat, and take a breath. We just want to ask you some questions."

"Right, right." She finally sat on the edge of the couch and shot us an embarrassed half grin. "I swear, I'm not normally a mess, but things have been a bit nerve-racking lately."

"Understandable," Zev said in a mild tone I hadn't heard from him before. "We don't want to add to your stress, but we were hoping you might be able to give us some insight."

She shifted a bit, rubbing her hands down her lap then back up. "On the project?"

"That and your working relationship with Jonas. We understand you've signed a confidentiality clause, and we will do our best to work around that restriction, but we'd like your perspective on this situation. Hopefully, your input will help us resolve your situation so you can return to your normal life."

It was remarkable to watch the scientist grow visibly calm as he spoke. The repetitive rubbing of her hands stopped, and her posture slowly straightened until she was studying Zev with a disconcerting intensity. The drastic behavior change struck me as odd, but as Zev seemed unconcerned, maybe I was being overly critical.

"Yes, of course. As I told Ms. Frost, I'm more than happy to answer any questions you have." She ducked her chin and tucked her hair behind an ear. "Well, any questions that I can legally answer."

"Of course," Zev murmured as he watched her. "It's our understanding that you and your team were working on the Delphi project, correct?"

She bit her lip and gave a hesitant nod.

Zev's friendly demeanor held steady. "After the death of Dr. Kaspar, it was just you and Jonas Gainer?"

"Yes. Losing Dr. Kaspar was quite the blow, but we were able to use her existing notes to move forward with our research. Jonas and I worked for months trying to piece together the information for a viable solution."

"According to Stephen Trask, based on Dr. Kaspar's research, Origin managed to create a working beta serum." There was no judgment in Zev's tone, no change in his expression, but he did pin her in place with an implacable gaze.

She gave a tentative half nod as if leery of her legal constraints, not that Zev was giving her any other option. "We did, yes."

"It's our understanding that your team tested that serum on animal subjects but encountered detrimental failure." Again, there was no condemnation in his voice, just an unspoken demand for answers.

Yet color still swept up her cheeks, and her glance shifted away. "I'm not sure... I can't..." She stumbled, her nerves rushing to the fore.

"Dr. Michaels," I interrupted, her nervousness uncomfortable to witness. "Please understand, Mr. Trask already shared this information with us. We are simply verifying the facts at hand."

She gulped then drew in a deep breath before straightening her shoulders and lifting her chin in a bid for composure. "Yes, we completed our first animal tests with mice during our pre-clinical-testing phase. However, it soon became clear that we were missing a critical component in the serum as the mice devolved rapidly and eventually died. There were also indicators that some of the test subjects had the ability to infect others."

My stomach bottomed out. "I'm sorry. The serum was infectious?"

Color came and went in her face as she all but wrung her hands. "For the most part, no. There was a single outlier in the initial tests—that's all. It was taken into consideration when Jonas and I reengineered the formula."

A single outlier was one too many in my opinion, but what did I know—I wasn't a scientist.

Zev didn't belabor the point. Instead, he asked, "And that reengineered formula... it worked?"

She met his gaze, and for the first time, her voice carried the hint of the steel that must have been required to hold her position. "That's difficult to say, as we were preparing to run our *in vitro* tests when the initial batch of serum disappeared."

"It disappeared or was stolen?" he pushed.

Frustration was evident on her face. "Whichever way you choose to label it, those vials were locked under maximum containment in the ABSL-4 lab the night prior, and the next morning, all three were gone."

Unfamiliar with the lab designation, I asked, "ABSL-4?"

"Arcane biosafety level four, the highest level of containment for biological labs specializing in magical agents." Her response was pure imperious instructor to peon student. "To bypass the security would require immense skill."

I barely refrained from rolling my eyes. "So you don't think Jonas took it?"

That earned me a fierce frown and a vehement, "Absolutely not, and it's laughable anyone would consider such thing."

"And why's that?" Zev asked.

"Because he was the conscience of our research team." After blurting that out, Dr. Michaels blinked and looked away, her hands resuming their restless movements in her lap.

Her wording struck me as curious. "How so?"

Her fingers stilled, clenched, and turned bloodless. "Jonas started with Origin as an intern, and when he graduated last spring, he was offered a full-time position on my... our research team."

I hadn't missed her pronoun slip on the research team, but she kept going before I could interrupt.

"Jonas was excited and focused on the project, willing to put in the long hours it required without complaint. He was the one who caught the discrepancies in Dr. Kaspar's notes. He brought them to my attention and voiced his concerns. Once I was able to confirm his discoveries, I took them to Mr. Trask." She lifted her head and met my gaze straight on. "Dr. Kaspar was brilliant and recklessly innovative, but she was ruthless in her determination to push the known boundaries of science. Jonas loved delving into the hows and whys of our projects, but he never lost sight of the human picture."

Taking the opening she provided, I asked, "If Dr. Kaspar

was the group's trailblazer and Jonas was the heart, what were you?"

She gave a mocking smile. "The balance."

Something about her, a subtle note I couldn't pin down, bothered me. Before I could dig any further, Zev spoke up. "Are you aware of Mr. Trask's suspicions about who's behind the theft?"

Her expression turned carefully blank, and her voice was cautious. "Yes, I am."

"Do you agree with his assumptions?" He watched her closely.

She held his gaze without flinching. "Mr. Trask has been faced with some alarming revelations in the aftermath of Dr. Kaspar's death, and I believe it hinders him from seeing the wider possibilities."

She'd sidestepped calling her boss paranoid with admirable ease.

Zev's half smirk meant he noted it too. "What kind of possibilities?"

"The Delphi project has the potential to alter the Arcane world in ways we can only begin to guess. There are many groups, and even more individuals, who would give anything, do anything, to ensure that they are the ones controlling that potential. It would not surprise me if there was more than one interested party involved in the theft."

Zev's lips flattened into a tight line. "You sound sure of that."

She looked toward the door, considering her response. When she turned back, it was clear she had something to share, something that made her uncomfortable. "Weeks ago, when LanTech officially announced it would be shutting down its lab, I was taking my lunch in a corner café near my office. A man sat down and asked me about my work. He claimed he'd been working on a similar project with LanTech, and he offered to share his notes with me for a price." She grimaced. "I politely declined his offer, explaining I was not interested in risking my job, or reputation, by dealing with someone with obvious mental-health issues and questionable morals. Then I left."

Hearing the condescension in her voice made it easy to picture her shutting down the man who'd approached her, but I couldn't help but wonder if she was really that altruistic. She said it herself—more than one person wanted to get their hands on the project. I found it hard to believe a smart woman like her, who understood the true impact of the serum, would really walk away from information that would allow her to complete the project. *Or am I just being overly cynical and paranoid?*

Zev pulled out his phone and thumbed the screen. "Dr. Michaels, would this be the man who approached you?" He held his phone out to Kerri.

She took it and studied the photo, lines furrowing her forehead. "Yes. He wasn't quite as put together as that, but that's definitely him." She handed the phone back to him. "Who is he?"

He took it. "He was one of the researchers at LanTech working with the information Dr. Kaspar provided." He angled the screen so I could see the file photo of Neil Pasternak. "And since then?" he asked Kerri. "Has he tried approaching you again?"

"No." She paused then asked, "Is he the one that's missing?"

I looked up from Zev's phone. "You heard about that?"

"Yes. We... Jonas and I knew LanTech had a research team working on a similar project and that Dr. Kaspar had sold proprietary information to them."

I felt my eyebrows lift. "And that didn't worry you?"

"Oh, we were worried initially. But it became clear we

were further ahead than they were on the project, especially when Origin secured funding that LanTech lost. Funding is the lifeblood of research units, and as LanTech was crumbling, Jonas and I knew we'd have a clear field for the serum." She worried her lip. "I remember hearing that shortly after LanTech announced it was closing, one of their researchers was killed walking home—a mugging or something. There were the expected whispers of conspiracy but nothing substantial." She rubbed a hand over her knee. "Still, Jonas starting walking me out to my car and insisting I ask security to escort me if he wasn't around. Both of us were a bit jumpy."

Studying her, I asked, "Did you think the mugging was connected to the project?"

She gave an uncomfortable shrug. "Not really, but it didn't hurt to be cautious."

"Understandable," Zev murmured. "Did you or Jonas notice anything unusual or worrisome?"

"No, but Origin did tighten our security as a precaution." She wrapped her arms protectively over her stomach, her shoulders curling forward as grief drifted over her face, leaving it more drawn. "It wasn't until Jonas was killed that I started believing we were being targeted. It was a tremendous relief when Mr. Trask arranged for this"—she waved a hand at the apartment—"and additional security."

"Just a couple more questions, Dr. Michaels, and then we'll leave you to your day." Zev brought his foot up and rested his ankle on his knee as he folded his hands over his stomach. "We're aware that Dr. Kaspar was a highly regarded Fusor mage and was known for her microlevel expertise. Did Jonas have an Arcane specialty as well?"

Her brow furrowed. "No, he held a minor ability as an electro mage. In his words, it was great for turning lights on and off but not much else. It was his dedication in the lab that made him stand out from the other interns. He was meticulous in his research and testing, perhaps to the point of being overly cautious. Not that that's a bad thing when it comes to science."

"And you?" I asked.

She blinked as if the question took her by surprise. "Like Jonas, I'm more scientifically focused, but I do have a low-level ability in pattern recognition. I find it comes in handy during the research phase of my projects."

Yeah, I can see that.

Zev gave her a polite smile. "I bet it does. One last question. You mentioned there were three vials taken?"

"Yes, it was enough to get through our in vitro testing, plus a control sample."

"How many doses would that be?"

"It would depend on the size and mass of the test subjects. If you're looking at lab mice, maybe five to six per vial."

That meant roughly eighteen Frankenstein critters could be running around. Unfortunately, Neil wasn't sticking to lab rats. "If it were to be used on something larger, say, humans...?" I asked.

She paled and gulped. "That's not... that wouldn't..." She took a moment to gather her composure. "Six to eight."

While I made the mental calculations, Zev asked, "How difficult would it be for someone with the correct skills and knowledge to replicate the current version of the serum?"

His question threw me for a loop, but when I got it, dread bloomed. Without counting the weird lab experiments from the hotel and warehouse, if Neil had also infected Chloe, Jonas, the sleeper, and himself, he was down to maybe two human-sized dosages. So long as no new batches of the serum were created, these experiments Neil was conducting could end with him, but if he, or anyone else, found a way to make more... the possibilities were nightmarish.

Kerri didn't rush to answer. Instead, she considered it for a long moment. "It would take months, possibly years, because they would have to reverse engineer the current serum in order to determine how to replicate it."

The lines on Zev's face grew more pronounced. "If they had access to project notes? Would that significantly speed up the process?"

"It could, or they could create another strain of the serum." Kerri studied us both. "Although it would be quite time consuming. Either way, it would be best to retrieve those vials as soon as possible."

"That's our goal, Dr. Michaels," Zev murmured before bringing the interview to an end.

He asked a few more questions about Jonas and his behavior before he died. Kerri wasn't able to share much other than that during the last few days, Jonas had appeared distracted, which was unusual when they were in the midst of a project. When it became clear she had nothing more to add, we took our leave.

We walked back to the SUV, and I said, "She's hiding something."

"Yeah, she is."

"So how do we figure out what she's not telling us?"

Zev stopped as we got to the SUV. "We start digging."

"On her?" I waited for him to unlock the car then pulled open the passenger door.

"On her and Neil." He held it open for me as I climbed in, his face hard. "Because somehow, somewhere, those two are connected."

Yeah, that's what I was afraid of.

CHAPTER EIGHTEEN

IT WAS HEADING into lunchtime when Zev pulled into a designated parking space across from the impressive collection of buildings known as Dueñas Park. Home to multiple corporate offices claimed by prominent Arcane Families, it dominated Medina Memorial Plaza with a dignified air. I followed him across the street along with a group of chattering office types. They turned left. We went right and took the cement stairs to the glass doors.

Six months had passed since my last visit, but nothing had changed. The lobby was the epitome of corporate bland. Abstract artwork hung on walls in muted colors. Silk plants were strategically placed, while plush chairs and magazine-strewn side tables offered a place for visitors to wait for acknowledgement.

Even the guard behind the high counter of the lobby desk was the same. As soon as he spotted Zev crossing the tile floor of the lobby, he came to attention. "Good afternoon, sir."

Zev barely broke stride as he dipped his chin in greeting and headed straight for the elevators. Not about to get left behind, I stuck to his side. The guard's gaze swept over me. I caught the beginning of a frown as he shifted position to come out from behind the desk.

"Ma'am," he said. It came out half question, half demand.

I slowed, but Zev, who had bypassed the main bank of elevators, looked back at the guard. "She's with me." His abrupt comment pulled the guard up short.

Zev missed the guard's nod because he turned back and stopped in front of a glossy door with no knob on the other side of the elevators. He pressed his palm against the wall, and a brush of power hit me as the security ward scanned his magical signature. The door slid silently open, and following Zev inside, I gave the watching guard a small finger wave and sly grin and earned a dark frown in return.

"You just couldn't resist, could you?" Zev asked after the doors closed.

"Nope." Perfectly pleased with myself, I grinned through the entire ride up.

The private elevator opened into a spacious office that could easily double as an apartment. Large tinted windows made up the far wall and showcased the landscaped beauty of the plaza below. To the right, a couch and two chairs created an inviting lounge space facing a large screen hanging on the wall. A glossy-topped wood-grained streamlined desk took up the space on the left and easily held three monitors. Behind it, floor-to-ceiling storage space reigned supreme— cabinets and drawers at the ends, split by bookshelves and a work counter.

All in all, it was stunning and not at all what I'd pictured when Zev said he had an office. Instead of having dungeon-like lighting, it was airy and bright. Plus, there were no blood-stained weapons lying about or a grim-looking cage tucked in a corner.

I let out a low whistle as I walked through the space. "Nice digs, Zev."

"Thanks." He tossed his sunglasses and phone on the desk. "I've got water and soda in the fridge." He pointed toward one of the cabinets. "Help yourself." He powered up his computer. "I'm going to see if Bryan got any video footage yet."

I beelined to the coffee maker on the corner of the work counter. "Something tells me I'm going to need the caffeine." I scanned the counter for necessary items.

"Drawer below," he instructed without looking up.

I pulled out the drawer and found beans, grinder, cups, and sweetener. "Cream?" I pulled out the grinder and the bag of beans.

"Fridge."

With the grinder doing its thing, I opened the cabinet to the left and found a small fridge tucked inside. When the grinder fell silent, I asked, "You want anything?" I started setting up the coffee to brew.

"I'll take coffee, black." He leaned over the desk, his fingers dancing over the keyboard. "Looks like Bryan sent over a few files."

I hit the button on the coffee maker. "Do you have another computer for me, or are we sharing?"

The sound of wheels rolling over tile had me looking over my shoulder to see Zev pull one of the chairs from the front of his desk over to his side and park it in front of the monitor on the end. Then he came in at my back and reached for one of the cabinets sitting high on the wall. "I've got it set up to double as a second workstation if needed." He brought down a slim keyboard and accompanying mouse. "I'll get it set up, and we can get started."

By the time our coffee was done, he had the second computer in place and a recording queued up. The middle screen had a browser window open, and Zev was logging into a system I didn't recognize. I handed him a cup of coffee then took my seat. "What's that?"

"The council database." The screen changed, and with a rapid series of clicks, he had multiple files open on the middle screen. "This is everything Trask and Clarke submitted to the council about the Delphi project." He opened a second window. "Arbiter database." Then he proceeded to click through a few more options, and more windows popped up. "This is what we know about Neil Pasternak."

I leaned over and studied the screen. Employee records, bank accounts, social media pages, interviews with known associates, and credit card statements. It was kind of scary how much information was on there. "Do they have this much on everyone?" If so, I really needed to rethink my electronic presence.

"No, only people we have an interest in."

That was not as comforting as he probably thought it was, but it was additional incentive for me to stay below the radar. "Right. Anything on Dr. Michaels?"

"Looking now," he murmured.

I turned back to my monitor, which showed a black-and-white low-resolution feed of a downtown sidewalk. "What did Bryan send over?"

"He managed to get the hotel's video feeds and footage from two nearby cameras from the north. He's still working his way along the most likely route from the hotel to the storage unit. If we come up empty, he'll expand his search."

Great. Here's hoping my few hours of sleep will be enough to see me through. "Any word from Imogen?"

He checked his phone. "Just a text saying she made the request to the coroner, and they hope to have results back later today. Might be tomorrow."

And I'd heard zip from Evan. If I was lucky, he'd turn up

something soon. "So for now, our best chance of finding Neil is hoping he shows up on camera?"

"Yes. Or him and Kerri."

I wasn't sure we'd get that lucky. "If the two are working together, I think Kerri's keeping her nose clean."

"Probably, but it won't do her any good if he decides to make a try for her."

"You think he'd be dumb enough to approach when she's got eyes on her?"

He sat back and sipped his coffee. "I think at this point, rational thought may be beyond Neil, and he'll do whatever it takes to get what he wants. Even go after Kerri."

"And what is it he wants?" When Zev raised an eyebrow in silent inquiry, I expanded. "If we're to assume he has the serum, what is his end game?"

"I'm going with the tried-and-true answer—he wants to get rich quick," Zev said dryly.

I wrinkled my nose. "All right, if we stick with that, then how is he planning on making his riches? According to Kerri, it's a limited supply, and creating more would take time."

Zev used his foot to rock his chair from side to side as he played along with my what-if game. "I'm sure there are enough unscrupulous parties out there that would pay a pretty penny for a magical steroid shot. Enough to ensure that if he and Kerri are working together, both of their futures would be secured financially."

"I'm not arguing that. I'm just wondering, if they're working together—or even if he's working solo—are there specific parties lined up? A waiting list? Or would they go the auction route? And if they do decide to go with the highest bidder, how do they get the word out?"

"My guess? Those would be the dead bodies we keep stumbling over."

"I don't think so." When he rolled his hand for more, I

said, "First, we're not even sure the deaths are connected to the serum. If they are, the message is buried and the connection lost under speculation. Second, say Neil is using bodies as examples. Wouldn't there be more on the streets? Isn't the whole purpose of this thing to disrupt Arcane society? Bodies dropping would do that."

Instead of brushing me off, he took my questions seriously. "Maybe he's working for someone, and that someone has him on a leash."

Okay, yeah, I can see that. If Neil found himself suddenly unemployed, it would make him ripe for picking by a discerning entrepreneur. "If that's true, I'm betting he's slipped that leash a couple of times."

"With Jonas," he noted grimly.

"And Chloe, yeah." I stared unseeingly at the screen. "Even then, it still doesn't make sense."

"Only because we don't have enough information." Zev sat up, set his coffee on the desk, and pulled his chair in. "Which is why we're here now. Time to put all the pieces together and figure out what he'll do next."

Resigned to enduring my frustration, at least for the moment, I made a noncommittal noise. "I have a feeling it's going to be a long day."

"Well..." He shot me a grin. "At least you get to spend it with me."

I lifted my cup and returned his grin with one of my own. "There is that." Then I settled in and started up the recording.

◆

A few hours later, Zev called in a delivery so we wouldn't have to leave—not that I would have minded the break—and we had lunch when it arrived. As I was finishing up the last of my

Philly cheesesteak sandwich, I got a text from Evan: *Check your inbox.*

I shoved the last bite in my mouth and wiped my fingers on a napkin before chucking it into the trash. Then I went to the computer and pulled up my email, swallowing the last of my lunch. I must have made a sound of surprise because Zev asked, "What?"

"I asked Evan to do a little digging for me. Looks like he found something."

As I scanned the contents, Zev dragged his chair over until our armrests bumped. I called Evan and put him on speaker, barely waiting for him to say hello before I asked, "Tell me what I'm looking at."

"Your request for info on your four names was fairly straightforward with only a couple of interesting blips. The biggest one is the email you're looking at from a Jonas Gainer to a Dr. Kerri Michaels dated the day before he died. Normally, I wouldn't bat an eyelash at it, but someone did a piss-poor job of deleting it from his email the day after he stopped breathing. As you can see, it looks like he wanted to discuss data discrepancies on a current project. Details are deliberately vague."

I ignored the not-so-subtle inquiry and considered this new puzzle piece. Jonas had already blown the whistle once, and that had triggered the events that led Origin to discover Lara Kaspar's duplicity. Now here he was raising the alarm for a second time, something Kerri had failed to mention. Clearly, Jonas had no trouble making waves, and it made me wonder how big those waves got before they sucked him under. Catching the grim lines on Zev's face, I could tell he was coming to similar unhappy conclusions.

On the phone, Evan was oblivious to our silent conjectures. "The most interesting bit in this email is who he blind copied."

My gaze shot to the email and the name highlighted in the recovered email header. "Stephen Trask."

"Which means whatever Jonas was concerned about had to be serious enough to involve the CEO of Origin. Then there's the fact that out of the four names you gave me, two are dead." He was quiet, probably waiting for me to say something. When I didn't, he continued. "Typically I wouldn't be worried about what you're up to, Rory, but I have to ask, are you good?"

"She's fine," Zev said before I could answer. He was glaring at the screen.

There was a pregnant pause on the phone, then Evan said, "Right. Moving on. Quick recap on the other names you gave me. Dr. Kerri Michaels. I wasn't able to find out much more than what you said you already had—her vitals, education, past job experience. Didn't find any formal complaints filed anywhere, and from what I can tell, she lives for her work. Much like her dead research partner, Jonas. However, he was considered an up-and-coming innovative mind in nanotech research. In fact, he contributed to a couple of highly regarded professional papers, mainly based on the cutting-edge projects he completed during his internship."

Hearing that, all the reasons why someone skilled in nanotech would be asked to join a project involving the creation of a world-altering serum made me swallow hard. I wasn't the only one haunted by foreboding. When I dared to look at Zev, I didn't think it was possible, but his face was even grimmer than before.

Not privy to our thoughts, Evan finished up. "Info on Chloe Sellares—also deceased, was fairly straightforward, no flags, and I included that in my second email to you. As for Neil Pasternak, I ran into blocks as soon as I tried to dig down. I didn't want to push it until I checked in with you."

I thought of all the data Zev already had on Neil and whoever might be behind those blocks. "Don't. We're fine."

"Right." Fortunately, Evan didn't push it and finished up his informal report. "Back to the blips. The second blip also came from Jonas. I did a basic phone trace. For the most part, you can pretty much set your watch by his routine. To and from home and work, a few side trips for food, tends to hit sandwich shops with the occasional splurge for pizza, artisan style with the weird toppings. There were a couple of coffee runs to a local shop, generally first thing in the morning. Hit the gym a couple times a week, probably to offset the desk time. But a week before his death, his phone put his location over by Salt River in a neighborhood that was not part of his regular haunts, nor did he make a return trip. It's in the secondary email as well."

"Thanks, Evan."

"I'd say anytime, but I know better." With that, he hung up.

I clicked over to the second email and read through the basic info Evan had gathered on Chloe, Kerri, and what little he had on Neil. When I got to Jonas, I zeroed in on the address Evan had mentioned. I plugged it into the maps site on screen, and a familiar beige building came up.

"Dammit," Zev muttered as we both stared at the screenshot of the building holding Neil's makeshift lab.

I rubbed my face, my head aching, my eyes burning. I knew what this meant. "Did we ever get any footage from around there?" I remembered that we intended to, but then Zev got called off and I headed over to Umber's. I couldn't remember if one of the others ever managed to get anything. The days were starting to blur—never a good sign.

Zev was working on his computer, scrolling through windows until he found the one he wanted. "Looks like Bryan got a couple, but I'll see if he or Imogen can get back over there and nose around, find out if anyone will talk." His fingers flew as he sent a group text from the desktop, and my phone buzzed a few moments after he hit Send.

This time, when we went back to the recordings, there was a low-level tension that followed, broken only when a return text came in from Bryan, confirming he'd go back to the neighborhood and see what he could turn up. Imogen's response followed a few minutes later, indicating she'd join up with him and help.

Zev and I spent the next few hours slogging through grainy video recordings and piles of information, some of it so mundane I wanted to stab my eyes out. I did find a couple of images that I thought might be Neil and Jonas, but the resolution was for crap, so I marked them for follow-up. Someone with more expertise than me could take the smudged figures and sharpen them into something recognizable. If they were legit sightings, we had Neil making his way from the lab to the hotel then disappearing the day before we came knocking at his home away from home. As for the possible Jonas image, it put him near the makeshift lab, but there was nothing catching him at the lab itself.

By the time evening closed in, I couldn't take it anymore. Bryan and Imogen kept sending in more and more footage until I dreaded the chime indicating incoming email. We made some headway, but there were still hours more ahead of us. My back ached, my head pounded, and my eyes were on fire, so I pushed up from the desk and stretched.

"You okay?" Zev eyed me from where he was sprawled out in his chair. His jaw was shadowed, and his eyes were red, proof I wasn't the only one suffering.

"I need a break."

He jerked his head toward the couch. "Use the couch. Take an hour."

Not about to argue, I stumbled over and fell face-first into the cushions. In moments, I was drifting, and it was a welcome relief from the headache and eyestrain.

I stayed in that place out of time until a weight shook my shoulder and Zev's voice brought me back. "Rory, wake up."

I blinked until Zev came into focus. When he saw I was awake, he turned back to the desk and starting talking. "Imogen's on the line with the coroner's report."

I swung my legs to the floor and pushed up with a groan. I stumbled after him and beelined to the coffee pot, listening to him talk to Imogen.

"Okay, Imogen, we're here. What did you find out?" Zev leaned against the desk, his hand pressed flat near the phone and his gaze on me as I emptied out the dregs and rinsed the coffee pot.

"The coroner is filing his report in the morning, but since he knew I wanted the results ASAP, he called." Imogen's voice held a rough edge, indicating that we weren't the only ones dealing with a long-ass day. "Physically, there's no connection between Chloe and Jonas's deaths, but he performed an Orenda exam."

I stopped prepping a new pot and looked at Zev, who explained, "The Orenda exam was developed by the First Nations as a way to test for the residual traces of magic on, or in, natural objects. It's a gold standard for magical forensics."

"It came back positive but unknown," Imogen said. "He then tested Chloe and Jonas's blood against the thing that died in the hotel room. There's no doubt that the magic used on that animal was used with both Chloe and Jonas too. Thing is, the coroner can't tell if the magic was introduced into their blood via injection or a magical attack."

"So there's a high chance Neil decided to use the serum on humans," Zev said darkly.

"Most likely," Imogen said. "Or Neil used it on himself and attacked Chloe and Jonas."

"The sleeper," I blurted as my brain snapped into gear, skipping steps and taking crazy turns that made scary sense. When Zev frowned at me, I explained, "The sleeper that attacked Umber, the one ACRT picked up. Any chance we can get our hands on a blood sample from him?"

"You think Neil dosed him?" Zev's tone was flat with skepticism.

"No... I don't know... maybe." I stumbled over the ideas slamming together in my head.

"Why would Neil waste his time with some random sleeper?" Imogen asked with a hint of frustration that I ignored.

"Look, I know it sounds crazy, but bear with me here, okay?" I set the coffee to brew and faced Zev, folding my arms. "If Neil injected himself and killed Chloe and Jonas, leaving magical traces behind, what's to keep the same thing from happening if one of Neil's animal experiments got loose and attacked a human?" It was easy to read the doubt on Zev's face, but I pushed forward, feeling like I was clinging to spiderwebs. "Neil's homemade lab, Etched Chaos, the alley where Jonas was found, the hotel—they're all within what, ten miles at most? Sleepers tend to stick to areas they're familiar with. They don't roam far. Then there's the timing of everything. Neil going under, Jonas getting killed, Umber getting attacked by the sleeper, all of that happened in the last..." I did a quick estimate. "Four days?"

"Something ripped out of cages in that lab." Imogen's words sounded forced, as if she didn't want to add credence to my suggestion.

Zev ran a hand through his hair and blew out a hard breath. "Dammit." He reached out to the phone and hit buttons until the sound of ringing filled the line.

"Yeah?" Bryan's grumpy voice answered.

"Got something to share." Zev proceeded to fill Bryan in on the conversation so far while Imogen and I listened. "On top of that, Jonas sent an email to Michaels and blind copied Trask, warning there were issues with the data on the project."

"What kind of issues?" Imogen asked.

"He didn't specify."

"That makes sense," she muttered.

"How so?" Zev glowered at the phone.

"I tracked down a friend of Jonas's, a buddy he works out with, and the last time he saw him, Jonas was acting squirrelly —the buddy's words, not mine. When his friend pushed for answers, Jonas admitted he was struggling with something at work and was trying to figure out who to share his concerns with."

"Are we thinking Neil killed Jonas, then?" Bryan asked.

"If he did, how did the two connect?" I asked.

"Maybe he approached Jonas like he did Kerri," Zev said.

"And what?" I asked. "Jonas turned him down, threatened to expose him, so Neil loses his mind and kills him?"

"I've seen crazier shit," Bryan said. "And if Neil's jacked up on that serum, there's no telling how messed up his mind is or what he's willing to do to get what he wants."

"And if someone else is pulling his strings, they may aim him at Kerri," Imogen added. "Especially since she's the last one standing and the only one who can replicate the formula."

Oh crap, I hadn't even thought of that. "How much security do you have on her?"

"I'll be calling in more," Imogen said grimly.

"All right, people," Zev said, regaining control of the conversation. "We've got a lot of strings floating around. Time to tie some off. Bryan and Imogen, I don't want you two solo, so team up and go back to Neil's place, tear it apart, see what you can find. If you strike out, go back to that damn lab and do the same there. Rory and I will finish up with the street cams and see if we can't track his ass to narrow down his hiding spot."

Orders received, Imogen and Bryan signed off. I stared at Zev in the heavy quiet, my stomach leaden and worry nibbling at my mind. "Zev..." I didn't know what I was going to say, but he seemed to.

"Don't speculate. It won't do us any good." He pushed off the desk and stopped in front of me, brushing his knuckles over my jaw. "Let's just focus on what's in front of us. We'll deal with the rest when and if it hits."

I held his gaze for a long moment before giving in. "Fine, but I want it noted for the record that I think this whole situation sucks."

That got me a faint grin. "Noted."

"Go." I waved a hand. "Queue up the next exciting rendition of Still Life on the Streets, while I get us coffee."

He turned back to the computer, and I did the only thing I could—I poured coffee and settled in for another torturous session of film watching.

CHAPTER NINETEEN

"I THINK MY EYES ARE BLEEDING." I sat back with the heels of my palms pressed against my burning eyes. My butt was numb, my lower back felt like a pretzel, and despite the copious amounts of coffee, my brain was blurry.

"Take a break," Zev suggested from his supine position on the couch, where he'd dropped about ten minutes earlier.

"Not sure that will help." Still, I pushed back from the desk and stood. After hours of sitting, my muscles weren't exactly cooperating. I tried to muffle a groan as I straightened and stretched, easing out the stiff kinks.

"Did you find anything?" he asked in a husky growl, the rasp of it sparking a couple of intriguing possibilities on how to get him to sound like that more often. The arm over his eyes shifted, his dark-chocolate gaze locking onto me. "Rory?"

I blinked. "Uh?"

His lips quirked. "Did you find anything?"

I rubbed my face hard. *Right, the street surveillance tapes that are my personal sixth level of hell.* Bryan and Imogen had supplied us with video from an auto garage that sat across the street from Neil's building. With the entrance to the lab being on the back side, there was no direct coverage, so we were piecing together what we could from the surrounding storefronts. It was spotty and haphazard, but I was impressed with how much footage they'd managed to get. Most of the owners were understandably hesitant to share, and after watching the comings and goings, I had a fairly good idea why.

I dropped my hands and meandered over to the sitting area where Zev lay. "Business at the auto shop is hopping from one to four in the morning, especially on the weekends."

His grin was faint as he angled his body to a sitting position, stretching those long legs out in front of him. "Chop shop."

"Yep. Plus, it looks like the local coffee shop doubles as the neighborhood's preferred pharmacy." After spending hours watching the recordings, it wasn't difficult to distinguish the street dealers happily providing customers with something more than caffeine.

He chuckled. "The coffee shop? Seriously?"

"You know how hard it is to get motivated. Sometimes you need something with a little more oomph than a cup of joe on its own."

He rubbed his chin. "I don't know why I'm surprised. In that business, the key to success is accessibility."

Yeah, hard to do business like that if no one can find you. Speaking of not being able to find someone... "Anything from Imogen and Bryan?"

Zev shook his head.

I turned and wandered over to the windows. Night had settled in, leaving the streetlights to paint the roads in a soft glow. A couple of hours back, Imogen had called in to let us know that she and Bryan had finished up with Neil's place and were heading over to the lab. They'd run into an overly curious neighbor at Neil's, which led to some fast-talking to ensure that the neighbor didn't remain curious. Once inside, they tore the place apart looking for anything that would give us a clue about where he might hole up or who he might be working with. Other than finding indications that Neil had a woman visitor at some recent point, they came up frustratingly empty.

The stagnant state of play left us all frazzled, something that became increasingly clear during our phone conversation with Bryan, when even his responses skimmed the line of rude to the point that Zev had called him on it. Twice. Maybe it was time for all of us to call it a day.

As if he could read my mind, Zev said, "They should be finished soon. Once they check it, we'll call it quits, try again tomorrow."

I angled and leaned a shoulder against the window so I was facing him. "Are we going back to Kerri?"

"For starters, yeah." He rubbed his jaw. "We need to know what discrepancies Jonas was worried about."

I grimaced. "Since she didn't mention the email in the first place, I'm not sure she's going to share."

A hard light gleamed in his eyes, and his face shifted from grim to determined. "Oh, she wi—"

His phone danced across the end table, cutting him off. He picked it up, looked at the screen, frowned, then swiped his thumb and brought it to his ear. "Imogen?"

When he straightened abruptly and shot to his feet, I went wired. His eyes came to me, but it was clear he wasn't seeing me, because he snapped, "Where are you?" He started toward the elevator, and I followed. "We're fifteen minutes out. Can you hold on till then?" He hit the button. "Right. Do what you need to. We're heading out now."

The elevator doors slid open. I stepped inside, and Zev came in behind me. He pocketed his phone and smashed the button for the garage, a frown darkening his face.

The mood roiling off him wasn't conducive to questions, but I had to know. "What's wrong?"

"Imogen thinks Bryan tripped a magical trap."

"At the warehouse?"

"Yeah."

That didn't make sense. "But we cleared it." I caught his look as it hit me. "Neil went back there, didn't he?"

Before Zev could answer, the doors opened, and he was out. I stayed at his heels as he ran to his SUV. The beep of the locks releasing came just before I demanded, "Keys."

He pulled up short and shot me a look. "What?"

"Keys. Transporter, remember?"

He tossed the keys toward me as I ran to the driver's side. By the time his ass touched the seat, I had the engine lit. I barely waited for his door to close before I reversed out of the space, aimed us toward the exit, and hit the gas, rubber squealing against the cement. My magic revved in time with the engine, shifting my perception to preternatural sharpness until the SUV and I were one and the same. Typically, I preferred the lighter handling that came with the sportier sedans, but the heavy SUV was surprisingly responsive. I ignored the curses coming from under Zev's breath as I wove my way through the decidedly slower traffic. Not that there was much, considering we were closing in on ten on a Thursday night.

I loosened my hold on my magic, letting it deepen the connection between the vehicle and me. Even in my heightened magical state, my pulse stayed level and my hands steady as my situational awareness expanded, enabling split-second reaction times. Magic-laced adrenaline raced through my veins, generating a high no street drug could beat. By the time I turned into the ally by the makeshift lab, my face ached from the wild grin stretching across it.

Throwing the SUV into park, I checked the time and

resisted pumping my fist in victory. *Seven minutes, twelve seconds.* I'd managed to shave off half the time. I turned my grin to Zev. "Yes!"

Even in the barely lit interior, he seemed a little pale. He uncurled his hand from the chicken handle and shoved open his door. "A little warning next time, Rory."

"Killjoy," I muttered as I got out and joined him at the hood. I clocked Imogen's two-seater a few spaces down. The SUV's headlights were aimed at the partially open door to the lab.

"Imogen? Bryan?" Zev called.

When no one answered, I exchanged a worried look with Zev. *That's not good.* My skin prickled as Zev pulled his magic up, the faint shimmer of blue erupting over his hands and flickering like silent flames along his arms. Untangling my magic from the SUV so I could snap my armor into place took me a few seconds, but once that was done, I reached out with my power, trying to get a sense of what lay in wait.

"Anything?" Zev's voice was low, staying just between us.

I shook my head and stretched my magical muscle a little more, ignoring the resulting ache. It wound its way inside and rippled outward like a puddle, slowing inching across the space. A sudden wicked sting, like a paper cut on steroids, made me hiss and pull back. "To the right back corner."

"Can you expand your shield?"

During our discussion about what I could and couldn't do with my Prism magic, I'd admitted to being able to cover a second person so long as they stayed within about six feet of me. "Yeah, but don't forget to keep close."

It took a bit of concentration, but I was able to shift my magic until it enclosed Zev. It was the weirdest feeling, as if I was trying to stuff two people into a suit made for one. I could feel it straining at the edges and made a mental note to practice, to increase not just my control but my speed, too, as both needed to be top-notch for this to work under fire.

"Ready," I said.

Taking me at my word, Zev moved forward, taking the lead, his hands at his sides, his magic roiling in readiness. He pushed the door so it swung inward and stepped inside. There was no need for a flashlight because the light of his magic was more than enough to illuminate our way.

I stayed right behind him, eyes peeled for an attacking Frankenstein cat-rat, hulked-out cicadas, Imogen, Bryan, or anything that moved. Nothing rushed forward—well, nothing physical, but something slammed against my Prism hard enough to force a grunt from me.

"Back right corner," I snapped to Zev.

The blue fire of Zev's magic lashed out and connected, igniting a silent explosion that sent Zev and me both stumbling back. Someone had definitely come back and laid a trap. My ears rang, and my thoughts felt muffled. An oily miasma of wrongness lapped at my magic, making my stomach churn.

"Zev?"

I could barely hear myself, so I was surprised to hear him ask, "You okay?"

"Not really." There was nothing to be gained by lying. "What the hell is that?"

He didn't bother with an explanation but focused on the immediate need. "Can you hold it back?"

"If you promise to do whatever you're going to do quickly." The slimy, unnatural whatever it was oozed against my magic, a sensation so disturbing that I shuddered and swallowed back an urge to vomit.

Inside the shield of my power, Zev's magic glowed brighter and began to writhe as if alive. It took a second for me to realize he was casting a counterspell to whatever was crouched in that corner. I narrowed my eyes in an effort to see what he was doing, but all I could make out were his arms, raised in a familiar mage pose—extended with palms forward. The pressure of his power shoved against mine, forcing me to make adjustments to the overstretched shield to accommodate it.

"When I hit one, drop the shield," he said. I wanted to protest, but he didn't give me a chance. "Three... two... one."

I dropped the shield. His spell shot forward with vicious force and hit the corner like a silent bomb. I slammed the shield back up as the magical impact wave shot back with stunning ferocity. The leading edge caught us, sending us sliding backward a couple of feet, but the shield buffered the main impact wave. When I caught my breath, I found myself crouched on the ground, arms above my head in a useless protective posture. In front of me, Zev was on one knee with a hand braced against the ground.

I lowered my arms and flattened my palms against the concrete. "You okay?" I croaked.

"I'm good." His voice sounded equally hoarse.

I realized the grossly disturbing presence was gone. "What the hell was that?"

His head hung down, his shoulders shuddering. "Someone tried to reopen the portal."

More than my stomach quailed. "So much for Neil being shit at spell work."

Zev's head rose, then he turned to look over his shoulder at me. His eyes burned with an unholy light that made my pulse trip. "I'm not sure this is Neil's handiwork."

Before I could ask why, a shriek broke through the night and was abruptly cut short. It sounded awfully familiar. "Was that—"

"Imogen!" Zev was on his feet and running for the door.

I quickly pulled my shield back before he could tear it apart and stumbled after him. I burst outside to see Zev loping along the cement block wall that separated it from the lot behind it. I picked up my pace as he disappeared into the shadows where the feeble lights didn't reach. With my luck, he'd disappear, and I'd be left alone with whatever the hell was out there hunting.

My feet pounded against the pavement. I could hear the muffled sounds of fighting, but I just couldn't pinpoint where they were coming from. Then blue-white fire split the shadows ahead, illuminating Zev and a pile of broken cement blocks at his feet. He clambered over the rubble with scary ease and disappeared on the other side, leaving only flickering shadows trailing his magic.

I hit the same spot and found that someone or something had crashed through the cement wall, leaving a gaping hole in its wake. Unlike Zev, I ended up using both hands and feet to get over the unstable pile of debris. Sharp, ragged edges shifted under my weight and sliced bloody nicks in my hands and wrists. Despite the nuisance stings, I skidded down the other side and straight into hell.

Zev, outlined in flaming blue, faced off with a nightmarish creature that left my brain scrambling for some kind of reference. Like a gross amalgam of human and beast, it towered over Zev. Inhumanly long arms ended in massive hands tipped with thick claws that rivaled the fangs of prehistoric saber-toothed tigers. One of those mammoth hands was swiping toward a figure desperately scrambling back while sending silver tongues of magic to try to hold the creature at bay.

I got closer, and that figure became Imogen, her lips curled in a snarl and her teeth bared, as she set loose another long-barbed streak of magic that lashed across the creature's torso. Under the disorienting strobe effect of dueling shadows and magic, the silvery spread of ice began seeping over the nauseating mix of scales and fur, only to disappear. The beast's head jerked back, and its mouth gaped, revealing a set of teeth that would shred bone and a thick black tongue, but while it appeared to be howling, no sound emerged. It swiped out at Imogen, who managed to duck but not fast enough. I watched in horror as she flew through the air and tumbled farther into the darkness.

Shit shit shit.

Terror locked me in place as my brain short-circuited. All I could do was watch helplessly as Zev rolled out of the way of a lethal strike from the spiked tail—a tail that shouldn't exist but was attached to bulging, muscled legs that were humanoid in shape and ended in split hooves. Zev shot back a blinding lash of magic. It wrapped around the creature's muscled legs and tightened. On the other end, Zev set his feet and yanked on the magical tether.

The creature's mouth opened on a silent roar as it fought for balance. It finally clicked for me that someone, probably Imogen or Bryan—*Where the hell is Bryan?*—had locked a muting spell in place. On that thought, my brain reengaged. I dashed around Zev, who was struggling in a magical tug-of-war with the creature, intending to get to Imogen out of the line of fire. Taking down a creature like that was outside my skillset.

As I ran, I caught a flicker of magic in the corner of my eye and realized writhing runes and sigils scored the ground. A couple of the markings looked awfully similar to those used in the lab, but under the circumstances, stopping to verify would be a lethally stupid idea. Before Zev lost what little control he had over the monster, I needed to get myself and Imogen clear. I slid to a stop near the shadowed lump in the dirt, ignoring the ache as the rough ground shredded my jeans and skin. I wrapped the two of us in my shield, praying it would hold if the monster decided to turn its attention to us.

Hoping for any signs of life, I ran my shaking hands over Imogen's still form. A surge of relief hit as her chest rose and fell under my palms, but it was short-lived. There was a violent shift in the air as the creature tore free of Zev's snare. Keeping one hand on Imogen, I twisted my head in time to see the creature rear back, claws raised, mouth open, fangs down, its lethal focus centered on Zev.

The creature lunged forward. Zev braced, and I didn't think—I simply reacted. With a half shout, half scream, I raised my other hand toward Zev and shoved my magic out, wrapping it around him, hardening it in desperation. It burst into place as the thick claws scraped across it. This time, the muting spell failed, and an ear-shredding whine of impact joined the horrific roar, ripping through the night. Magical sparks flew under the claws with each strike. My skin lit up with a thousand needles from head to toe, setting off a white starburst of pain. Red welts erupted over my exposed skin, but I dug deep, refusing to buckle under the pressure. The shield shivered but held.

Enraged, the creature grew frenzied, nearly mindless. Each strike reverberated through the psychic link of my magic with an unrelenting savagery. It left me unable to do anything but endure, and I wasn't sure how long I would be able to manage that. Ice-cold fingers took hold of my wrist, locking tight around it. Then a wave of frigid power hit me, stealing my breath. Instead of fighting it, I embraced it, and on blind instinct, I wove the two magics together, strengthening Zev's protection.

In the minute respite granted by the unexpected boost, Zev hastily etched a primitive Arcane circle in the dirt with a rock. Then he sank his magic into it, cycling his power until his figure turned into an eye-searing human candle. "Now!"

His command rang through the night and reverberated in my skull until my bones ached with the power behind it. I dropped the shield. Zev sent his magic out. The blue-lit magic took on the amorphous shape of a multiheaded hydra,

It wrapped around the maddened creature like a fiery being of myth and squeezed. The flaming reptilian heads struck in unison. The creature bellowed as magic writhed in a violent storm around it. Then with a thunderous clap, Zev's hydra and the nightmare creature exploded, leaving my vision spotty and the air heavy.

A scream of rage broke through the night, and it came from Bryan, who stood in the spot where the creature had been. But it wasn't the Bryan I was familiar with. Instead of the charming laid-back man, he was bloodied and crazed, trapped in a blue-tinged mesh of magic like some demonic fish. His clothes were ripped and stained, his hair stood on end, and his face was a twisted, animalistic mask of fury and madness. He struggled against the magical net with single-minded intensity. The minute Zev pushed to his feet and slowly approached, that focus locked onto him.

I could hear Zev's voice, low and calm, as he tried to connect to Bryan, but something inside me warned that it wouldn't work. That same something had me scrambling to my feet as it started screaming that Zev wasn't safe. I half ran, half stumbled toward him. "Zev! Wait!" My voice was a broken croak and didn't reach him, but my movement caught Bryan's attention.

He stared at me, and even from where I stood, I could see that the whites of his eyes were bloodred and there was nothing sane behind them, just cold maliciousness. Power crashed against my shield, and at my feet, Imogen whimpered. I grimly kept moving forward and was almost in touching distance of Zev when Bryan struck again, this time throwing a spell toward Zev. My reaction was instantaneous and my magic even faster. Bryan's magic struck out, and my power caught it, twisted it, and sent it back, all of that happening between one breath and the next. Whatever spell Bryan had thrown hit him full-on. He screamed, his body going rigid, seizing for a few seconds. Then he fell motionless.

In the still night, a gasp sounded from behind me. I stood there in horrified realization, staring at the lifeless body at Zev's feet. *Oh shit. I just killed an Arbiter.*

CHAPTER TWENTY

THE NEXT COUPLE of hours passed in a blur, and when they came back into focus, I was sitting in a plush waiting room on a private floor in a medical building frequented by Arcane Families.

"Here." Zev handed me a paper cup filled with water.

Perched on the edge of a small couch, I took it and was surprised to note that, unlike everything else, my hands were rock steady. I sipped and eased the gritty soreness in my throat. "Thanks." It came out rough.

He settled next to me, his weight sinking the cushions enough that I had to lift the cup so it wouldn't slosh over the sides. He was so close his thigh brushed mine. "You need to update Sabella." His voice was low, as if he didn't want to be overheard, but we were the only two in the room.

I blinked. "What?"

He reached out and turned my face toward him, his gaze locking with mine in such a way that I couldn't escape his seriousness. "Call Sabella."

The fog that had settled around me began to drift away, leaving behind an unwelcome clarity. Shit was about to hit the fan, and I needed to cover my ass. I should have done that first thing, but in the rush to get Imogen help and keep the mess in the lot on the QT, time had gotten away from me.

I handed him the cup and scrubbed my sore palms over my face, only then realizing they were scraped up. "Sabella, right." I looked at the door inset with a narrow window and saw the rush of activity outside. "Can you make sure no one comes in?"

He studied me then nodded. "Yeah, but don't take too long."

I gave him a nod as he got up, set the cup on one of the small tables, and walked out. He took up a sentry position outside the door. I pulled the scrying stone out from under my T-shirt and gripped it gently. This time, activating the magical connection was as simple as focusing my intent, mainly because self-preservation was a fantastic motivator.

"Sabella, I need you."

A breathless moment of silence passed, then her voice filled my head. *"What's wrong?"*

"Bryan Croft is dead."

Her psychic stillness raised the hair on my arms. *"How?"*

Although her one-word question held an intensely deep foreboding that left me shaky, I managed a stoic response. *"I killed him."*

A flash of shock erupted and was replaced by a cold curiosity. *"Explain."*

I did, ending with, *"Bryan's intent to kill Zev was clear, and my reaction instinctive."* It was the only excuse I could give, mainly because it was the truth.

"And Imogen and Zev witnessed this?"

The addition of Zev in her question pulled me up short. *Right, I kind of skipped the part about Zev knowing my secrets during my previous check-in. Dammit.*

"Yes," I answered.

"You're sure? Because you don't sound sure."

I dragged my free hand through my hair, fisted it at the base of my skull, then released it as I carefully navigated the looming pit under my feet.

"Zev is definitely aware. Imogen might have been a bit out of it, but I think it's safe to assume she has enough pieces to put it together."

"And where are they now?"

I looked at the door and saw Zev's broad shoulders and back blocking out most of the window. *"Zev's holding everyone at bay for me, and Imogen is being checked out by a Family doctor."*

"I see." Her psychic presence faded somewhat, as if she had mentally left the room.

I waited—not patiently, I might add—for her to return. To combat the need to crawl out of my skin, I began to pace. With each successive pass, my anxiety rose until finally, I couldn't take it anymore. *"Sabella, they're going to come for me."*

The familiar sense of age and power returned in a strangely comforting wave. *"Calm, Rory."*

I pulled up short. *"Yeah, considering I killed the Clarkes' Arbiter, calm is not an option."*

"First, your actions are justifiable. Second, if Zev's standing guard, I think it's safe to assume he's waiting for more information before reacting. As for Imogen..."

Needing a nervous outlet, I curled my hand in a fist and thumped it rhythmically against my thigh.

"They won't be releasing Imogen until morning," she continued. *"The most she can do is report what happened to Stephen, and if her recall of events is anywhere close to yours and Zev's, the Clarkes may be upset, but it was their Arbiter who attempted to kill another Arbiter. As my proxy, you're fully within your rights to defend the others, even should one of them be the threat."*

I wished I could feel as confident as her on this. *"How can you be sure?"*

"You're asking me, of all people, that question, dear?"

Despite the hint of humor in her question, I backpedaled a bit, as I was not keen on pissing her off—I just wanted to make sure I didn't end up in a cell. *"Please, Sabella. I need to know what kind of damage control I need to instigate."*

"I've already started it." Her mental voice turned brisk. *"I touched base with critical people to ensure that the situation remains contained and they understand that you belong to me. It will buy us time. Mind you, not much, but enough to see through this investigation."*

"And after the investigation?" I couldn't help but ask, even as I hated the hint of pleading buried in the question.

Her sigh was almost audible. *"We'll deal with that when it's time. For now, we must remain focused on your rogue scientist. And, Rory..."*

"Yes."

"Keep your mouth shut, and stay with Zev, no matter what. Do you understand?"

"Yes." I swallowed hard. *"Thank you."*

"Don't thank me yet, darling. I have a feeling things are going to get very interesting for us both soon." With that, she added, *"Be careful."*

"I will."

Then Sabella was gone, leaving me alone in my head. I considered slipping past Zev and getting the hell of out of town but figured the odds of doing that successfully were crap. I tucked the scrying stone back under my T-shirt, went to the door, and pulled it open.

Zev turned, his gaze taking in my face. "You good?"

"For now."

"Mr. Aslanov," a male voice called.

I peeked around Zev to see a nurse in muted-color scrubs heading our way, wearing a polite smile and a sharp gaze.

Zev moved enough to give me space to step out, but I didn't take it. Instead, I stayed behind him as he said, "Yes?"

"Ms. Frost is asking for you and Ms. Costas." His gaze shifted to me. "Ms. Costas, I assume?"

I nodded.

He stopped a few feet away. "Good. If you'll both follow me?"

The nurse led us down the hall, past a couple of nondescript doors closed against the curious, and stopped by the one near the end. He took hold of the handle, paused, and warned us in a low voice, "Don't take too long. She needs rest." With that, he pushed the door open and waited to the side as we moved into the room.

The lights were low, and a half-drawn curtain blocked the view to the bed beyond. The door closed behind us as Zev pulled aside the curtain and went to the foot of the bed. "Glad to see you're still alive."

I came up behind Zev and stood awkwardly by the curtain. Imogen lay half-reclined with a couple of lines, most likely painkillers, running from her arm to the IV stand next to the bed. Under the fluorescent light at the head of the bed, with her dark hair pulled back, her normally pale skin carried a waxy cast and her unusually light eyes appeared fever bright.

Those eyes landed on me as she moved a bit as if trying to get comfortable. They didn't waver even when she winced. "I suppose I should say thank you."

I managed a stiff shrug but said nothing—probably my best bet considering the rabid speculation in her eyes.

"At least now I understand why Sabella chose you."

Taking Sabella's warning to heart, I stayed mute. Undaunted, Imogen continued to study me. Maybe she was used to people crumbling under her scrutiny. If so, she was bound for disappointment because self-preservation was a wonderful motivator. Borrowing a trick from Zev's playbook, I buried my agitation and worry deep behind a disinterested mask.

"You up for telling us what happened?" Zev asked, cutting through our silent standoff.

Her white-lined lips curved slightly, and there was nothing nice about it, but she fortunately turned her attention to Zev. "I'm not exactly sure. Bryan and I spent most of our day retracing what we could of Neil's tracks, strong-arming people to get the security tapes where we could, and going back through Neil's house. All of it turned up great gobs of nothing useful, which left us both fairly frustrated."

"I caught that earlier, when you two checked in before heading to the lab. I figured if you struck out there, we'd be calling it a night."

She nodded and began plucking at the sheet at her waist. "To be honest, Bryan was pissing me off, and I was looking forward to calling things to a halt." She grimaced and moved her head in that way people did when they weren't comfortable with their own actions. "We'd gotten in a couple of arguments, nothing major, but I called him out on his attitude because it was getting old."

"Was that normal for him?" I asked.

She flicked her gaze to me then shifted it to Zev. "No. Actually, Bryan's the one you want at your side when things start to slide to shit because he keeps things tight." She shook her head, and a flurry of emotions fluttered over her face too fast to read. "That should've been my first clue something was up."

"Hindsight's twenty-twenty. You know that, Imogen," Zev countered. "So Bryan's behavior was off, and you two went to the lab."

"Actually, Bryan's behavior started changing on the way to Neil's house. It got worse as the evening wore on, so by the time we hit the lab, our aim was to finish up as soon as we could."

"What happened at the lab?" Zev asked.

"He snapped." Imogen's reticence disappeared as her Arbiter persona took front and center. Her face and voice hardened into a cold professionalism. "We got there, and it looked exactly like how we left it. It wasn't until I was inside that I realized someone had been there."

"How?"

"That broken circle—someone had started restoring the runes. They were shaky as if whoever was laying them wasn't quite sure what they wanted, which meant they would be volatile and unpredictable if set off. I went to warn Bryan, but he stepped on one before I could pull him back. There was a punch of power that knocked me back. I barely got my balance back before Bryan rushed me and had me up against the wall, trying to choke me. Even as I fought him off, I realized it wasn't him."

"How?"

"His eyes." She frowned. "The whites were lined with veins of red, and his pupils were blasted wide until only the black remained." She shuddered. "As much as that freaked me out, it was clear he was under some kind of thrall."

"You got away."

She managed a jerky nod. "Yeah, and I headed outside so I'd have room to maneuver. Unfortunately, what followed me wasn't Bryan. It was that thing..."

Which reminds me... "I thought Bryan was a Mirage, not a Charmer."

Zev angled so he could address me and Imogen at the same time. "He was a master Mirage mage, but it wouldn't surprise me to find out he carried a minor ability as a Charmer."

A grim realization hit me, but it was Imogen who voiced it. "What attacked us wasn't a minor ability, Zev."

He studied her. "What are you saying?"

Imogen held his gaze without flinching. "If Bryan was

infected with the serum, it had to be during the initial search of that lab, and whatever magic we tripped finished what it started."

"That weird cicada," I muttered, and when both Arbiters turned to me, I finished my thought. "When we first searched the lab, that mutant cicada nicked him. How likely is it that Neil did something so that thing could inject enough of the serum to cause a reaction in Bryan?"

Imogen and Zev looked at each other in silent conversation. Finally, Zev said, "It would make sense, especially if Neil was experimenting with delivery systems for the serum. Dr. Michaels mentioned there was a singular result where they were able to transfer the effects between subjects."

Imogen's nod was slow, considering. "It would also explain his deteriorating attitude. Once he stepped on that rune, it flipped the last trigger."

"How would Neil know to go back there?" I asked. That would have been crystal-ball-level knowledge.

Zev paced at the foot of Imogen's bed. "I'm guessing that was more a Hail Mary type of move—restoring the runes in case someone came back to discourage anyone from poking around."

"And Bryan had the misfortune of being infected and tripping it?" Imogen asked.

I wanted to add, "What she said." Instead, I watched Zev, and so did Imogen.

He stopped at the footboard and rubbed the back of his neck. "Unfortunately, yeah." He looked at the woman in the bed. "If it had been you, who knows what result the rune would've triggered." Something moved over his face, but from my angle, I couldn't read it. Then he turned to me, and all I saw was ruthless resolve. "We need to head back over there and examine those runes."

"Actually," Imogen interrupted, her hand rising as if to

hold him back. It dropped back onto the sheet. "That will have to wait because I got a message from Kerri, and it seems Neil's been a very busy boy tonight."

"Is she okay?" I asked.

She looked at me. "For now. Security is on alert, but she's understandably rattled." She directed the next bit to Zev. "I need you to escort her to another secure location."

He folded his arms, frowning. "Me?"

Imogen's eyes darted to me and back to him. "Well, you and Rory. They won't let me out until tomorrow, and I'm not comfortable leaving her with just the standard security team. Not with all that's gone down tonight."

Zev considered her request. "How about this? Rory and I will get Kerri settled in, and then Rory can stay with her while I go back to the lab."

I was shaking my head before he finished. "Uh-uh, nope. No one is going anywhere alone, not anymore. The lab can wait."

His eyebrows rose, and his jaw took on a familiar jut, his displeasure with my solution obvious. "We can't have anyone else tripping over those runes."

"I don't think that's a problem since the only one who keeps returning to the scene of the crime is Neil. And if he's reaching out to Kerri, it's because he wants her to run so he can chance getting to her." It was my turn to be obstinate. "I don't know about you, but I'm done chasing Neil. It's time to bring him to us."

"She's right, Zev." Imogen's startling comment had us both turning to her. Exhaustion and pain had taken her waxy skin tone to gray, and it was clear she was about to succumb to whatever painkillers the hospital staff was pumping into her veins. "Go guard Kerri—use her as bait. If we're lucky, maybe you'll get a chance to grab Neil."

"Fine." He scowled before giving in. "Can you give your team a heads-up that we're on our way?"

The bright gleam in Imogen's eyes had faded and turned blurry. "Yeah." She twisted as if to reach for the side table but hissed in pain.

Zev cleared the far side of the bed. "Stop. I got it." He handed Imogen her phone and waited while she texted.

When she was done, she handed it back to him and lay back. "As soon as they let me out of here..." She finally began to slip under.

"Got it." Zev shook his head in clear exasperation and lowered the top of the bed until Imogen was lying flat. He dimmed the light so she could rest. Without a word, he and I left Imogen's room to play bodyguard and bait a mad scientist.

◆

Our drive to Kerri's took place in near-total silence as neither one of us had much to say. I couldn't speak for Zev, but the confrontation with Bryan replayed on an endless mental loop, leaving me strangely numb. It seemed like no time had passed before we pulled into the neighborhood where Kerri was currently stashed and our SUV's headlights swept over the familiar SUV parked at the curb.

Zev pulled in behind it and shut off the engine. I sat there, staring unseeingly through the windshield, listening to the ticking of the cooling engine. A hand landed on my thigh, and I jumped.

"Rory? You okay?" Zev was crouched in the open passenger door, squeezing my thigh gently and watching me closely.

"Yeah." I covered his hand with mine and held tight. I shoved through the weird dissociation until the world resettled into familiar clarity. "Yeah," I repeated, my voice rough. "I'm good."

He waited a moment before taking me at my word and letting me go. He rose and moved away from the door so I could get out. Then I followed him through the quiet complex to Kerri's back fence. I absentmindedly wondered why we couldn't use her front door, but then she was there, face pale, eyes wide, holding back the vinyl slats and pulling back the sliding glass door to let us in.

"I thought Imogen would be coming." Panic added a higher pitch to her voice.

This time, Zev didn't wave me through but took the lead, disappearing inside. I'd done enough escorting to know he was ensuring that no threat lingered inside, which left me to answer Kerri. Uncertain how much had been explained to her, I stuck with, "Imogen's been unavoidably detained. She asked us to escort you to a new location."

Her eyes darted toward where Zev had disappeared and back to me. "Oh, okay."

Zev said, "Clear" in a low voice, and I stepped inside, letting Kerri close the door behind me. I spotted a small duffle bag, with a laptop case on top, waiting by the couch. "Why don't you grab your stuff, and we'll get you out of here so you can sleep tonight?"

I got a jerky nod from her, but instead of doing what I asked, she stood there, wringing her hands, while Zev spoke quietly into the phone, probably updating the security team outside.

I swallowed a sigh and reached for patience, reminding myself that she had good reason to be freaking out. Even if she'd teamed up with Neil at some point, facing him down now was a daunting proposition. "Kerri," I said. She didn't respond. "Dr. Michaels."

That worked. She blinked at me like an owl before

comprehension set in. "Right, my stuff." She looked around as if just realizing where she was. Spotting her bag, she rushed over and grabbed it.

Zev looked at me as he tucked his phone away. "Outside is clear, so I told Trask's team to head over and make sure the new place is still secure."

That meant we had to leave immediately. "We'll be right behind you." I turned to Kerri, "Follow Zev, Dr. Michaels."

He slipped out the patio door, and I waited until Kerri scurried behind him before bringing up the rear. We retraced the path back to the SUV. Even though I kept an eye on our surroundings, it did nothing to dull the itch along my spine. It made me reconsider carrying my firearm on a constant basis, but it wasn't like bullets were much use against magic. Still, having the weapon in hand would have been comforting.

We made it to the SUV without incident. Zev got Kerri settled in the back, and I took the front passenger seat, mainly because I still felt unsettled, which was not a good state to be in when operating a vehicle. When Zev navigated the neighborhood and took a roundabout way to the main street without the GPS's assistance, I realized he knew exactly where he was going.

He pulled out onto University, which at that time of night was fairly quiet. I twisted in my seat to see Kerri. With the intermittent wash of streetlights, she slipped in and out of shadows, making it difficult to read her expression.

"Can you tell me what happened tonight, Dr. Michaels?" I asked.

She angled toward me. "I was working on things when I got an email from Jonas." She motioned to the laptop case on top of her travel bag. "It was so unexpected that I opened it before I could rethink the wisdom of doing so."

Yeah, getting an email from a dead man would do that to a porson.

She clutched her hands in her lap, which set my teeth on edge for some reason. Ignoring my irrational reaction, I prompted, "What did it say?"

"It was a video clip." Even in the uncertain light, I could see her swallow before she looked out the window. "At first, I didn't understand what was happening, but..." Her voice trembled and broke. Before I could snap something bitchy and tell her to pull her shit together, she said, "It was Jonas, but he was upset, arguing with someone out of frame. He kept demanding that they explain the reports."

I didn't think I could endure a traumatized recitation of events, so I asked, "Do you still have it on your laptop?" When she gave me a jerky nod, I managed a small smile that I hoped was reassuring instead of just me gritting my teeth. "Could I see it?"

She twisted in her seat belt and, with a few stilted movements, pulled her laptop out of the bag. "Yes, sure. Here, let me get it up for you."

Zev remained silent as she pulled up the video for me, but I knew he was listening closely. Kerri handed me the slim laptop, and I turned back in my seat, setting it on my lap. She had the email open and the video up. Whoever had recorded this had done so covertly because Jonas was in the frame, but he wasn't captured straight on. The recording device, most likely a phone, was angled down low, probably so Jonas didn't realize he was being caught on tape. Making a mental note to forward this to Evan in hopes that he could pull information from the metadata on the video or email, I hit Play.

Jonas's panicked voice filled the interior. "I'm telling you, someone changed that report, because those indicators are completely off. If the project moves forward using that information, it could be disastrous."

Despite the odd angle, I could see how nervous Jonas was. He shifted constantly, unable to stand still, and his gaze kept jumping around. There was the sound of a door slamming open followed by a blast of electronic music with a driving beat and then what sounded like a couple of drunken kids trying to figure out how to keep the door open so as not to get locked out. Jonas half turned, looking behind him, and the frame jerked as well as if following the movements of whoever was recording it.

Jonas turned back, pale but determined, and hissed, "We have to let Mr. Trask know and stop this before someone gets hurt."

Before our amateur filmmaker could respond, an argument broke out behind Jonas. He turned, and the footage jerked then got shaky, making it difficult to see anything. There was a glimpse of weed-choked asphalt and then the flash of a familiar pile of broken pallets, like those in the alley where Jonas had died. Dread settled like lead in my stomach, making it cramp. The audio became muffled, but I could hear the tone of the voice change from nervous to angry to scared. Then a scream ripped through the laptop's speakers. When the video pulled back into focus, I watched in horror as a demonic fire consumed Jonas like a Roman candle. His screams continued for agonizing seconds, then he fell silent. The video stopped.

The horrific afterimages lingered. I looked up at Zev and whispered, "Holy shit, Zev."

Then something slammed into the SUV and upended everything.

CHAPTER TWENTY-ONE

A HAMMER BASHED against my skull, making it hard to think, and something was dripping down my face, but no matter how irritating it was, I couldn't seem to lift my hand to brush it away. In fact, every time I tried, my body rebelled with a series of screaming complaints. For a long, suspended moment, I was tempted to retreat back to the comforting darkness lurking at the edges of my mind, but the compulsion to move held it in check.

Despite the debilitating ache in my head, I managed to pry my eyes open. A haze filled the air, and something white was trying to smother me. Above the weird suffocating cloud, the light from a streetlamp spilled through cracked glass. Even weirder, there was a pole in the middle of the SUV's hood. My thoughts finally connected. Zev driving. Kerri in the back. Watching the video of Jonas. Turning to Zev, then...

Dammit, we've been hit. Zev! Panic trumped pain, and I batted away the slowly deflating airbag, sucking air into my tight chest. "Zev," I croaked, but there was no answer. My movements grew more frantic as I shoved the airbag aside and twisted against the seat belt locking me in place. Fire scored around my ribs, and my breath stalled.

Zev was slumped over the wheel, only his seat belt and the airbag holding him upright. The bits of safety glass from the driver's-side window covered him like a glittery blanket. His door was buckled, and the cab's roof was a lot closer than before, indicating we'd rolled at some point, which explained why my body felt like it had been run over. I managed to get my seat belt to release and twisted in the seat, desperate to check on Zev. Distantly, I could hear myself calling his name.

Ignoring the collection of aches and pains, I managed to get my hands on him, and I curled my fingers around his neck as I used my other hand to lift his head up. The steady beat of his pulse softened my initial panic, but the obvious lump just above his temple kept it close. I cradled his face with one hand and used my other to check for broken bones or any unexplained bleeding. Only after I'd confirmed that the bump appeared to be the worst of his injuries did my surroundings trickle in.

First came the sound of a nearby argument, the words not quite filtering, although I could tell that one was female and the other male. I looked at the back passenger seat where Kerri had been and saw the door bowed in but no Dr. Michaels. "Kerri?" I called out even as I realized the back passenger door was wide-open.

If she was able to get out of the SUV, she had to be okay, and I needed help. "Kerri, help me with Zev."

"Rory," she said from behind me.

I turned to see her wrenching open my door. "Are you okay?"

Exasperation flashed across her face. "I'm fine obviously."

The borderline-bitchy comment made me want to kick her in the face, but since I needed to get Zev out of there, I refrained. "Good. Help me get Zev out."

With a frustrating lack of urgency, she glanced at Zev and frowned. "I don't think it's smart to move him."

Not about to argue with her, I snapped, "Just help me."

She sighed. "If you insist."

There was something off in her voice, but I didn't have time to process it. "Who were you arguing with?"

I never got the answer because a few things happened at once. My neck prickled with awareness of an approaching threat that had nothing to do with magic, Zev gave a soft groan, and some man cursed behind me as hands yanked me back out of my seat and away from Zev.

With no magical threat incoming, instinct and Guild-mandated defense training kicked in with a vengeance. Despite the waves of pain set off by being jerked backward, I still managed to slam my head back and connect. The painful impact left my head spinning even more as a curse echoed in my ears, but muscle memory had me swinging out in an awkward elbow strike and back fist. There was a grunt, but my unbalanced position meant there wasn't enough power behind my moves to do much other than piss off whoever was trying to grab me.

"Hurry the hell up."

I didn't recognize the voice as I struggled to get my legs untangled from the wrecked SUV, and then an arm wrapped around my throat and waist, dragging me back. I clawed at the arm at my neck, skin tearing under my nails, as I tried to get a grip to rip the arm away. Another vicious curse hit the air, then something pinched my thigh. I freed one foot and managed to brace it against the center console and shove back. The abrupt move freed my other leg, but lines of agony seared through jeans and skin as it scraped along something sharp. Legs no longer trapped, I tumbled backward out of the SUV, helped along by whoever had grabbed me. We fell back, and I landed on someone hard enough to elicit a pained grunt.

I flailed, throwing elbows and knees where I could, desperate to get away. Finally, I was able to twist out of the hold. I scrambled up, or at least I tried. I pushed to my feet, but my legs were rubber, and numbness crawled through me.

"Wha... what the hell?" I managed a couple of fumbling steps before the ground rose up to meet me, and everything went dark.

◆

The next time I opened my eyes, I knew I was in deep shit. This time, there was no disorientation from a crash to contend with. Instead, one moment there had been nothing, and the next, I was awake, shoulders screaming, wrists aching at my back, and cheek pressed against a cold, hard surface. Even worse, my skin crawled under the touch of an unfamiliar magic. Not some minor spell either. The discomfort was so acute that it was like lying under a blanket of razor-sharp needles, risking a full-body puncture experience with every exhalation. That disturbing sensation cleared my head faster than a face full of icy water.

Fortunately, my ability had managed to kick in while I was out, enough to keep the worst of the threat at bay. Now that I was awake, I sank more power into my shield, thickening it into a magically impermeable armor. If I was lucky, it would be enough to keep me alive and relatively unharmed. If not, well, maybe I could buy myself enough time to figure a way out of this mess—so long as they didn't decide to shoot or stab me first. Although based on the crawling reddish-purple lines of power visible from my position on the floor, physical threats were the least of my worries.

Shit shit shit.

There was so much power slithering across the floor that I was clearly lying in an Arcane circle. This was not good. Neither was the silence that suddenly replaced the indistinct murmurs that I hadn't noticed until they fell silent. Feet moved across the floor and came closer. Trussed up like I was, there wasn't much I could do but wait for whoever it was to make the first move. It didn't take long.

"I'm glad you're awake," Kerri said, her voice unnaturally cheerful, none of the annoying nerves from our previous interactions in evidence.

My hands were bound behind me, and I lay in a magical cage in the middle of the floor, making sitting up difficult but not impossible. It took longer than I wanted, but once upright, I didn't bother trying to stand. Not only was my body one big aching bruise, but my head was spinning badly enough that me getting to my feet would just end with a face-plant.

On the other side of the circle, Kerri watched me. Under the bright fluorescent lights, it was easy to see the bruise coming up along her neck and a cheek. Her pants were torn, revealing a white bandage wrapped partway up her calf. I got some minor satisfaction in knowing she hadn't escaped the crash unscathed. Too damn bad it hadn't knocked her out like it had Zev and me.

Thinking of Zev sent my pulse racing, but with Kerri watching, I tamped down my panic. Once I got out of whatever the hell this was, I could deal with Zev and all the rest. Heart rate back under control, I aimed a glare at Kerri. "What the hell is going on?"

Her expression remained coolly clinical. "What's most important for you to know is that you are going to help us finalize the Delphi serum."

Choking back a bubble of hysterical laughter, as I was sure that wouldn't be appreciated, I managed to croak, "Us?"

"Us." This time, a man's voice answered. It belonged to a man who stopped at Kerri's side and folded his arms.

For a killer, he looked fairly normal if not a bit ragged on the edges. His hair was a lank mess. Bags big enough to hide a body in hung under his bloodshot eyes, and with the way he was clenching and unclenching his hands, I felt safe assuming his nerves were shot to hell. That would be completely understandable for someone who'd spent the last couple of weeks killing people, herding mutant scientific experiments, trying to dodge pursuing Arbiters, and most likely serving as patient zero for an unstable serum. The deep, bloody gouges on his arm made me happy, but it wasn't enough to stop my rising apprehension when I put a name to the scowling face.

"Neil, you're a hard man to track down."

A glint of crazy stared back, signally that his veneer of normalcy was on the verge of shattering, but none of that leaked into his voice. "I've been busy."

Yeah, that's the goddess's own truth. Kerri's familiarity with him as they stood close to each other, staring at me with matching reptilian gazes, slammed the final piece into place. *Say hello to Team Mad Scientists.*

I looked from Neil to Kerri. "You were never Neil's next target."

Her pleasant expression didn't waver, but the cold gleam in her eyes grew sharper. "No, I wasn't." Neil gave an uncontrolled jerk as if to lunge toward me, but Kerri put a hand on his arm, effectively holding him back. She continued to lightly brush her fingers against his quivering skin. That simple touch revealed that they were more than just partners in crime. "Neil would never hurt me, but we needed Origin to believe it was a possibility."

Great, so not just working together but sleeping together too. Lovely. A spot of warmth flared just under the neckline of my T-shirt. My gaze shifted to the magical lines caging me, and I tried to figure out what Kerri was up to, but they remained steady. When the burst of warmth came again, I realized it was from Sabella's necklace, not Kerri.

A flicker of hope rose. If I was being tracked, I needed to buy time, which meant keeping these two talking. "Why is that important?"

Kerri gave me a puzzled frown, clearly not expecting that question. "Excuse me?"

I wasn't sure what she didn't understand. It was a legit question, but clearly I was missing something. "You two managed to kill off your research teams and get control of the serum, so why not disappear and wait it out? Why risk getting the Trasks' attention, much less the council's, by setting the serum loose on the streets? And then killing an Arbiter? That guarantees you'll spend your lives looking over your shoulders. Why not just take the serum and wait it out?"

"Wait it out?" Kerri sounded like an amused parrot as she dropped her hand from Neil's arm.

"Yeah, wait it out." With exaggerated patience, I said, "Neil hunkers down with the serum, you wait for the dust to settle with Trask and Origin, then you quietly slip away into obscurity. You and Neil rendezvous later and do your evil-villain routine, probably selling it to the highest bidder, and then retire to some remote island where they serve fluorescent fruity drinks with little paper umbrellas." Of course, that was the most stereotypical scenario ever devised, but there was a reason such plans were the gold standard. "What's that saying? 'The simplest solution is generally the easiest'?"

"You think you have us all figured out, don't you?" Her amusement was clear.

Not even the tiniest bit. There was no way to unravel the depth of crazy these two were swimming in, but I had a feeling I'd be treading those waters soon enough.

As if to emphasize that point, Kerri shared a chuckle with

Neil before turning back to me and shaking her head. "Nothing is ever that simple, Ms. Costas."

That spot of warmth just under my shirt remained steady, and I clung to the hope it offered, praying that whoever was on the other end got here quickly. In the meantime, I'd keep playing twenty questions.

"So tell me, what am I missing?"

Neil shot Kerri a look, and when he turned back to me, he wore a smirk. "Let me guess—science was not your best subject."

If he wanted to sling insults, I was all for it. "Like interpersonal communication wasn't yours."

My insult wiped away his smirk, and he glowered at me, a hint of red there and gone in his eyes. Kerri murmured his name and gave him a warning headshake, reining him in yet again. His jaw flexed, and his hands fisted, and I had a moment to worry that he was about to slip Kerri's leash, but then he spun and stalked back to the table strewn with lab equipment.

Kerri watched him go, and only when he rummaged through the glass tubes, held them up for scrutiny, then typed something into the computer did she turn back and focus on me. "Are you familiar with the research world?"

I shook my head.

"There are two major sources of funding for research— private funds and public funds." She settled into lecturer mode with unsurprising ease. "The Delphi project was privately funded and initially had massive support, mainly because Dr. Kaspar was lead researcher and had stellar credentials. Then she was killed, and her questionable behavior came to light. This did not go over well with the initial investors. In fact, they were quick to distance themselves from the whole embarrassing dilemma, and suddenly, their pockets weren't so deep. That was a blow, especially as we were on the cusp of a breakthrough, but then, when her research was taken by the Cordovas and restricted..." Anger darkened Kerri's face. "We couldn't let the project get mothballed. It was too important."

More like your ego couldn't handle the blow. But saying that out loud wasn't in my best interests. It was fairly clear where she was so eagerly going, so I nudged her along. "So you decided to find an alternate form of funding?"

The anger drifted away, replaced by a calculating satisfaction. "Someone once said, 'Action precedes funding. Planning precedes action.' I not only planned, but I acted, and in return, I secured the funding necessary to make the Delphi project a reality."

That didn't sound good at all. I could think of one group that had deeper pockets than the Arcane Families. But as the argument between Leander Clarke and Stephen Trask had proven, their existence was up for debate.

Wanting confirmation, I asked, "From whom?"

Her smile was sly, but she ignored my question and headed to where Neil was working. From my position on the floor, it was hard to see much other than that they were studying something. She asked him a question I couldn't make out. He nodded and handed her something, which she pocketed.

Kerri looked up to find me watching. "Do you know the most rewarding part about research?" She didn't wait for my response as she moved around the table. "It's discovering all the unexpected turns that your work can take, which then leads to the most opportune doors. For example, when your current formula creates terminal results, it's vital to have an antidote before you present a finished product. And to create that antidote, you need a nullifying agent."

Ugly suspicions crawled closer, and the second half of her

initial statement came back to me: *"You are going to help us finalized the Delphi serum."*

A glimmer of understanding sparked a panicked mental litany of curses. My voice was tight as I repeated, "A nullifying agent."

She made a quiet hum of agreement as she grabbed a syringe from a white container on the table and held it up where I couldn't miss it. "It was the last and most difficult piece to identify, a component that could counteract the magical trigger in the serum. We were working on the solution just before LanTech closed its doors. We would've moved the research quietly over to my lab at Origin, but then Neil had to disappear when his coworker ended up being mugged, and questions started being asked."

"Mugged?" There was no stopping my disbelieving snort or the look I shot to Neil. "Try murdered, right, Neil?"

Neil's face flushed red, but Kerri wasn't looking at him— she was still looking at me. Her eyes narrowed, and she set the syringe down before turning to a guilty-looking Neil. "What is she talking about?"

Neil kept his focus on the work in front of him, his color high, as he avoided Kerri's eyes. "I have no idea."

At that, I laughed outright, deliberately widening the fracture between the mad couple. "Please tell me you don't believe his bullshit."

An animalistic snarl broke from Neil, his attention snapping to me with murderous intent. For a brief second, the monster under his skin peeked out, the underlying threat so clear I was happy to be inside the dubious protection of the circle. Refusing to reveal how his reaction rattled me, I continued to poke. "What happened, Neil? Did you think Chloe was going to share her concerns about the project? Did you jump the gun to make sure she stayed quiet?"

At his side, Kerri shot him a dark look. "Tell me you didn't kill that girl."

In a flash of violence, Neil threw a test tube against the wall. Before the jangle of broken glass faded, he was in Kerri's face. "She had a report on the computer, predated with her last day and ready to be delivered to Clarke. I erased it but knew it wouldn't be enough. We needed more time, so I made sure we got it."

Instead of quailing under his looming threat, Kerri stared at him for a drawn-out moment, tension creeping higher with each second. Finally, she said, "Clean that up, and get the vector ready."

He held her gaze for another heart-stopping moment then dragged his hands through his hair and spun away to follow her orders.

Interesting.

Kerri took something I couldn't see from the drawer, picked up the syringe, and headed toward me. She stopped just outside the reddish-purple glow of the circle and took a seat on the ground. "To return to our earlier conversation on nullifying agents, Ms. Costas, *you* are nothing short of miraculous."

The emphasis on "you" made my stomach bottom out with dread. The warmth from Sabella's necklace remained unchanged, and I desperately wished my hands were free because holding it would make me feel tons better. It was a pathetic security blanket, but still...

Instead, I cleared my throat and managed what I hoped was a nonchalant tone. "Not sure why you think that, as I can't see how a Transporter can help with a magical steroid serum."

That earned me a quick reproving glance. "Let's not play games. It's such a waste of time." Reprimand delivered, she touched a spot to the right of her knee. Magic flared and spilled into a smaller circle I hadn't noticed earlier. "Your performance with the illusion mage—Bryan, wasn't it?—was impressive. At least, according to Imogen's call with Mr. Trask." She gave the barest sneer when she said Trask's name.

Kerri ignited a series of runes inside the smaller circle she sat in. From my position, it was difficult to see them or the spell she was casting. Casting circles were meant to magically contain another mage, and a well-trained caster could also use the circle to boost their magic. Unfortunately, I had no idea what the deal was with two circles, but whatever she was up to, it was clear I was running out of time and on my own.

"I don't know what Imogen said, but I think you have the wrong idea about me."

Kerri just smiled. "Well, we'll find out, won't we?" She pulled an uncut crystal from her pocket. Holding it in one hand, she bent forward and touched one of the glowing sigils on the outer ring of the circle, then she looked at me. "As trite as this sounds, I must warn you that this may hurt."

CHAPTER TWENTY-TWO

KERRI MUTTERED SOMETHING, and the reddish-purple lines flared to a deep orange as power raced through the circle. With nowhere to go, I poured more strength into my shield and braced for an attack. Instead, a crushing wave of magic rose and slammed into my Prism with bruising force. Considering the smothering weight of power bearing down on me, I could tell that Kerri was well trained. The fact that I wasn't currently imitating a human candle, drowning in a room with no water source, or being torn apart by vicious winds or some creature's claws and teeth meant that the magic she commanded did not belong to an offensive element.

Despite the heavy weight of pressing power, my shield held fast because at its heart, magic was based on will, and I could be a stubborn bitch when necessary. If surviving was simply a matter of who could outlast whom, I had faith that I could walk away from this. But simply outlasting Kerri wasn't an option because, well... Neil. I snuck a look at the table and found him watching, lips stretched in a malicious grin. Yeah, he was going to be a problem.

Focus on the immediate threat.

Heeding the reminder, I decided to start evening the odds. First up, I needed to pinpoint what kind of mage Kerri was so I could revert her magic and shatter the circle. Considering that my knowledge of offensive magical abilities was sorely limited, identifying her magic was going to be a challenge. Granted, if I dropped my shield, I *might* be able to figure it out, just maybe not before I stopped breathing. My brain raced, considering and discarding various options. There was something about her magic, about this circle, that eluded me. So I started over at the basics.

For me, rebounding magic was instinctive, or at least, it had been up until that moment. I needed to figure out the trigger, but it was difficult to concentrate with the annoying unintelligible whispers and pitiless painful pressure clawing at my mind. Her attack wasn't physical in the traditional sense. Yes, it felt like needles were piercing my skin, but the unrelenting grip on my skull was even more worrisome. My headache had returned with a vengeance and brought along extra help, making it hard to think. Whispers, like a badly tuned radio, ate at the edges of my mind.

Hard as it was, I forced myself to concentrate. I blinked through the haze of pain and found Kerri sitting cross-legged on the other side of the circle, her palms pressed into two sigils, both burning orange. The same flaming orange filled her unblinking stare, which she aimed at me as her lips moved with words I couldn't hear.

Disconcerted, I closed my eyes and sank deeper into my magic, belatedly wishing I'd researched offensive spells for Prisms first instead of the defensive stuff. I tried to figure out what Kerri was actually doing. I lost track of time and of my body as I swam through those metaphysical depths. It was like pushing through a deafening storm of wild, unpredictable winds and currents. Trying to pick my way through was a chancy tactic, but my only other choice was to go down and stay down.

Yeah, that isn't really an option.

I kept fighting, but it was getting harder and harder. Holding her back wasn't working, I needed a closer look at her magic. Desperate, I took a risk and let a tiny crack emerge in my shield. Kerri's magic wasted no time sniffing it out, then it began seeping through my shield. The whispery noise increased, fracturing my concentration, and something sank sharp teeth into my brain, like a barbed hook. My shield squeezed around the thin crack, but no matter how hard I tried, I couldn't get it to close all the way. Hissing, I lifted weighted lids, opening my eyes, and was surprised to find Kerri kneeling right next to me. I tried to move, but my body didn't respond.

She touched my face. I could barely feel it, but I sure as hell heard her murmur, "Stay."

I tried to jerk away from her touch, but again, my body didn't respond.

She lifted an uncut crystal, positioned it just above the center of my chest, and whispered, *"Quaerite, et invenietis reditus."*

Seek, find, and return what? Before I could figure out the answer, light erupted from the crystal, and a sharp pain tore through my chest, centered where she held that damn crystal. My spine bowed, and I couldn't hold back a whimper. *Damn that hurts.*

"Still." She set down a now glowing crystal and lifted a syringe.

I was frantic to get away from her and that needle, but my body didn't fucking move. This time there was another, less painful sting as she sank the needle into my arm. *What is she doing to me?* Panic rose, scrambling for purchase, but I ruthlessly squashed it under desperate determination. A tangled snarl managed to escape my frozen vocal cords.

Her gaze flicked up, and my breath caught as that orange flame burned bright and steady in the depth of her eyes. "Quiet. Still."

This time, her commands shoved against that spiked barb in my head, and the knowledge finally clicked. Kerri wasn't a minor pattern mage—the bitch was an Auctori mage, someone who could influence thoughts and actions.

She lifted a syringe, now filled with my blood, and smiled with satisfaction. "Perfect." She set it on the floor next to me and then turned back to pat my face with an infuriating insolence. "We're almost done."

She dug into her pocket and pulled out another syringe, this one filled with a pale-green liquid. My heart raced, and trapped in my unresponsive body, I could hear myself screaming in rage and fear.

I felt another prick, and then she was gathering the empty syringe, the glowing crystal, and the second blood-filled syringe before getting to her feet. "Stay here, and be good."

Seething, I watched her cross the circle and step out, taking both the crystal and the syringes over to where Neil waited with barely concealed impatience. Anger rose with every heartbeat, so deep it was frightening. There was no knowing how long it would take for the injection to take effect, but until it did, I would make damn sure Kerri regretted it. With single-minded focus, I went after the psychic barb, determined to turn the tables on Kerri. On closer inspection, I was thrilled to discover the barb wasn't as deeply rooted as—I hoped—Kerri expected. That would explain why her control only extended to my physical body and not my mind.

Unfortunately, there was a tether attached to the barb, and I quickly understood it was her direct line of control. My body might not obey me, but my mind and magic would, and that was my loophole. I would need to reconfigure the magic of the mental barb so the next time Kerri pulled, it would snap back into her gray matter, shifting the control to me.

Spurred on by fear and frustration, I narrowed my focus and slipped into the magic. With teeth-gritting focus, I began recrafting the barb's intent. It wasn't easy, especially as I had to be mindful of not tripping the tether. Plus, I was trying not to think about what was currently coursing through my veins. I had a few breath-stealing moments when Kerri's attention shifted to me as she made sure I was where she wanted me before she went back to whatever she was working on. Each time that happened, I lightened my touch but didn't stop. Finally, it was done.

I'd only get one shot at this, and it was going to hurt. First things first, I needed Kerri back in the circle because the minute she triggered the barb, it would tear free from me and zip along the tether back to her. I wasn't sure the barb would cross the casting lines if she was physically outside the circle. So like any good bait, I tripped that psychic tether, mimicking an escape attempt.

Sure enough, her head jerked up, and her gaze narrowed. Still frozen in place, all I could do was glare back. She grabbed something from the table in front of her then said something to Neil, who flicked a look my way, shook his head, and went back to his computer and slides. Kerri, a frustrated frown on her face, rounded the tall lab table and headed for me, light catching on something silver in her hand. I held my breath and her stare as she touched the wards and stepped into the circle. The magical cage resettled behind her.

She cocked her head, crouched at my side, and tapped my cheek with the razor-sharp blade of a scalpel. "What are you doing?"

Everything slowed and crystalized at the same time, a sensation eerily similar to what I'd experienced when I changed from driver to transporter. Her magic slid down the tether, and the barb quivered in reaction. I braced as little white starbursts spotted my vision, and I mentally started my countdown. Her magic closed around the barb and pulsed. The barb trembled then jerked free with an agonizing tearing sensation. It shot back along that tether with stunning speed, taking my magic with it, and sank deep inside Kerri. Fire erupted in my face as Kerri's hand jerked, dragging the tip of the scalpel along my cheek.

The invisible cage on my body disintegrated. I turned my head and said, "Quiet." Kerri's eyes widened, and her mouth opened in a silent gasp. "Still," I hissed.

She began to topple backward, but I was already moving. With my hands still bound behind me, I awkwardly got to my knees and shuffled over. When I was close, I bent down, getting eye level with an immobilized Kerri. She stared at me with a mix of fear and anger, and I could feel her fighting against the barb. She was damn strong and knew what she was doing, whereas I was winging it and pissed. Still, I would bank my fury against hers any day of the week.

Staring deep into her eyes, I ruthlessly flexed my magical hold and hissed, "Release me."

She jerkily rolled up then crawled around me so she could slice through the ties on my hands. The sharp scalpel made quick work of the bindings. My arms dropped, and the painful rush of returning blood left me clenching my teeth. The barb wiggled harder as Kerri took advantage of my momentary slip in concentration.

She slashed out with the scalpel, but I was already rolling away from the wicked strike, tightening my grip on the magical tether. "Stop."

Kerri crouched on the floor, frozen, a hand raised for a

second strike, teeth bared, and a furious light in her eyes. Distantly, I could hear Neil saying something, but since it would take some time for him to bypass the circle, I concentrated on Kerri. I clumsily got to my feet and wrenched the scalpel from her hand, feeling better with an actual weapon.

Staring down at her, I ordered, "Sit."

With stiff movements, she sat. I risked checking where Neil was and found him outside the outer ring, red-faced and furious. Between his hands, a sickly yellow orb tinged in black formed.

I scanned the inner runes, and recognizing one for strength, I stepped over and sank my magic into it. Maybe I was angrier than I realized, because a powerful wash of silvery magic swept through the circle in a thunderous wave, drowning out the orange flame and replacing it with a Prism shield that took my breath away.

Okay, that's new.

I didn't get much time to appreciate the massive shield before Neil looked at Kerri and snarled, "Now."

He threw his sickly-looking magic at the shield. It hit and erupted into a storm of red, purple, and black at the same time that Kerri tried to reclaim the barb. Power roared in my head, and my grip on Kerri's tether tightened so fast and so hard that a low moan escaped her unmoving mouth and a red-tinged tear leaked from her eye. Seeing it satisfied the feral part of me, and I didn't let up.

No way will I lose control of that bitch now. As for Neil... Buoyed by an intoxicating rush of power, I stalked to the edge of the circle until I was as close to him as I could get. He was partway through another cast, but I deliberately looked at the fading tendrils of his last spell, which was being absorbed by my magic, leaving nothing behind but my beautifully strong Prism.

I then turned back to his red-ringed gaze, crossed my

arms over my chest, and smirked. "Go ahead, asshole. Throw another one, and see what happens."

The implied threat was enough that he paused, hand in midair, his gaze skating from me to Kerri and back. "You can't stay in there forever."

I shrugged just as Sabella's stone gave a warm pulse. At the same time, something small and furry scurried across the floor and charged up Neil's leg. He gave a short yelp and kicked out, trying to dislodge the brown desert rat trying to gnaw its way through his calf. I started laughing as his kick grew more frantic, but he finally managed to dislodge the rodent. It hit the floor, landing in the narrow space between me, the circle, and Neil. There was a brush of familiar magic as Neil kicked out one last time. The rat darted away and disappeared through an empty doorway I hadn't noticed before.

My smile gained teeth, but I kept talking to Neil, refusing to reveal that Zev was somewhere nearby. "Was that one of your experiments?"

Neil's lips curled, and his hands brightened as he gathered his magic. This time, it was a writhing knot of inky-black red-eyed snakes. Or something that resembled snakes. A whimper sounded from behind me, but I didn't dare take my attention from Neil. His arms shifted, but before he could unleash whatever the hell he held, blue-tinted lightning whipped around his torso, spinning him around to face a furious Zev.

Neil's face contorted with rage as the writhing magic he held bent and reshaped, clashing with Zev's magic. I didn't get a chance to enjoy the fight because Kerri got desperate, throwing everything she had into reclaiming her magic. I lost my slippery hold on my temper.

Pain exploded in my skull, and I spun around with my own roar of rage, reaching for my magic. When it answered, a distant alarm told me that something was wrong, but my need to hurt Kerri shoved it away. I latched on to the magical tether and let loose. My magic tore along the tether, whipped around the barb, and tore apart Kerri's pathetic attempt with incendiary power. A far-off scream sounded nearby, but caught in the overwhelming flood of magic, it barely penetrated.

It didn't take me long to realize I was in trouble. My magic was loose, gaining strength too fast for me to reclaim control, and I was drowning under the unrelenting onslaught. My vision whited out, and I could barely feel my body. I was nothing but an anchorless mind caught in a storm of power. If I was lucky, I'd get snagged by a metaphorical tree until it passed, hopefully leaving behind enough tatters I wouldn't end up a vegetable. I did my best to survive the raging winds even as it tore bits and pieces away. I narrowed my focus to simply enduring and wasn't sure how long I'd drifted in the colorless winds when the first brilliant fork of lightning caught my attention.

It was so unexpected and bright that I thought it was an illusion. I stared into the haze, wanting to catch another glimpse. Then it came again, this time a little bit closer, leaving a fascinating trail of blue in its wake and bringing a voice with it. "Rory! Snap out of it, dammit!"

Recognition hit and, with it, a burst of determination. "Zev?" My voice was just a croak, nowhere near loud enough to be heard above the storm. I tried again. "Zev?"

This time I got an answer. "Rory, listen to me. You need to let go."

Let go of what? I didn't know if I asked the question out loud or not, but I must have, because Zev said, "Whatever connection you have to Kerri, let it go!"

Who's Kerri?

"Rory, are you listening to me?" Panic rode Zev's voice,

and it was so unexpected that it felt like a mental head slap. "For fuck's sake, you've got to let go before it's too late."

Reality snapped back with painful clarity. Kerri. The barb and tether. The injection. The circle. *Shit.*

Heeding Zev's urgency, I frantically searched for the glowing tether, only to realize it was coiled up my arms like incandescent ivy. The magic churning through it burned so bright that it was blinding. With rising desperation, I began to tear it down my arms as Zev continued to yell at me. It was difficult and painful, but I managed to block his voice out so I could concentrate on loosening the magical bindings. Moments later, the last fiery ties of power fell free, and I found myself on my knees next to a slack-faced Kerri in the middle of a burning Arcane circle, feeling curiously hollow.

"Rory!"

Light and shadows flickered across my vision like a manic strobe, and I narrowed my eyes against the bright kaleidoscope of magic that had replaced the previously placid power lines of the Arcane circle.

"Zev?" *Damn, my throat hurts.* I coughed and tried again, "Zev?"

"Rory, hurry."

I turned toward his voice and finally saw him, caught on the outer ring of the circle. He stood there, hands extended, muscles straining, his body outlined in the same intense blue from the earlier lightning storm as wild magic flowed around him in mesmerizing currents. There was something familiar about his pose, but it kept slipping through my fingers.

"What's going on?"

"Get up and help me reverse the circle."

I swayed on my knees, his words bouncing around my skull without settling.

"Rory, dammit, snap out of it and get up!"

My brain might have been skipping, but his harsh demand brought me to my feet. "I'm up."

I rubbed my face hard, feeling a sting and smearing something along my cheek. I dropped my hands and looked around, the strange sense of distance dissipating fast as the world came back into focus. And it wasn't pretty. The reason for Zev's strange position clicked into place. He was trying to channel the raging power whipping through the circle.

"What do you need me to do?" I asked.

"Like we did with the Drainer's Circle. Take the opposite point."

As soon as I heard "Drainer's Circle," I was on my way to the position opposite Zev, memories of how we broke Lena free of the lethal spell chasing me. As I got close to the circle's edge, something shifted inside me, but with Zev's urgency pushing me forward, I ignored it and stepped into the current.

Magic rushed me, flooding into the previously hollow spaces, filling them between one breath and the next. My vision whited out as power seared through me with vicious force. I did my best to ride out the volatile magic, desperately trying to gain some kind of hold, but it was like trying to catch lightning. I lost track of where I was, and my sense of self was precarious, but I grimly held on, breathing my way through the initial onslaught. My awareness came back in pieces, and as soon as I had a tentative hold, I caught Zev's eye.

"Are you ready?" he asked.

Truthfully? No, but this is as good as it's going to get, so it will have to do. "Yeah," I gritted out.

I could feel him attempting to corral the magic, to pull it back and make it obey. I did my best to mimic him. It took a few moments before I could determine that we were dealing with multiple magics fused together.

As I added my strength to his, I couldn't help but ask, "What happened?"

Despite the draining fight, Zev managed to answer, "Neil."

The part of my brain not occupied with saving our asses put the pieces together. Neil was a Fusor mage, and the spell he'd tossed at my Prism must have melded my magic, his magic, and whatever remained of Kerri's magic into one frightening element. *Oh shit.* I wasn't sure Zev and I would be enough to stop this mess. "Tell me what to do."

In the flickering light of the magic, Zev's face was drawn and sweat dripped from his temple, but his eyes burned with a deep determination. "Can you reach your magic? Pull it back to you?"

I changed focus, reaching for that familiar energy. I found it tangled with something dark and twisted. I called it back, doing my best to pull it free. It wasn't easy, each inch a hard-won battle, but I kept at it, determined not to lose. Neither Zev nor I could afford the consequences. My muscles shook under the strain, and I could feel a warm trickle from my nose and ears. Even knowing what that meant, I couldn't stop. If I did, Zev would pay. My legs weakened, and I sank to my knees, still fighting.

Then I heard another voice, one I hadn't expected. "What the hell?"

I lifted my head to see a wan Imogen come to a stop next to Zev, who looked as bad as I felt. She rushed around to a midpoint between Zev and me, her gaze on the floor. Whatever she was looking for, she must have found, because she stepped into the circle and added her magic to ours. It was the shift in power we needed. With her help, we managed to tear apart what Neil had fused together and sink each magical power line through the now-fragile runes. My magic bucked under my grip, but I held tight, determined to lock it down.

By the time I threw the last lock home, I could barely think, much less move. The last vestiges of magic faded away, and with the circle now still and silent, I finally let go, barely feeling anything as my body gave in and sank under the encroaching darkness.

CHAPTER TWENTY-THREE

AWARENESS SEEPED IN, a drop at a time. First to penetrate was the faint rhythmic beeping. It was annoying, but I was too tired to make it stop. Then came snippets of voices, the words fragmented and meanings unclear. I slipped back under, and when I rose again, I was met with a low hum of aches and the larger discomfort of an unrelenting itch that crawled over every inch of my skin. I went to scratch, but my arm weighed a freaking ton. Grunting with effort, I peeled my eyes open only to be greeted with an eye-watering glare. I turned away, screwing my eyes closed to escape.

"Turn 'em off." My tongue got tangled on the words, and an undecipherable mumble emerged. But someone must have translated, because the light pressing against my lids disappeared.

This time, when I got my eyes open, it didn't hurt. I blinked, shifting shadows into discernable shapes like the railing on the bed and the blocky machine emitting those annoying beeps. A hospital. I was in the hospital. The beeping sped up, there was a dull clunk, and then something warm and firm squeezed my hand. I lifted my gaze, and it collided with the deep, relieved chocolate depths that belonged to one person: Zev.

My rising anxiety slowed and then receded, taking that damn itch with it. I swallowed, not that it did much for my dry mouth, so I tried to lick my lips and ran into the same problem. Zev reached over, grabbed a plastic cup with a straw, and held it up to my mouth. Leaning forward set off a chain reaction of low-grade aches. *I'm thirsty, dammit.* It took a second to remember how to suck, but when it finally clicked, cool water hit my parched mouth and slid down my sore throat. I almost cried in relief.

"Slow, babe." His voice was low with an underlying roughness I didn't understand.

When I finally curbed the worst of my thirst, I lay back and watched him set the cup aside. He picked up a remote and hit a button. The bed under my head rose, angling me just enough to make it comfortable. He tossed the remote onto the table and nudged it back a bit so he could drag his chair in close. The entire time, he kept my hand in his, not that I gave him much choice.

He sat back down, dropped the side rail, and settled in. Then he brought our laced hands up and brushed a brief kiss to the back of my hand. "Hey there."

"Hey," I said in a husky voice.

His lips curved up, and that relief from earlier made a comeback, lighting the dark chocolate of his eyes to more of a warm and comforting milk-chocolate color. "How are you feeling?"

"Like crap." There was no sense in lying. I was, after all, in a freaking hospital. "What happened?"

His fingers tightened on mine, and his smile grew a little tight. I did, however, get another absentminded brush of his close-cropped beard against my hand, a touch I was quickly becoming addicted to. Instead of answering, he said, "How about we start with the last thing you remember."

Hmm. That sounds ominous. "Imogen riding to our rescue." Memories flickered and steadied. "We got the circle drained, didn't we?"

The deep lines in his forehead eased, and so did some of the smaller ones around his eyes and mouth. "Yeah, we did, but it wasn't easy. If she hadn't shown up..."

He didn't have to finish, because I remembered my growing dread when the fused magic struggled against our hold, almost as if it had morphed into its own entity with its own twisted agenda. That made no sense since magic wasn't an intellect, just a manifestation of a mage's intent and will. But there was one thing that might explain the power's weird behavior.

"Neil's last spell?" I asked.

"At best guess, yes." Zev's fingers tightened on mine then relaxed as a hardness swept through his face.

As a minor Fusor mage, Neil shouldn't have been able to pull off a spell of that caliber. A rush of questions begged to be asked, but it hurt to talk, so I kept it short. "Serum?"

Zev did another brush of my fingers against his jaw, the rasp of the soft bristles making my skin jump. "I think so."

I lifted my gaze from that strangely intimate touch and met his eyes. "Did you ask?"

His lips flattened, and he shook his head. "Didn't get a chance."

I could only think of one reason he why he wouldn't. "Dead?"

"Yeah." He anticipated my next question before I could ask it. "Kerri's alive, but she's not talking either."

Something in his voice added an unexplained layer to his statement. I frowned. With his free hand, he gently traced the furrows on my forehead, his eyes focused on the movement. When his gaze returned to mine, it carried a puzzling wariness. "I don't know what happened between you two, but she's in a vegetative state, and the healers aren't sure she'll ever recover."

Stunned, I wasn't sure how to react. Part of me felt justi- fied, since she'd invaded my mind and all but held me captive in my own body. If I added in all the lives she'd ruined or helped ruin, her current state was like fate's way of evening the scales. Still, I thought maybe I should feel something besides a distant sort of regret. Maybe I would later, when I wasn't attached to an IV and lying in a bed. As if a switch was tripped, I remembered the needles Kerri had jabbed into me, and a whole new set of worries popped up.

I squeezed Zev's fingers until he looked at me, and I asked the first question to spin free. "What day is it?"

"Sunday. You've been out just over thirty-six hours." That explained the dark circles under his eyes, the lines on his face, and the relieved expression when I first woke up. "I... we were worried you'd be out longer."

I held the pronoun slip close, saving it for later. "Kerri injected me. What wa—"

"We don't know," he said, his voice staying low and a warning glint in his eyes. "The hospital tests came back negative."

"But the ser—"

The monitor's beeps sped up, and he leaned in and cut me off with a soft press of his lips to mine. When he drew back, the beeps were for a whole different reason. "The tests were clear, Rory." He kept his voice soft, quiet, just between us. "There's no sign of anything out of the ordinary floating through your veins."

I knew what he was saying, but fear wasn't letting me go. "Bryan—"

He squeezed my hand. "Imogen asked the hospital to

compare your tests to ones taken from Bryan and the others. You're fine."

I wasn't sure I liked the idea of Imogen having my blood, and that must have been obvious because Zev cupped my face, holding me still as he stared into my eyes. "She got to the doctor before I could, but I had the samples and results sent to Sabella as soon as it was done. Sabella gave the doctor permission to share the results, but that's all Imogen has. Sabella has everything else."

I would rather Sabella have that kind of information than Imogen, but honestly, I would have preferred that neither the test nor the samples existed. As relieved as I was about the results, it couldn't smother all my worry. "Then what was in that syringe?"

"I don't know." He studied my face as his thumb swept over my cheek. "Hey, don't borrow trouble."

"She's awake!" The excited cry came from the door, and Lena rushed into the room, Evan trailing behind her.

Zev dropped his hand and barely managed to stand up before she all but shoved him out of her way and deftly maneuvered around the IV line. I swore there were tears in her eyes. She wrapped me up in a careful hug. "Oh my God, Rory, I'm going to kill you if you ever scare me like that again." Her voice was strained.

I managed to return her hug as I buried my smile in her light-auburn hair. "Hey, it's okay. Obviously, I just needed a nap." I winced at my lame attempt at humor, but seeing Lena so frazzled brought home how serious the whole situation must have been, and I was at a loss to know how to comfort her.

She knew me well enough not to call me on it. Instead, she simply squeezed me one more time before letting me go and taking charge. "Right, then," she said briskly with no signs of her earlier distress. She straightened then turned to

Zev. "You, go home, take a shower, and change. Evan and I will stay with Rory until you get back."

"Lena-bee," Evan chided as he stood near the door. "Cut the man some slack, yeah?" He used a finger to nudge his glasses up the bridge of his nose before aiming a smile my way. "Hey, Rory, nice to see you awake."

I gave him a tiny grin and matching finger wave. "Thanks, Evan."

"All right, boys and girl," Lena cut in then pointed at Zev. "You, be gone."

Faint amusement danced over Zev's face, erasing some of his exhaustion. "You're kicking me out?"

Lena was unrepentant. "Yes, that's exactly what I'm doing. Now, shoo." She waved him toward the door.

He held his position and simply arched an eyebrow at her. Watching them made me giggle, but when Zev looked at me, I said, "Go on, Zev. It's fine."

"You're sure?" His hesitation was clear.

"Yeah, I'm sure." I lifted the hand attached to the IV. "It's not like I can go very far."

He dropped his arms, moved around Lena, and leaned in to press a kiss to my forehead. When he pulled back, he said, "I'll be back soon."

There was so much in his eyes and his voice that it brought a lump to my throat and poured warmth into my hidden hollow spots. I reached up and cupped his face. "I'll be here when you get back."

He gave me a short nod, straightened, and told Lena, "The nurses should be swinging by in just a bit. You might want to ask them to bring her something more to drink."

"I've got this, Zev," Lena said gently. "You have a ride here?" When he shook his head, she looked at Evan and got an answering nod. "Let Evan take you home."

Arrangements made, Zev and Evan left. A wave of exhaustion swept through me as I settled back into the bed. I wasn't sure how long I'd be able to keep my eyes open, but when Lena dragged Zev's chair over and sat close, eyes on mine, it was clear she wanted to talk.

Blowing out a breath, I stared back. "What?"

"Are you really okay?" There was a mix of worry and apprehension packed into her question.

"I'm good. Promise." When she continued to study me, she did not look reassured, which wasn't a surprise, really, since she knew what this assignment had involved. I reached out, caught her hand, and squeezed. "Seriously, everything's okay."

She looked toward the empty doorway, deep in thought. My neck was starting to ache, so I shifted carefully to my side until I was facing her. When she turned back, she said, "Is it?" Before I could answer, she kept going. "I know you think Sabella's protection will keep you safe, but..."

Not sure where she was going, I stayed silent.

"He wouldn't leave your side." Her gaze rose to mine. "From the moment he rushed you in here, until now, he wouldn't leave you. When that Imogen chick showed up and started demanding things from the doctor, Zev shut her down, hard." Hearing that made something inside me warm. But Lena wasn't done. "That kind of diligence generally comes up when the danger level hits the red zone, so I need to know, Rory—are you really okay, or are you in too deep?"

Lena was my best friend, and I wouldn't disrespect her by brushing off her concerns. We both knew they were valid. Anytime Arcane Families got involved, risks became the norm. It was like some unwritten law. But even after the last few days and the fact that my secret was slowly but surely becoming not so secret, I couldn't walk away. And not just because of Zev.

I shot a look at the empty doorway, ensuring that no one

lingered in the hall, then turned back to her. "The currents are rough, but I'm keeping my head above water. I've got both Zev and Sabella making sure I don't go under."

"Zev I get, but Sabella..." Lena shook her head. "No matter what you think, she's not doing this out of the kindness of her heart. She's getting something out of protecting you."

"I know." And I did, no matter what Lena thought. I had no illusions about Sabella. When those with power stepped lightly around someone, that would be the one person you needed to watch the most. And as risky as it was to keep Sabella close, it was also the only way I could keep an eye on her.

"About Zev," Lena said, abruptly switching topics.

"What about Zev?" I returned cautiously, not comfortable with that gleam in her eye.

"So..." She drew out the word. "Things seem to be getting deep with your tall, dark, and broody shadow."

Heat rushed up my face, and Lena laughed.

"Now that's a good sign," Sabella said from her position at the door. Dressed in tailored slacks and a silk blouse paired with a hip-length sweater that looked soft to the touch, she was the epitome of class. She was holding a bouquet of purple-and-blue flowers in an elegant vase.

"Are those for me?" I awkwardly rolled to my back.

Lena rose and did her best to help me as Sabella came into the room. "Of course."

Between Lena and me, we got the head of the bed raised until I was sitting up—well, for the most part. My head swam a little, but Sabella's presence required my attention. Lena stepped back so Sabella could set the vase on the table near the bed. As Sabella took off her sweater, Lena, standing behind her, raised her eyebrow in silent question and pointed to the door.

I managed a tiny nod because I figured there were a few things Sabella and I needed to talk about without an audience. "They're beautiful. Thank you."

Sabella touched my shoulder and smiled. "You're ever so welcome." She looked around, spotted the empty chair, and like Lena and Zev before her, pulled it close and settled in, folding the sweater over the arm.

Lena headed to the door. "I'm just going to grab a nurse and see if I can get you something more than water to drink, Rory."

"Thanks, Lena," I called as she left. I turned to Sabella. "I owe you a big thanks."

Faint puzzlement marred her face. "For...?"

"The scrying stone."

"Ah yes. It was rather helpful in tracking you down." She eyed me closely. "Zev mentioned things were rather dicey when he arrived."

I grimaced. "That's one way to put it."

"You disagree?"

I shook my head. "No. In fact I'd go one step further and label things as dire." I cleared my throat. "So thank you for ensuring that he got there in time."

She reached for her sweater, dug into a pocket, and pulled out the necklace in question. She handed it to me. "You'll probably want it back, then. I asked Zev to retrieve it from the items the hospital collected when you arrived, as I wasn't comfortable with it getting lost."

"Zev said you have my blood tests and stuff as well?" I asked.

Her gaze sharpened. "I do."

"Guess that's another thank-you I owe."

"No, Rory, you don't." Her voice was resolute, her expression intent. "You're my responsibility. You work for me. As such, unless you indicate otherwise, whatever you share with me stays private. Ms. Frost might have been working under Stephen's orders, but it does not excuse the blatant disregard of your privacy. I've never approved of Stephen's single-minded focus, and after this, I don't see that changing."

I dropped my gaze, nervously tipping the necklace from hand to hand. "About the tests..."

"What about them?"

I caught the necklace in a tight fist and met her eyes. "I know they came back negative, but Kerri injected me with something. If she gave me the serum—"

She raised a hand, stopping me from continuing. "Do you feel different?"

I shook my head.

"Are you sure?" She watched me. "Reach for your magic."

I followed her directions, feeling the power rise slowly to my call.

"Is it different?"

I spent a minute or two poking and prodding, but other than being understandably sluggish, it seemed as normal as it could get. "No."

"Then perhaps you're borrowing trouble."

I bit my lip then winced because it was chapped and sore. "She said they wanted me for my magic so they could create an antidote to the serum."

"That may have been their intent, but there was nothing salvageable in that lab, Rory."

I held her gaze, praying I wasn't putting my faith in the wrong person. "Swear to me."

Instead of getting upset with my demand, she seemed proud of me, as if my small defiance pleased her. "I swear, Rory Costas."

Knowing that was the best I would get, I dipped my head in acknowledgement.

Sabella was quiet for a moment then said, "I'm surprised Zev isn't here."

My lips twitched. "Lena kicked him out."

Amusement lightened Sabella's eyes. "Good for her. Well, while you're still awake, it's best to let you know that as much as I'd prefer to dispense with the follow-up meeting, Stephen and Leander felt a recap of events was necessary. As you are an essential witness to the happenings, the meeting will be postponed until your release."

"Got it."

"All right, choose your poison." Lena swept into the room juggling three cups. "Apple juice, ginger ale, or water?"

"Whatever's wet and cold will work."

Lena lined the cups on the table and let me loose. She and Sabella turned on the TV and dialed in a home-renovation show. By the time I sank back into my pillow, I'd managed to join in on the debate between shiplap and wainscoting but lost the battle with sleep somewhere around the granite-versus-marble discussion.

CHAPTER TWENTY-FOUR

THREE DAYS LATER, I was back in the conference room at Seraglio Siena, but instead of sitting off to the side and observing, I had my butt planted in a chair to Sabella's right. Between the dark looks Leander Clarke kept aiming my way and Stephen's unrelenting stare, I began to believe Lena was right to be worried. Even though I was seated between Sabella and Zev, I still felt like I was treading water in the middle of a shark-infested ocean.

On the way into the meeting, I'd asked Sabella how much detail I would be required to reveal. She correctly read my concerns and explained that Bryan's death, while highly regrettable, was viewed as justifiable considering the threat level he presented at the time. Therefore, the Clarkes could not hold me responsible. As for my potential contributions to an antidote for the serum, she said, "Keep your answers vague, and let me handle the rest." I wasn't as confident as she that such an approach would work, but I would do my damnedest to follow her directions.

Once the meeting was underway, Sabella did a remarkable job keeping the discussion civil. Zev, Imogen, and I walked the others through the investigation and our resulting reports. Emilio, Leander, and Stephen all listened closely as we laid out the various connections, from Neil targeting Chloe after her inadvertent discovery of discrepancies to Jonas's deadly confrontation with Kerri, ending with our conclusions that Kerri or Neil—or both—had used the beta version of the test on animals and unwitting humans with disastrous results.

I couldn't help but notice Stephen's barely concealed speculation and excitement when we explained that the beta version serum appeared to work, at least initially. Under the cover of the table, I fisted my hands in my lap to keep from slapping that look off his face. The fact that Bryan had paid the ultimate price for Stephen's driving need to play Arcane God infuriated me to no end. I wasn't the only one who picked up on his reaction. Emilio watched the head of the Trask Family with a hard-eyed cool calculation that made me wonder if Zev might be getting a new assignment soon. Leander appeared to be torn between taking his anger out on me and taking it out on Stephen. Strangely, Imogen stayed unruffled at Stephen's side, outwardly oblivious to the undercurrents, but I didn't believe it. I caught her staring at me and Zev, something working deep in her cool eyes.

The underlying riptides in the room threatened to suck me under, but every time I thought I would go down, Zev or Sabella managed to keep me afloat. When I was recounting the confrontation with Bryan, Imogen had no qualms about implying that I was a Prism, but when Sabella pressed for proof, Imogen reluctantly admitted she had none as she had been knocked unconscious during most of the fight, coming to only toward the end when Bryan struck out at Zev. Her recollection of what actually happened was blurry, but she remembered Zev facing down Bryan, me yelling, magic clashing, then Bryan dropping at Zev's feet. Sabella asked Zev to recount the incident, and he did so, neatly tailoring the story so it sounded as if Bryan's death was an accidental byproduct of Zev and me working together to keep Bryan at bay. I let him and Sabella do their thing until Imogen reluctantly conceded that perhaps her assessment was incorrect.

There was a heart-stopping moment when Leander asked me point-blank, "Ms. Costas, are you a Prism?"

I didn't want to lie, because that would end badly, but I wasn't ready to expose myself either. So heeding Sabella's advice, I held his gaze and politely answered, "Mr. Clarke, I am a Transporter, something you're more than welcome to verify with the Guild." That wasn't the whole truth, but it also wasn't a lie.

When it came time to recount what happened when Kerri and Neil dragged me away, Sabella kept her questions simple, which allowed me to do the same for my answers. I shared that Kerri had managed to listen in on Imogen's call to Stephen and used her assumptions about my abilities as a basis for her next steps.

This time, it was Stephen who interrupted. "You said she took samples from you?"

"She drew blood from me, yes," I admitted.

"Did she give you the serum as well?"

I looked at Sabella, who inclined her head, giving me the go-ahead to address that question. I turned back to Stephen, met his overly eager gaze, and locked down my urge to tell him to fuck off. I was proud of how calm I sounded when I answered, "Not that I'm aware of."

"That's not a no."

"That's an 'I'm not insane with magic, and my lab tests all came back clean,'" I shot back with borderline civility.

His mouth tightened, and his hand resting on the table fisted, but Imogen touched his arm, and he visibly relaxed. "I apologize, Ms. Costas, but I wanted to ensure that we won't be facing another situation like that with Mr. Croft."

Patronizing jackass. I managed something I hoped was close to a smile but might have fallen short. "I think we're all safe, as I am not fighting the urge to kill anyone at the present time." *Not kill but maybe strangle.*

Sabella spoke before Stephen could push it and asked me to finish. I did my best to wrap it up, concluding with Kerri's explanation for why she and Neil decided to steal the serum. Fortunately, that shifted the conversation away from me as Imogen took over. It seemed that while I was in the hospital, she managed to retrace the money trail of Kerri's mysterious backers, only to end up at dead end after dead end. Not unexpectedly, Leander was all over that, claiming once again that it was additional proof of the Cabal's involvement and existence.

Even though no one asked me, I was on Leander's side, and while no one else may have voiced similar beliefs, it soon became clear that Stephen, Leander, and the stoic Emilio were no longer calling the shots.

"Stephen, Leander, you requested this investigation," Sabella stated as she folded her hands on the table. "Based upon what we heard here today and the combined reports of the Arbiters and Ms. Costas, it is obvious that the Cordova Family had no involvement whatsoever in any part of this. Agreed?" When Leander and Stephen agreed, she continued. "As for your insistence on continuing with the Delphi project after the council advised you to stop, and your unauthorized use of proprietary information in that endeavor, both LanTech and Origin must answer to the council. Therefore, the presence of Stephen Trask, Leander Clarke, and Clarke's LanTech partner, Oliver Nilson, are mandated by the council in three weeks' time. Information will be couriered to each of you." Then Sabella turned to Emilio. "The council extends its invitation to you should you choose to witness the hearing."

"We appreciate the council's invitation, and contingent upon my schedule, I may accept," Emilio said.

Stephen turned an interesting shade of red as he shoved up from the table, Imogen rising at his side. He visibly fought back his temper before choking out, "We're done?"

Sabella inclined her head regally. "For now, yes, we're done."

Stephen shot a glare at Emilio and slid his gaze over me. At the roiling darkness in his eyes, the hair on my arms rose. I had no doubt I had gained if not an enemy then extremely unwanted attention from the Trasks. Imogen looked at Zev, then to me, her lips curving in a cunning smile, then she followed Stephen out.

Leander was slower to rise, but instead of being angry, his face was pale and drawn, almost as if he aged years in the last few minutes. It was clear he understood the gravity of answering to the council and was not looking forward to any of it. Still, he gained points in my book when he turned to Emilio and said, "While I won't regret requesting this investigation, I do offer my sincere apologies for the inconvenience this may have caused your Family and hope you understand this was not done out of maliciousness."

Emilio studied the older man from his seat while the silence stretched between them. Finally, he sighed. "Apology accepted, Leander."

Leander turned to Sabella and sketched a half bow. "Thank you for your time, Sabella. Perhaps our future meetings will be under less distasteful circumstances."

"I truly hope so, Leander."

We all watched in heavy silence as Leander left. Once the door closed behind him, Emilio said, "Well, that was..."

"Interesting?" Zev drawled as he pushed his chair back and stretched out his legs.

"Telling, I think," Emilio corrected cryptically. He turned to me, and I was surprised when he asked, "How are you doing, Rory?"

I sat there feeling shaky as the adrenaline that had kept me going drained away. It seemed to take my verbal filter with it. "I think I'm in trouble."

Sabella reached over and patted my arm. "You'll be fine." Then, proving I wasn't the only one who'd noticed Trask's weird behavior, she said, "Stephen's going to have plenty to worry about soon enough. Besides, he knows better than to go up against me."

"Or me," Emilio added as he got up from his chair.

I blinked at him. "I'm sorry?"

He pushed his chair in and leaned against it, arms folded along the high back. "Your help when Jeremy was taken, and again here with this, is something I and my family will not forget." He straightened, walked over to Sabella, and offered her his hand. "I believe I owe you a lunch, beautiful."

Sabella's smile was dazzling as she took his hand. "Yes, you do." She rose to stand next to Emilio then turned to touch my shoulder. "You're off the clock, Rory." She moved to Zev, who'd risen, and brushed a quick kiss against his cheek. When she pulled back, she shared a knowing look with me and Zev. "I'm sure I can trust you to get her home safely?"

"Of course," Zev said then exchanged brief goodbyes with Emilio.

I sat in my chair, stunned, as Emilio and Sabella walked out, leaving me alone with Zev. When they disappeared through the door, I turned to Zev and tipped my head back so I could see his face as he stood next to me. "What just happened?"

He dropped to a crouch next to my chair, his hand

covering mine, which was knotted in my lap. The warmth of his touch chased away the strange jittery feeling that threatened to take over. "You've officially entered the game." Despite his gentle touch, his voice carried a ruthless edge. His lips curved, but there was more resignation than amusement in that small movement. "I did warn you."

I twisted my hand around until I could weave my fingers through his and hold tight. "Yeah, you did." I dropped my gaze to our intertwined hands and swallowed hard. "It's just..." I wasn't sure how to finish, but it didn't matter.

He hooked a finger under my chin and tipped my face up, his dark eyes roaming over my face. "You're going to be fine, Rory. You're not alone."

The dark looks from Trask, Imogen's weird behavior, and even Clarke's understandable anger over Bryan's death had all managed to bring home the reality of my theoretical future, and the picture that formed was scary as shit. Maybe it was because I didn't feel a hundred percent after my time in the hospital, but I had some doubts about my ability to survive what was coming next. For the first time, I let those doubts lead, wondering if the threat of Sabella would be enough to hold things at bay, if Emilio's claim came with strings I could accept, and if Lena was right and I was in way over my head. Even worse, I wondered if when push came to shove, Zev would stand with me or if I was just a momentary challenge for him.

My worry must have been obvious because Zev's harsh features softened. He untangled our hands and cupped my face, taking my mouth in a tender kiss. His touch and taste held the waiting reality at bay, replacing it with a different kind of promise, one that I desperately wanted to hold close.

My hands curled in Zev's shirt and tugged him toward me as my mouth opened under his gentle onslaught. Our tongues tangled—mine frantic, his soothing—until my desperation dulled under a rising need for more. I willingly got lost in his kiss. When Zev finally lifted his head, he was breathing hard, and hunger rode rough on his face. I realized my hands were buried in his hair and I was about to fall out of my chair and into his lap.

He rested his forehead against mine. "So, now that the job's done, you ready?"

Not quite following, I drew back with a puzzled frown. "Ready? For what?"

He pressed his lips against mine then stood up, hand out to help me stand. "For our next adventure."

His answer was nicely vague. I took his hand and let him pull me up. "Which one?"

He curled his arm around my waist, keeping me close as we headed for the door. "The one where I take you out on a real live date that doesn't include murder, mayhem, or magic."

"That's a thing?"

"Mm-hmm. I promise you'll like it."

"Sounds delightfully boring."

He shot me a wicked grin that made much more interesting promises. "I assure you, it'll be far from boring." His grin turned into a comical leer. "Besides, you owe me one."

The reminder of the favor I'd promised when he helped me save Lena had me giving a fake sigh. "If you insist on cashing in such a valuable marker, you'd better not disappoint."

He threw back his head and laughed. Watching him, I figured disappointment would be the least of my concerns.

◆

- YOU HAVE ARRIVED AT YOUR DESTINATION -

◆

Thank you for taking a ride with RISKY GOODS. Rory and Zev will return for their final leg of their trip in **LETHAL CONTENTS.**

Now available in Kindle Unlimited!

◆

Want to know how Rory and Zev met? Then don't miss out on exclusives & new release information by subscribing to Jami's newsletter at: https://www.sub-scribepage.com/Jami-Subscription-Books

Do you want to share your exciting discovery of a new read? Then leave a review!

Or you're welcome to swing by and visit Jami's website at: http://jamigray.com

◆

If you're interested in a detour, turn the page and explore Jami's other series.

KYN KRONICLES SERIES

Urban Fantasy/Paranormal Romance Series

Welcome to a world where the supernatural walks alongside humans, their existence kept secret behind the thinnest of veils. Now modern man's scientific curiosity is determined to rip that curtain aside, revealing the nightmares in the shadows.

Binge the series today at
www.amazon.com/dp/Bo7MDWGTRT!

◆

SHADOW'S EDGE

Raine's spent a lifetime hunting monsters, but can she stop her prey from exposing the supernatural community one bloody corpse at a time?

SHADOW'S SOUL

When a simple assignment turns into a nightmare, can Raine and Gavin unravel old vendettas before they both pay the ultimate price?

SHADOW'S MOON

Compromise isn't in Warrick's vocabulary and Xander won't abandon the hunt. As the line between instinct and intellect blurs, will they survive the fallout?

SHADOW'S CURSE

When the queen of chaos locks horns with death's justice, Natasha and Darius set a dangerous game in motion, leading two predators into a lethal dance of secrets.

SHADOW'S DREAM

Tala can't forget the past. Cheveyo can't change it. As the dreams they shared linger, can they escape the encroaching nightmare before it's too late?

Stay tuned for the final installment arriving late 2021

PSY - IV TEAMS BOOKS

Welcome to a world where facing danger requires the unique skill set of the men and women of Jami Gray's PSY-IV Teams. As sparks, and bullets fly, love, action, and adventure will target these unique couples as they race through each breath-stealing operation.

Binge the series today at
https://www.amazon.com/dp/B07D4H14DR

  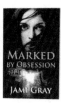

---◆---

HUNTED BY THE PAST

Cyn & Kayden

To escape a killer from their past, can a reluctant psychic trust the man who walked away?

TOUCHED BY FATE

Risia & Tag

A seer's secrets become her only bargaining chip in a high-stakes game of lies and loyalty determining her fate.

MARKED BY OBSESSION

Meli & Wolf

A woman in hiding. A telepath who sees deeper than her scars. Can they forge a bond stronger than the obsession stalking them before time runs out?

FRACTURED BY DECEIT

Megan & Bishop

After a brutal attack by a telepath, Megan turns to Bishop for help, but how does he keep her safe when she's threat?

LINKED BY DECEPTION

Jinx & Rabbit

Forced to play intimate criminal partners, will Rabbit & Jinx risk turning illusion to truth as they race to untangle a web of conspiracies and lies?

FATE'S VULTURES BOOKS

Post-apocalyptic Romantic Suspense Series

Known as The Collapse, the ravaged aftermath of Mother Nature's fury colliding with man's merciless need for survival has left civilization teetering on the brink of disintegration. Decades beyond the first brutal years, there are those who believe there is a possible future worth fighting for, worth dying for. Betrayed but not broken, they hold to their code, one considered outdated and useless. Loyalty to each other, shields for those without, warriors born and bred.

Ride along with FATE'S VULTURES and binge the series today at www.amazon.com/dp/B07PHM191J

◆

LYING IN RUINS

Charity & Ruin

On a shared mission of vengeance, who will tear them apart first—their suspicions or their enemies?

BEG FOR MERCY

Mercy & Havoc

Will an assassin and a mercenary find their balance on the thin line of loyalty, or will it snap under the weight of their wary hearts?

CAUGHT IN THE AFTERMATH

Vex & Math

Caught between a looming conflict and the fallout of a brutal betrayal, will they survive vengeance's aftermath?

FEAR THE REAPER

Lilith & Reaper

To ensure a future for those they've sworn to protect, two adversaries must navigate a minefield of past betrayals and broken promises to defeat a common enemy, before it all goes to hell.

This complete series is available wherever books are sold!

ARCANE TRANSPORTER BOOKS
Urban Fantasy Series

Binge this complete urban fantasy series thrill-ride today!

Need to ensure you delivery, magical or otherwise, makes it to its destination? For guaranteed delivery, hire the best in the west, Rory Costas, Arcane Transporter. (Independent contractor - not responsible for damage incurred in transit.)

Check out this series at
https://www.amazon.com/dp/B088FCSVKB

◆

GRAVE CARGO

When a questionable, but lucrative delivery job takes an unexpected turn, will Rory survive the collision or crash and burn?

RISKY GOODS

A dead mage, a missing friend, and an unpredictable alliance merge into a volatile package sending Rory careening through the Arcane elite's deadly secrets.

LETHAL CONTENTS

A failed assassination, a kidnapped ally, and a treasonous scheme pit Rory and Zev against a devious enemy determined to watch Arcane society crash and burn.

ABOUT THE AUTHOR

"Taking a refreshing approach to fantasy magic, this fast-paced, economical thriller is told from a highly likable perspective." —Red Adept Editing

Jami Gray is the coffee addicted, music junkie, Queen Nerd of her personal Geek Squad, Alpha Mom of the Fur Minxes, who writes to soothe the voices crammed in her head. You don't want to miss out on her multiple series that combines magical intrigue and fearless romance into one wild ride -- Arcane Transporter, Kyn Kronicles, PSY-IV Teams, or Fate's Vultures.

Printed in Great Britain
by Amazon

83504001R00180